STATE OF MIND

A Virgil Jones Novel—Book 13

THOMAS SCOTT

For information contact:

ThomasScottBooks.com

Linda Heaton - Editor

HIGH ROAD PRESS

VIRGIL JONES SERIES IN ORDER:

State of Anger - Book 1

State of Betrayal - Book 2

State of Control - Book 3

State of Deception - Book 4

State of Exile - Book 5

State of Freedom - Book 6

State of Genesis - Book 7

State of Humanity - Book 8

State of Impact - Book 9

State of Justice - Book 10

State of Killers - Book 11

State of Life - Book 12

State of Mind - Book 13

State of Need - Book 14

JACK BELLOWS SERIES IN ORDER:

Wayward Strangers

Updates on future novels available at:
ThomasScottBooks.com

For Jack —
Gone, but not forgotten

Mind

/mīnd/

noun:

The element of a person that enables them to be aware of the world and their experiences, to think, and to feel.

––––––––––

"Life is a state of mind"
—Jerzy Kosiński

––––––––––

"I don't know how many times I have to say it, Virg: It's all connected."
—Mason Jones

CHAPTER ONE

Everything seemed wrong somehow. The sky wasn't where it belonged, and he was blind in one eye but had no memory of how that had come to pass...only that it had. He was dressed for cold weather even though the day was sunny and mild. A manufactured wind blew hard across his face, pulling his cheeks back so far that his teeth were visible, at once a grimace of righteousness and fear. He knew he was about to die but didn't know why, only that it was a conscious choice he'd made so that others might live. His heart ached with losses of the past —a woman whose name he couldn't recall no matter how hard he tried—and to a lesser extent, the loss that was yet to come.

The distance between the boats was less than a quarter of a mile. Gunfire could be heard...even over the roar of the wind, and something else that should have been familiar but wasn't. When he looked up expecting to see the sky, he saw only water. He hung upside down, suspended by thick leather straps that dug into his shoulders and made it hard to breathe. He could see himself, visible in the water below, a blur of his own face across the breaking waves. The familiar black patch that covered his bad eye was tucked behind his goggles, the elastic straps digging into the side of his head. It was all a flickering image that held little meaning, if any. *Just like my life until now,* he thought, though he didn't know why that particular phrase took root inside his brain.

A man and a woman he thought he knew were on a boat watching his approach. He couldn't remember their names, but as he passed overhead, the man in the boat raised his arm and waved. He desperately wanted to know who they were, but he was out of time, and they were already out of sight. And then, in a moment of clarity he was back inside himself, in control of what he was doing, and what was coming.

He rolled the aircraft upright and climbed, banking around toward the trailing boat. Tears escaped his good eye and puddled at the bottom of his goggles. When he had the altitude he needed, he pushed the throttle all the way forward and pointed the airplane toward the men in the boat. Though he didn't think he'd fear the end when it came, the sound of his own scream filled the cockpit right up to the moment of impact.

And then there was nothing.

MURTON WHEELER SAT UP IN BED, HIS HANDS SHAKING, his body covered in sweat. His wife, Becky, placed her hand on his back. "Same dream?"

Murton nodded. "Yeah. Ten days in a row now. I feel like I might be losing my mind."

"Can you tell me about it?" Becky said.

Murton took a deep breath, then stood from the bed and moved around the room. "What's to tell? You've heard it as many times as I've experienced it."

"But every time there's something more. What was it this time?"

Murton leaned against the dresser, wiped his face with his hands, then said, "I'm not sure. The whole thing happens so fast, it's hard to keep track of."

"You were flying the plane again?"

"Yeah, I'm always flying the plane. Except I don't realize it at the moment. And this time I was inverted. I saw myself in the water below. I was wearing an eye patch. I'm not sure how to explain it. It was me, but it wasn't me...if that makes any sense."

Becky walked over and took her husband's hand in her own. "Close your eyes."

"I really don't want to do that, especially right now."

"Murton Wheeler, close your eyes."

Murton looked at Becky for a moment, then did as he was asked. "Now what?"

"Describe the man in the plane. You said it was you, but it wasn't you."

"I know what I said, Becks, but the images reflected off the water's surface were too blurry." Murton opened his eyes and said, "I can't do it."

"What about the man in the boat?"

"What about him?"

"You told me a day or two ago that you knew who he was."

"That's not entirely accurate," Murton said. "When I saw him, I thought I should know who he was, but I don't."

"Except you saw him."

"I did, but it was like seeing someone drive by at eighty miles an hour. I only caught a glimpse."

"But you've had ten glimpses so far."

"I know. Let's hope there isn't an eleventh."

"You also said there was another woman...not in the dream, but one whose name you couldn't recall."

"And I still don't. Not now, or in the dream itself. It probably doesn't matter. I never even saw her. It was more of an impression. What are you doing?"

"Getting dressed. I've got an idea."

"Care to let me in on it?"

"Call Virgil and tell him you're going to be in a little late this morning." Virgil Jones was Murton's adoptive brother and his boss at the Major Crimes Unit with the Indiana State Police.

"Why?"

"Because we're going to talk to someone."

Murton shook his head. "I am not going to a shrink, Becks. We've already talked about that."

"I know we have. We're going to talk with someone else. Call Virgil, then get cleaned up."

MURTON CALLED VIRGIL AND EXPLAINED WHY HE WAS going to be late. "Becky wants me to talk with someone, but she wouldn't say who."

Virgil let out a little chuckle, then said, "That sounds like our girl. Same dream, huh?"

"Yes, and it's driving me nuts."

Virgil laughed again. "I'll bet she's taking you to see a shrink."

"I'm glad you find this whole thing so amusing," Murton said. Then, "How much?"

"How much what?"

Murton rolled his eyes into the phone. "How much money? You said you wanted to bet."

"It was a figure of speech, Murt."

"So put your money where your speech is, and give me a figure. I know you can afford it."

Virgil could. He and his wife, Sandy—the lieutenant governor of the state—were wealthy. The whole thing happened by chance after they adopted their eldest son,

Jonas, whose parents had been murdered a few years ago. "Okay, how does ten bucks sound?"

"Like you're afraid of losing," Murton said.

"Make it a hundred, then."

Murton said, "Deal," then hung up.

As it turned out, Murton should have made it a thousand.

———

VIRGIL SET HIS PHONE DOWN ON THE KITCHEN TABLE next to his plate, then finished his eggs. When he looked up at Sandy, he saw her head was tilted to one side, her eyebrows raised. "What?"

Sandy smiled at her husband. "Don't 'what' me, mister. That sounded like Murton. Is he still having that dream?"

Virgil nodded. "He is. I'm starting to get a little concerned. Becky is taking him to talk with someone."

"A shrink?"

Virgil shrugged. "I don't know. She wouldn't say." The family pet, Larry the Dog, came walking by, glanced at Virgil's plate, and wagged his tail. Virgil gave him a scratch on the head, then set his plate on the floor.

"If you keep doing that, he's going to get fat," Sandy said.

"He's sort of hard to say no to."

They sat quietly for a few minutes, then Sandy said, "I'll bet she's going to take him to see a shrink."

Virgil, who knew an opportunity to cover his bet when he saw one, said, "I doubt it. How much do you want to bet?"

Sandy went for the hundred as well. "Why are you giving me an evil grin?"

"Because now the bet is between you and Murt. I just covered my ass either way."

That's when Jonas walked around the corner. "Swear jar."

Virgil shook his head. "Nope. No way. The word 'ass' isn't swearing."

Jonas gave Virgil a look, then said, "Uh, yeah, Dad, I think it is."

Virgil, who hadn't won a swear jar argument since its inception, wasn't backing down. "Nope. It's in the Bible, so it doesn't count."

Jonas shook his head like he couldn't believe his father would use that kind of excuse. "That's lame. You know what we should have? We should have a lame jar too."

"Sorry, buddy. It is what it is," Virgil said.

Jonas shrugged in mock defeat, then turned to Sandy. "Hey, Mom?"

"Yes, sweetheart?"

"Remember when Wyatt was a baby and wasn't in big-boy pants yet?"

"Of course," Sandy said. "What about it?" Wyatt was Virgil and Sandy's youngest son who had made the transition to Sponge Bob underpants a little over a year ago.

"Well, I was wondering why every time you changed his diaper, you had to sprinkle some of that white powder on his ass." Then he looked at Virgil. "What? It's in the Bible. You said so yourself."

Virgil stood, took a dollar from his pocket, and put it in the jar. Then he turned to Jonas and said, "That's not funny, young man. It's a word for grownups, Bible or not."

"I guess I missed that part...about the grownups. Maybe if you—"

"Jonas," Virgil said.

"Yeah?"

"Go get ready for school."

"Okay. Love you, Dad."

"Love you too, buddy."

Sandy was sucking on her cheeks so hard it looked like she didn't have any teeth.

———

MURTON AND BECKY WALKED INTO THE BAR, A JOINT called Jonesy's Rastabarian, which was owned by Virgil and Murton, along with two of their best friends, Delroy Rouche, and Robert Whyte. Delroy and Robert were native Jamaicans who Virgil and his late father, Mason, hired years ago to help run the bar. Together they'd managed to turn an ordinary downtown tavern into one of the most popular Jamaican-themed bars in the Midwest. Robert ran the kitchen, the sous chefs, and the rest of the backend, while Delroy took care of the bar and the wait staff.

Virgil and Murton also owned a private investigations firm that Becky ran from an upstairs office over the bar. She handled all the research for the state's Major Crimes Unit, and was paid off the books through the MCU's discretionary fund. The entire arrangement was a little circular...some would even say shifty. But because Virgil and Murton reported directly to Governor Hewitt (Mac) McConnell through his chief of staff, Cora LaRue, if anyone thought the setup was shady, they kept their opinions to themselves, lest they face Cora's wrath, which was legendary.

When Murton and Becky walked into the upstairs office, they found Chip Lawless, one of the MCU crime scene technicians waiting for them. "What are you doing here?" Murton said.

"Good morning to you, too," Lawless said.

"Don't be too hard on him, Chip," Becky said. "He's had a few rough nights."

Murton turned and looked at his wife. *"A few?"*

Becky gave him a fake smile, then turned to Lawless. "You bring the kit?"

Lawless nodded and tapped the case sitting next to him on the sofa. "Ready when you guys are."

Murton dropped his head and let his chin rest on his chest. "We're doing an Identikit on my dreams?"

Becky crossed her arms and said, "It's either that or the shrink. You choose."

Murton shook his head. "Becks, you know as well as I do that these types of drawings aren't nearly as effective as everyone thinks. This isn't television, you know."

Lawless opened the case and began setting up the equipment. "That's not necessarily true, Murt," he said. "The technology has come a long way. We use a system from the UK called EvoFIT. It's being used by police forces around the world with great success."

Murton was skeptical. "Oh yeah? What's so special about this system?"

Lawless explained while he got his gear ready. "This particular type of recognition composite system doesn't require you—or, uh, whoever—to have good recall of a face, unlike the traditional feature methods that require you to explain, for example, how big someone's nose is, or the shape of their jawline. Plus, it's quicker than the older, traditional methods."

Murton glanced at the clock on the wall. "How much quicker?"

"Quite a bit," Lawless said. "As I said, EvoFIT uses a different approach. I'll show you several faces containing random features, like eyes, noses, and mouths. What you'll do is select a few of these faces that are most similar to what you recall. Then, I'll mix and combine the selected faces together to produce another set for selection. We'll repeat this process a number of times, which will narrow the results and allow the composite to evolve until we've got a match. It's really pretty cool."

Murton waved the explanation away. "Okay, okay, let's get on with it already. You sound like part of the sales department."

"I hope we can get something out of this," Becky said.

Lawless jerked his thumb at Murton. "Me too. This one here seems a little cranky."

A LITTLE MORE THAN AN HOUR LATER THEY WERE DONE. Lawless had produced two composites, one of the man in the plane, and one of the man in the boat. He hooked his equipment up to Becky's color laser printer, and the result was a realistic likeness that was almost as clear and crisp as a photograph.

Murton looked at both composites for a few minutes and had to admit that they were impressive. He set them on the table that fronted the sofa, then leaned back and closed his eyes.

"Do they look right to you, Murt?" Becky said.

Murton nodded and spoke without opening his eyes. "They do look right. In fact, they're damned near perfect. The problem is, I have no idea who they are. Other than in my dreams, I've never seen either of these men before."

CHAPTER TWO

The boys, back together again.

None of them had ever been to Indiana or even bothered to look at it on a map. There were four of them, each a professional in their own way. Each had done time over the course of their lives, and every last one of them vowed they'd never go back. The peeling paint, the cold steel bars of the cage, the narrow cots and lousy food, the guards and their spring-loaded saps, and the fights in the yard, every waking moment hell on earth. But still, they needed to make a living, their monthly nut no different from anyone else's, which is to say, everpresent.

Their specialty was banks and credit unions, specifically ones in rural areas all across the country—from the upper northwest to the lower southeast. They went in with good intel, kept a strict watch on the clock, and got out quick.

Almost every alphabet agency in the country was looking for them, from the ATF, DEA, DHS, FBI, right down to the Department of Veteran's Affairs. The veteran's affairs people were on the list for the simple reason that one of the last jobs they pulled had been well outside their wheelhouse, knocking over a VA clinic near Carson City, Nevada, walking away with enough meds to take down a herd of wild elephants. As it turned out, no elephants were ever harmed but a VA employee was killed during the heist, and the drugs were later wholesaled by a trusted source on the Vegas strip for over a half-million. A week later they split it five ways, and they all walked with a cool one hundred grand for about two days worth of planning and fifteen minutes of execution.

They came from different corners of the country, two of them from the deep south—one near the panhandle of Florida, the other from Baton Rouge—one from North Dakota, another, LA. They took their time between robberies, varied their targets and methods, kept their heads down, their mouths shut, and their burners charged. Most of the money they earned went into cryptocurrency via untraceable offshore accounts. They were building for retirement, and they were almost there. A few more jobs—one in particular—and they'd be done, living off the interest and sipping rum punches in places like Belize or Madrid.

They were brought together as they always had been by the leader of their group, a smart, take-no-bullshit woman who lived in Cortez, down between Tampa and Sarasota, along Florida's Gulf Coast. She ran a bar called Slips—the name more of a reference to the waitresses' attire than the location of the bar—even though the bar itself was in such disrepair it was dangerously close to slipping into the marina.

Her name was Kelly Snow, her surname a bit ironic because she'd never seen a white flake in her life...at least the kind that fell from the sky. A Florida haircut kept the sweat off of her neck, a slight gap between her two upper front teeth made her look approachable when she smiled, but her bitter dark eyes said go away if she turned them on someone she didn't want around.

Snow hadn't built the bar business herself. She'd inherited it from her father, Fred Snow, who made claims back in the day that when Hemingway wasn't in the Keys, he'd cruise north and stop in to get good and plowed between novels. It was all bullshit because the math didn't work out on the ages between her father and Hemingway. What wasn't bullshit was the fact that dear old dad had done some federal time for letting a kilo or two of coke float through the bar every now and again to help make ends meet.

When the DEA caught on and pressed Fred Snow's wife about the drugs, she was as high as a rock star at the end of a year-long tour. When told of her options—few that they were—she sang like a squeaky hinge that hadn't seen a can of WD-40 in its entire life. She testified against her husband who promptly ended up in jail, and after a while, when the dust of the entire affair had settled, everything was fine.

Until he got out ten years later.

Fred Snow took a cab from the federal pen and went straight to the nearest hardware store. He bought the biggest ball-peen hammer he could find, then went home and bashed the living bejesus out of his wife for ratting him out to the feds. When the neighbors heard the screaming—most said it was really only one short yelp, the kind a dog might make if it got shot—they called the police, who found Fred standing there hunched over his wife's dead body, screaming at her like a madman, the hammer—still slick with blood—hanging from his hand. He'd beaten her so severely that one of the crime scene technicians noted in his report that the floor and ceiling reminded him of a Jackson Pollock painting that had been done with only one color.

The case was eventually closed, the wife was buried, and Fred got to ride the electric slide for first-degree murder. And the daughter, Kelly Snow? Well…Kelly ended up with a bar called Slips.

LOOKING BACK, KELLY ALWAYS KNEW HER FATHER WAS A little greasy. The kind of guy who'd do whatever it took—legal or not—to get the job done. A Florida shit-kicker, in other words. Kelly hated him for what he had done...actually felt her love of him click off after he'd killed her mother. One second it was there, and the next it was gone, like someone had simply flipped a switch. And whenever she thought of her now-dead mother, the only times she could reference in her brain were the ten years her father had been in prison for hustling the coke. Those were the semi-good years...the ones where mom was clean and happy. But after the killing, the hate began to consume Kelly Snow. Ultimately, it changed her into someone else entirely. Someone just like her father.

WITH EVERYONE IN HER FAMILY DEAD AND GONE, AND the business now her own, beyond the hate she carried around, she came to understand two things: Running a bar along Florida's Gulf Coast wasn't as easy as it appeared. There was always something...staffing and payroll issues, food deliveries and liquor distributors who wouldn't give an inch on payments, and worst of all, taxes. All kinds of taxes. Income taxes, payroll taxes, state taxes, federal taxes—every last nickel due on either a monthly or quarterly basis. The taxes were eating her alive like little government fire ants that scurried and bit and chewed at her until she thought she might scream. It was no wonder the old man had been running some blow through the joint every now and again. If he didn't, they might not have been able to eat. It made her question herself in ways she didn't like to scrutinize with any amount of depth or regularity.

No matter. If she didn't figure something out, Slips would be shuttered, and she could not let that happen. So Kelly Snow, full of anger and hate—not to mention her father's genes—figured it out.

———————

SHE DIDN'T FOOL HERSELF BY TAKING ALL THE CREDIT because the whole thing happened purely by chance. She was locking up one night, the bartenders and waitresses all gone, the floors mopped, the chairs upended on the tables, the toilets scrubbed, the kitchen cleaned—like that—when a man came up behind her outside the bar and asked for a drink.

"We're closed," she told him. "We open back up tomorrow morning at ten." She turned the key in the deadbolt to make her point, then tried to sidestep the man. She actually thought she would have to fight him off, but then he did something that surprised her. He stepped back, his palms out in a peaceful gesture, a warm smile radiating from his face under the glow of the multi-colored lights strung overhead along the marina's dock.

When she finally took note of the man's narrow shoulders, his thinning gray hair, and the way his eyes looked like ping pong balls behind his thick glasses, she knew she wasn't dealing with someone looking to hurt her...she was looking at a harmless old man.

"Please. A drink and a word are all I ask. I knew your father." His accent was slight, but noticeable. "He did some work for us many years ago."

"He's been dead for a while now," Snow said.

"I'm aware," the man said. "That is why I wish to speak with you."

Snow laughed. "Not interested, pal. My old man was a jerk, and he died in prison after beating my mom to death. And if that wasn't enough, I ended up with this dump, which, from a financial perspective is about to slide into the Gulf if I don't do something, and quick."

"I'm aware," the man said again. Then he reached into his pocket and pulled out a plain white envelope. He handed it to Snow and said, "This is simply for listening to what I have to say. I would like to make a proposal. If you say no, I will walk away and you'll never see me again. But if we sit and talk, the amount in that envelope is nothing compared to what I could arrange for you."

Snow looked inside the envelope and saw a neat stack of hundred dollar bills, banded and stamped like they'd just been pulled from a bank vault. She thumbed through the bills to make sure they were all the same denomination—they were—and that the amount stamped on the band was correct. "Ten grand to listen?" The skepticism in her tone was obvious.

The man smiled at her again. "Yes, simply to listen. Now, about that drink?"

Snow gave him a long hard stare, stuck her tongue between her teeth and lower lip, then unlocked the door.

Once they were inside, the man introduced himself only as Alberto. "My surname is of no importance. You may call me Bert, if you wish."

Snow put the envelope in her purse, then walked it behind the bar. "What'll you have?"

"Rum. Whatever your best might be. On the rocks, if you please."

Snow made the drink, set it in front of Alberto, then thought, what the hell, and poured one for herself. After taking a few sips, she looked at the strange man in front of her and said, "Okay, Bert, I'm doing what you asked. I'm listening, and that means I'm earning the money in the envelope you gave me. So, what's this all about?"

CHAPTER THREE

Alberto finished his drink in two long swallows, then pushed his glass forward a fraction, an indication he wanted another. Snow poured him a double, then crossed her arms and waited.

"You may not remember, but you and I have met before."

"We have?" Snow asked.

"It was many years ago. I would come in and talk business with your father, and you would be sitting right down there at the end of the bar. Sometimes you would help the workers clear the glasses and the dishes from the table."

"I do remember being here—even though I shouldn't have been inside because I was too young—and I do remember doing those things...but I'm afraid I don't remember you."

Alberto gave her a nonchalant shrug. "It is of no importance, really. A simple statement of fact."

"If it's of no importance, why do you bring it up?"

"I suppose it is an attempt to validate myself with you...to prove that I worked with your father. He was very helpful to us over the years." Alberto touched the tip of his nose with his index finger. The message was clear.

"I'm sure I wouldn't know."

"Ah, but you should. It was your mother who talked to the police, not your father."

"And he killed her because of it."

"That is not the point."

"Then what is?" Snow said, a little frost in her voice.

The frostiness didn't seem to bother Alberto. "The point is your father never talked to the authorities. Not one single time. Even when they were strapping him into the chair, he never said a word about our operation. The DEA had put a deal on the table for him. If he talked, it would have saved his life."

"Then why didn't he?"

Alberto picked up his glass and took a drink of his rum before he answered. "Because it would have ended yours. The people I formerly represented were ruthless if crossed. It was my job to make it clear to your father that if he kept his mouth shut, you would be left alone and cared for. It was also my job to make it clear that if he tried to cut a deal, that you would be...mmm...eliminated. In short, your father saved your life."

Snow listened to what Alberto told her, and she realized as he was speaking that they were moving down a dangerous path. "You're saying you would have killed me if my dad tried to make a deal to save himself?"

Alberto was a professional, so he was only mildly offended by the statement. He swished his index finger back and forth between the two of them like a windshield wiper. "Not at all. It wouldn't have been me. But there would have been someone at one point or another, and nothing I could do would have stopped it."

Snow took a sip of her own drink and said, "So what is it you want from me?"

"In a word? Leadership."

Snow laughed out loud. "Then you've probably got the wrong woman. My leadership skills are driving this bar so far down the drain it's embarrassing for the sewer system."

"I believe you underestimate yourself," Alberto said.

Snow gave him her hard-eyed stare and said, "How about we get down to it?"

"I no longer associate with the men who supplied your father. In fact, I am out of the drug business altogether. I am too old for such foolishness these days. The drug trade...it is a young man's game."

"Then what do you do?" Snow asked.

Alberto looked over the tops of his glasses and considered his answer. "I suppose you could say I am in the intelligence-gathering business. With the right group of people, it can be very lucrative."

"If it's so lucrative, why do you need me?"

"I've already answered that," Alberto said. "I need a leader."

"What happened to your last one?"

"Nothing...except perhaps age itself. You're speaking with him right now."

"And you want me to take over for you?"

Alberto gave her the swishing finger again. "No, not take over. Rather...fill in for me. As I said, age is not something working in my favor."

"You're actually being pretty vague, Bert."

"Then let me be clear. I have the names of four men who will work for you." He held up a finger to make his point. "Not with you. For you. They are skilled men at what they do, each with their own individual talents, but they cannot do the job alone. On their own, they lack direction. You will put them on your payroll here at the bar so they can keep the IRS at bay. And while they can be trusted, they are not what you would call management. They are strictly labor."

"And you want me to be the management?"

"Of course."

"Why me?" Snow asked.

"You need the help. You said so yourself. Your father proved himself to be a trustworthy associate. I'm simply keeping my end of the arrangement, as I told him I would."

Snow leaned across the bar and got right in Alberto's face. "What are we talking about here, Bert?"

Alberto looked at his watch. "I'm afraid I have another meeting to attend. One that can't be missed. Always the consequences in my line of work. I'm talking about you running your own crew, just as your father did. Quick jobs, good intelligence, and, if done properly, very little risk. There would be some travel required."

Snow was already shaking her head. "I don't want to get involved with drugs."

"This is not drugs, I assure you."

"Then what is it?"

Alberto finished his drink, then said, "This we will discuss in detail tomorrow evening at the same time, but only if you wish to proceed."

Snow thought about it for a few seconds. She looked around the bar and thought about the bills and the taxes and the payroll and the almost—but not quite yet—bad roof and said, "So I'll see you tomorrow."

Alberto gave her a tight nod and said, "Good."

She let him get almost all the way to the door before she said, "Hey, Bert?"

He turned and said, "Yes, Kelly?"

"Bring another envelope with you tomorrow, or you can forget the whole fuckin' thing."

Alberto's face lit up with a huge smile. "You see? Management. Had you not asked, I wouldn't have shown."

He closed the door softly as he left. When Snow picked up the glasses to put them in the sink behind the bar, her hands were shaking.

THAT HAD ALL BEEN FIVE YEARS AGO...THE MEETINGS AT the bar with Alberto, the envelopes, the planning, the strategizing. She asked for a month to think it over, and Alberto agreed. And she *did* think about it. She thought about it so hard it made her head hurt. She wanted the month for two reasons: One, she had just been handed a total of twenty grand, which was enough to cover the bar for thirty days...maybe forty-five if she stretched it, but she was sick of stretching it. The other reason? She didn't want to end up like her old man, locked away for doing something stupid.

But when Alberto told her what she had to do, she thought—putting morality aside for a moment—it didn't sound too difficult, and the risk was so low, especially for herself, she found it almost impossible to refuse. And, she had to admit, the whole idea of it sort of turned her crank. As for morality?

Morality could go fuck itself.

THINGS STARTED TO GO BAD AFTER THE HEIST AT THE VA clinic. They got the money from the sale of the drugs, but of the four men who made up Snow's crew—Jimmy Bray, Alex Carver, Bobby Stout, and Victor Potts—Carver was becoming a problem. Not only had he beaten the clinic worker to death during the robbery, but he was also running his mouth and flashing a little too much cash. And, he was beginning to show up late for their planning meetings.

They were sitting in Slips after hours, waiting on Carver, who was a half-hour late. Snow was behind the bar, keeping the beer flowing and trying to keep everyone else at ease, especially Alberto.

When Snow caught his eye, Alberto tipped his head away from the others...an indication he wanted a private word. She followed him to the back of the bar.

"Carver has become a liability," Alberto said. "The killing of the worker at the clinic has drawn the authorities deeper into their investigation. It is exactly the kind of attention we do not need...especially now. The Indiana jobs we have lined up were going to be our exit strategy."

Snow nodded in a noncommittal way. "I know, but the thing is Bert, the VA job was in Nevada, we're sitting here in Florida, and the cops are clueless."

"Maybe not as clueless as you'd like to believe."

"Meaning?"

"I have many sources, as you know. My friends at the treasury have connections within Homeland Security. I was informed that when our boy Carver beat this man to death, some DNA was recovered. It is only a matter of time before they match that with what they have on file in the federal prison database."

"He didn't do federal time," Snow said. "He did state time down in Louisiana. We might be okay."

Alberto bared his teeth at her, and Snow didn't like it. "We would definitely be okay if the five of you hadn't gone off the rails and taken a job I knew nothing about."

"It was quick, easy money, Bert. No different from the banks and credit unions."

Alberto still had his teeth out. "It was completely different, and you know it. We've been coasting...*coasting* along comfortably for over five years now with the intelligence I provide. When you stepped outside the lines, you put us all at risk. Do you think the authorities will stop the DNA comparison at the federal level? When that turns up dry, they'll go state to state. And they have thousands of people with computers to do that kind of work. It will take them no time at all."

"What are you suggesting?"

"Carver is out. There is no other way."

"He's not going to be very happy about that."

Alberto put his hand on Snow's shoulder. "I'll be as gentle as possible. He will see the light, I assure you."

Snow shook her head. "I don't think he'll want to give up his cut of the Indiana jobs."

"I will make arrangements to keep him quiet. This can

be done. Tell the others to pack their things, clean out their hotel rooms, and head for the condo in Indianapolis. Do it now."

Snow did as she was told, and five minutes later, Bray, Stout, and Potts were out the door. When she walked back to where Alberto had taken a seat, she said, "What about me?"

"You will leave tomorrow and meet the boys in Indiana. For now, I would like you to wait here with me. When Carver arrives, I believe he'll handle the news better if you are present."

AN HOUR LATER CARVER FINALLY WALKED THROUGH the door, a little drunk and a little high. He looked around the empty bar, then turned toward Snow. "Hey, Kelly. Where is everyone? Hell, I'm usually the last one here."

Alberto was behind the bar, washing the glasses in the sink. "Not usually, my friend. Always. It has become your habit. The others will be along shortly. Come. Sit. We have much to discuss."

Carver gave Alberto a half shrug, pulled out a bar stool, and sat down. "Think you could get me a beer and a shot, Bert?"

"Of course, my friend," Alberto said. He reached into the cooler and pulled out a bottle of beer, cracked the cap, and set it on a napkin. "Here is your beer." Then he pulled out a silenced .22 from under the counter and shot Carver twice in the chest and once in the head. As he fell backward, Alberto smiled and said, "And there is your shot."

Snow put a hand to her throat, then looked at Alberto. "Bert?"

"It had to be done. He would have taken us all down. Quickly, lock the front door. We don't want any unexpected visitors popping in right about now, do we?"

Snow looked at Carver's body for a few seconds, then said, "No, I guess we don't."

CHAPTER FOUR

S now locked the front door, then went to the supply closet to get a bottle of bleach, along with a mop and bucket. When she came out of the closet, she found Bert letting another man in through the back door. He looked as solid as a slab of granite, his face lean and angular behind a thick heavy beard. He held one shoulder slightly lower than the other, and he walked with a particular gait...throwing one hip forward before moving his leg. Snow thought it looked like a manufactured swagger of sorts. His nose was slightly crooked and bent out of shape as if he'd taken a hard hit at some point in the past. His whole presentation and appearance gave off a certain vibe, one that Snow found mildly appealing. Nevertheless, she looked at Bert and said, "Who the hell is he?"

"He will be Mr. Carver's replacement." Then, "Why are you laughing?"

Snow shook her head and pointed at the body on the floor. "Jesus, Bert, five minutes ago you popped the guy, and now you're calling him Mr. Carver?"

"Respect for the dead, dear. It is not something to be taken lightly."

"Says the guy who killed him. You still haven't answered me." She pointed at the other man. "You... what's your name?"

"Duncan. Jeff Duncan. But everyone calls me Cap."

Snow frowned. "Cap? How'd you get a nickname like that?"

He walked toward Snow and extended his hand. "You must be Kelly. It's nice to meet you. To answer your question, I served in the military. Held the rank of Captain until I got out."

Snow shook his hand, then said, "Why'd you leave?"

"I was shot in the shoulder. That's why it always looks like I'm listing to port. There's also this." He reached down and pulled his pant leg up just enough to reveal the prosthesis. "Took it right above the knee."

Snow glanced at Duncan's artificial leg, then said, "That must have been painful."

"I've been through worse."

"Your shoulder?"

Duncan looked away in thought, his eyes flat. "In a manner of speaking."

Snow wasn't quite sure what could have been worse

than losing half a leg, but the look on Duncan's face told her not to push the issue, so she left it alone.

Bert cleared his throat. "Cap has a van outside. Are there any security cameras we need to be aware of?"

Snow let out a snort. "Around here? If we did have any, they'd be the first thing someone would steal. Maybe the only thing."

"Very well," Bert said. He turned to Duncan. "Cap, you can handle the disposal?"

"Of course," Duncan said. He bent over and grabbed Carver's legs and dragged him toward the back door, leaving a reddish-brown streak on the floor trailing the body. Before he went out, he turned and caught Snow's eyes. "I look forward to working with you." Then he hauled the body outside, lifted it into the back of the van, and drove off.

Kelly Snow watched him pull away, then locked the door. When she looked at all the blood, she put her hands on her hips and shook her head. "I'll be here until morning cleaning this up." Then, with no segue whatsoever, she looked at Alberto and said, "So, I guess you're in charge of personnel now?"

"'Now' has never been part of the equation, my dear. I've always been in charge of personnel. That includes you."

"Whatever. A little heads-up would have been nice, Bert. I don't know anything about this guy."

"He seems to have caught your eye. It was written all

over your face. In any event, you know everything you need to know. He can be trusted, I assure you. He comes with the highest of recommendations. And do not worry about the floor. It will be taken care of. I'll expect to see you at the Indianapolis condo by tomorrow."

Snow tossed her hands in the air, then let them fall against her sides. "Who's going to take care of all this blood?"

"Give me your keys. I will handle it."

Snow gave him a curious look, then reached into her pocket and handed the keys to Bert. "Don't drink all the rum," she said. "I'll see you in Indy."

Bert watched her go, waited ten minutes to make sure she wasn't coming back, then took out his phone and called Duncan. "Did she see you?"

"Nope. I was parked behind the strip mall on the next block, although I have to say, it makes me a little nervous sitting here with a body in the back of the van."

"Very well. And not to worry. Bring the body back here along with the other supplies I asked for. We will take care of two problems at once." He unlocked the back door, then went behind the bar and poured himself a shot of rum while he waited.

———

DUNCAN WALKED IN THROUGH THE BACK CARRYING two five-gallon plastic gas cans. He set them on the floor, then walked over to the bar, upended a mug, and drew himself a beer from the tap. He sat down next to Alberto and said, "I've got to be honest with you, Bert. I'm a little concerned."

Alberto took a small sip of rum, then said, "About?"

"A couple of things. This crew has been together for quite a while. Do I have that right?"

"You do. What of it?"

"I'm wondering how Carver's exit and my entrance are going to be received."

"Snow will handle the boys, I assure you. With the exception of the VA heist and the trouble that has caused for us—me in particular—I've never had any reason to doubt her leadership."

"If you say so," Duncan said.

"I do. You said there were a couple of things that concerned you. What is the other?"

"When you hired me, you said that the Indiana jobs were your exit strategy."

"And they are," Alberto said. "Even if that was not the case, I'm afraid that Mr. Carver's indiscretions have made it all but impossible to continue."

"Well, Bert, that creates a little problem for me. You guys have been going at this for five years. I'm the new guy, which means your excellent intelligence aside, I don't have as much bank as everyone else."

Alberto sipped at his rum, then nodded thoughtfully. "Of this, you are correct. But I assure you, after the

Indiana jobs you will not be short on cash for a very long time. What you do after that is none of my concern. I will be sitting on a yacht in the French Riviera, a beautiful woman on my arm, a glass of wine in my hand, and not a care in the world."

Duncan laughed without humor. "Yeah, and I'll be sitting in a trailer by the river, a dog at my feet, watching a flat-screen TV. Am I getting through to you here, Bert?"

"Your point has been made, but it is futile to discuss it further. The intelligence I've gathered for the upcoming jobs is in the trunk of my car. First thing tomorrow morning it will be aboard a private jet I've chartered out of Ft. Myers." He pulled out a boarding pass for Duncan. "This will get you to Indianapolis." Then he handed him a slip of paper with the condo's address. "Your new friends will be waiting for you when you arrive. I've been told the accommodations are quite luxurious."

Duncan looked at the boarding pass and saw that it was for a coach ticket at the back of the plane. He put it in his pocket without saying anything.

"So after these jobs, I'm out," Duncan said. It wasn't a question.

"After these jobs, we are all out, my friend."

They sat quietly for a few seconds, then Duncan said, "Ask you something, Bert?"

"Of course."

"If these jobs are the last ones, why not send the intel

with Snow and head for the Riviera now? Don't you trust her to give you your cut?"

Alberto looked at nothing for a moment, then said, "Trust is such an interesting construct, is it not? It permeates our lives, sometimes open and apparent for anyone to witness, other times hidden or secreted away, revealed only when we are at our most vulnerable. Trust, I've discovered, is nothing more than the measure of who we think someone else is. Sadly, we are often mistaken."

Duncan put a whisper of sarcasm in his voice. "Geez, Bert, you should have been a poet."

Alberto laughed. "I have been many things to many people throughout my life. I do not think anyone would ever call me a poet." He tipped his head back and finished his rum. Then he held up his empty glass and said, "But I appreciate the compliment."

"You're welcome," Duncan said, "though if I'm being truthful, it was really more of an observation. Say, any chance I could catch a ride on that private plane you chartered? No disrespect, but it's better than screaming babies and emotional support animals back in coach."

"I prefer to travel alone, I'm afraid."

"Me too," Duncan said. Then he grabbed Alberto by the back of the neck and slammed his head on the bar top over and over until his face looked like a plate of Chef Boyardee Beefaroni. He let the body slide to the floor, then went through Alberto's belongings. He found a silenced .22—not Duncan's preferred weapon of choice, but he'd deal with that later—a fat roll of hundred dollar bills, his cell phone, flight itinerary, and car keys.

He dragged Carver's body back inside, dropped it like a piece of meat next to Alberto, then picked up one of the cans of gasoline and began pouring it all over the bar. When the first can was empty, he picked up the second and used half of it in the bar, then poured a trail out the back door, right up to the van. He used the remainder of the can on the inside of the van, then tossed the can into the water next to the pier.

He pulled Alberto's keys from his pocket and hit the button on the fob. He heard two quick beeps to his left, and when he turned that way, he saw the parking lights of a silver BMW flash. He ran to the car, popped the trunk, and quickly rifled through a fat expandable envelope, one that contained all the intelligence Bert had gathered for the upcoming robberies. He left everything in the trunk, slammed the lid, then got behind the wheel and pulled closer to the van and the building.

Then he took a lighter, lit the boarding pass Alberto had given him, and dropped it out the window. He was half a mile away when the marina lit up behind him, the flames licking out of the building and across the bay. The whole thing reminded him of things he didn't want to think about. He reached up and slapped the rearview mirror away, and headed toward Ft. Myers.

Coach, my ass, he thought, then laughed like a mad man, which, of course, he was.

CHAPTER FIVE

Virgil walked into the MCU facility, an old post office building just south of the city's not-so-infamous Spaghetti Bowl, a never-ending series of loops, on-ramps, and exits that had—at one point in the past—put the city's engineers to shame. The bowl had since been demolished, and the spaghetti had been rebaked into something more modern and palatable. But the name of the area remained in the minds—if not the hearts—of the city's longtime residents, and Virgil thought it always would.

As the lead detective of the MCU, Virgil ran the show. But lately, things were beginning to take on a different flavor around the shop, mainly due to Virgil's soft heart, and what felt like his never-ending presence down in Shelby County, where, together with his friend and business partner, Rick Said, he owned a sonic drilling natural gas extraction company... one that had made him wealthy. But that was only part of the story.

When Ben Holden, the sheriff of Shelby County died, Virgil and the rest of the MCU were deep in the weeds trying to root out a group of killers who were tearing the county—not to mention half the state—apart by manufacturing and selling crystal meth. Virgil took it upon himself to have one of his men, Ron Miles, fill in as acting sheriff until the case was wrapped up. All of the bad actors were either captured or killed, but in the end, Miles was gunned down and died as well.

Virgil had been heartbroken and still was, but he wasn't alone in his grief. The Shelby County Sheriff's department secretary, an older, fiery redhead named Betty, had taken the deaths of Holden and Miles just as hard, if not harder than Virgil. She resigned from the department after both men died, and moved back to Indianapolis to be closer to her children. Life was short and fragile, and no one knew that better than Betty.

Except Betty's children, it turned out, had busy lives of their own. They appreciated the fact that she wanted to be closer but they had jobs and responsibilities that took up most of their time. With no grandchildren on the horizon yet, Betty-the-mom ended up bored with nothing much to do all day and night. How many times could you go to the zoo and watch a bunch of drugged-out monkeys napping in the trees?

When she asked for her old job back, the new sheriff, Carla Martin—a former DEA agent and current girlfriend to Tom Rosencrantz, one of Virgil's detectives—told her the position had already been filled. Betty drove back to the city and decided, rather begrudgingly, to accept her new station in life. Then, one day the finger of fate reached out and something happened that no one—Virgil in particular —would have ever thought possible. Except Virgil being Virgil, should have known it would turn out the way it did.

The MCU's departmental secretary's husband got transferred to the west coast, and that left the MCU in a bit of a bind. He and Rosencrantz were talking about it one night at the bar when Rosencrantz told Virgil he'd heard that Betty was looking to get back to work.

"Oh, man, Rosie, I don't know," Virgil said. "She's sort of...uh...brassy."

Rosencrantz frowned at him. "Who isn't?"

"Lots of people," Virgil said.

"That's not what I meant," Rosencrantz said. "My point is, who doesn't have some sort of quirk, or whatever, that you have to work around? Look at Ross." Andrew Ross was the junior member of the MCU squad and Rosencrantz's partner.

"Ross? What about him? He's a great guy and a perfect cop."

Rosencrantz laughed. "I'll be sure to mention you said so." Then, before Virgil could respond, "Ross is as strong-willed, opinionated, and direct as anyone you've ever known. Tell me I'm wrong."

"I can't...mostly because it's true." Virgil took a drink of his Red Stripe, then said, "But Betty? Really?"

"Are you telling me you can't handle her?"

"Of course not."

"Then what's the harm? Give her a shot. She's been a law enforcement departmental secretary most of her adult life. Show her how the phones work and where the printer is, and she'll be off and running."

"Show her how the phones work?" Virgil said.

"Figure of speech, Jonesy."

"Let me think about it, huh?"

"You're the boss," Rosencrantz said.

"Not if I hire Betty."

BUT VIRGIL DID THINK ABOUT IT. HE THOUGHT ABOUT it until the entire MCU was in chaos, meetings were missed, and departmental reports weren't filed with the prosecutor in a timely fashion. Finally, Virgil's own boss, Cora LaRue, stepped in and put her foot down. The message was clear, as it usually was when Cora was involved. "Hire someone, or I will."

WHEN VIRGIL WALKED INTO HIS OFFICE, HIS NEW secretary gave him a head-to-toe look. "What?" he said.

Betty had her eyeglasses hanging from a chain around her neck. She reached down, perched her glasses near the tip of her nose, then said, "Do you always dress like that?"

Virgil pulled his chin into his neck, then looked down at his white T-shirt to make sure it didn't have a stain or something. "What's the matter with the way I'm dressed?"

"Well, let's see: You're wearing blue jeans, a white T-shirt, and hiking boots. As one of the top law enforcement officials in the state, I'd think you'd want to try a little harder. Ben always wore the uniform."

"Uh-huh. I'm not Ben."

Betty made a funny noise with her lips and said, rather dryly, "I'm aware. I always thought you dressed the way you did because you were trying to blend in with what I imagine you consider 'the hicks' down in Shelby County."

Virgil took a deep breath. "Betty—"

"Don't interrupt me. I'm not done. Why not take a lesson from your brother, Murton? Now there's a man who knows how to dress for work."

Virgil sucked on his cheek like he had a bad tooth.

"What's wrong? Do you need me to make you a dental appointment?"

"No, I don't need to see the dentist. My teeth are fine."

"Speaking of Murton, where is he this morning?"

Betty said. "Also, I can't find Chip. Everyone else is present and accounted for."

"Thank you, Betty. I'll color myself informed," Virgil said, not quite realizing he was beginning to sound like Ben Holden.

Betty wagged a finger at him. "Don't sass me. I didn't take it from Ben, and I'm not about to start taking it from you. I'm only doing my job. Where's your gun, by the way?"

"In my holster. Why?"

"Where's your holster?"

"I'm left-handed, so I wear it on my right hip, in the cross-draw position," Virgil said. *I'm thinking about shooting myself with it right about now. Maybe I'll take out Rosencrantz first.*

"Good. See that you keep it on you at all times."

"Betty, I know how to do my job. You don't have to tell me when and where I should carry my gun. Speaking of jobs, don't you have something better to do than pester me about my wardrobe and weapon?"

"Yes, I've got plenty to do, and if you'd leave me to it, I might actually get some work done."

"Carry on, then."

Virgil turned to walk away, but he'd only taken two steps when Betty said, "Where are you going?"

"I'm going down to the bar."

"At this hour? They have programs for people who have that sort of affliction, you know."

Virgil sighed. "Betty, I don't have an affliction. I own the bar, and I also have an office there. The phone is ringing. Maybe you should answer it."

"So now you're going to tell me how to do my job?"

"I am the boss," Virgil said. Then he hurried away like a teenaged girl who'd just seen a spider.

Betty laughed quietly and said, "We'll see about that, won't we?" Then she picked up the phone. "Major Crimes Unit. How may I direct your call?"

VIRGIL WALKED INTO THE BAR THROUGH THE KITCHEN and spent a few minutes speaking with Robert. "How's it going, Chef?"

"Everyting irie, mon. You?"

"I'm well. Came down to check on Murton." *And to get out of the office.*

"I tink he still upstairs with Becky and Chip. Delroy say they doing some kind of art project or someting like dat. You want someting to eat, you?" The kitchen was already alive and noisy, the sous chefs working hard to prepare for the upcoming lunch rush.

"No thanks. I'm still working off breakfast."

"Okay. You let me know if you change your mind, you."

"Thanks, Robert. I'll see you later."

When Virgil walked into the patron area of the bar, he

saw Delroy was busy on the phone, so he gave him a nod and headed toward the stairs. That's when he heard Delroy say, "Hold on, you."

Virgil walked behind the bar and poured himself a cup of Jamaican Blue Mountain coffee from the pot, then waited. When Delroy finished his call he looked at Virgil. "Dat da repairman about the cooler. It acting up again."

"I thought you had him replace everything."

Delroy shook his head. "Dat what I thought too, mon. But either the parts don't hold up, or da last guy didn't know how to do his job, him. Anyway, it someting about coils and cooling fans and caterpillars dat Delroy know nothing about. We need to have it looked at again."

Virgil gave Delroy a kind laugh. "I think the word you're looking for there is capacitors, not caterpillars. Anyway, you run the joint, Delroy. Do what you've got to do."

"I will, but dat not what I wanted to ask you about."

"What is it?"

"I'm worried about Murton, me. He not himself."

"He's had a few rough nights. Bad dreams and that sort of thing. Don't worry, it'll work itself out, I'm sure."

Delroy waved Virgil's words away. "I know all about da dreams, me. But I tink it deeper dan dat. I tink you do too."

"What do you mean?"

"He hasn't been da same since he kill dat rasshole who murdered all those young girls. I tink the dreams are trying to tell him someting, but Murton too stubborn to see it...or admit it."

"Murton has his own way of working through things, Delroy. He always has. He'll work his way through this as well."

"I hope you're right, you." Just then the phone rang. Delroy glanced at the caller ID and said, "It the repairman calling back. He probably want to talk about how much the caterpillars cost."

Virgil clapped him on the back and headed for the stairs, a smile on his face, full of the life energy he drew from the people around him. Then he thought of Betty. *Well, most people, anyway.*

WHEN VIRGIL WALKED INTO THE OFFICE, CHIP WAS busy packing up his gear. "Hey, guys. What's going on?"

"Becky had an idea," Murton said.

"Robert said you guys were doing some kind of art project or something," Virgil said.

Becky had her feet propped on the corner of her desk. She dropped them with a thud, then said, "I thought if Chip could put a composite together of the men in Murton's dreams, it might help him figure out who they are."

"Any luck?" Virgil said.

Murton shook his head. "Nope. I've never seen them before."

Virgil scratched at the back of his head. "Mind if I take a look?"

Murton pointed at the table in front of the sofa. "Help yourself."

Virgil walked over to the sofa, sat down, and then carefully examined the pictures. He looked at them for a long time. When he turned to Murton, he gave him a curious look and said, "You say you've never seen either of these men before except in your dreams?"

"Yeah, that's what I said...about three times now. Why are you looking at me like that? You're sort of pale. If you weren't already, I'd tell you to sit down."

"You've seen at least one of them, Murt. I guarantee it."

Murton sat down next to his brother and looked at the composites. "Which one?"

"In a minute," Virgil said. Then he turned to Lawless. "Chip, get your gear back out. I want to try something."

"Why am I not surprised?" Lawless said.

Virgil shook his head. "You've been hanging out with Ross again, haven't you?"

Lawless didn't answer and began setting the equipment back up. Murton looked at Virgil. "What's going on, Jonesy?"

"You told me you saw yourself reflected in the water.

You also said there were two people on the boat. A man and a woman."

"That's right," Murton said.

"Why didn't you do a composite of her as well?"

"I keep telling everyone—though not many people seem to be listening—that it all happened very fast. It won't do any good for me to try and come up with a likeness of the woman because I never got that good of a look. It was a glimpse, at best. I don't think I can do it."

"You're not going to do the next composite, Murt," Virgil said.

Lawless stopped mid-setup. "Who is?"

Virgil looked at the pictures on the table and said, "I am."

CHAPTER SIX

Duncan spent the night in a cheap motel near the airport, courtesy of Bert's pocket money, then went shopping for clothing that would be more suitable for private air travel. With that done, he went to the airport, parked in the long-term lot, carefully wiped down the car—couldn't really do anything about the DNA—then gathered the file folder, his gun, along with everything else he needed and nothing he didn't. Then he took the flight itinerary and looked at the name Alberto had used to charter the jet. When he saw the name, he smiled to himself. Alberto knew how to cover his tracks. He pulled out Bert's phone and called the air charter service listed on the itinerary. The woman on the other end of the line answered with a dopey, well-rehearsed greeting. "Good morning, it's a great day to fly with Global-Air by your side. How may I direct your call?"

Duncan dropped what he hoped was a little sophistication into his voice. "Good morning, this is Bernard Alexander. I have an aircraft on standby for departure to Indianapolis in less than an hour."

"Of course, Mr. Alexander. The aircraft is ready, and the flight crew is at your disposal. Is everything in order?"

"I'm afraid not. A scheduling conflict has developed on my end. I won't be going to Indianapolis myself. I'll be sending one of my associates in my place. I hope that's not a problem."

"Since you've pre-paid, it's no problem at all, sir. For security purposes, could I have the confirmation number listed on your itinerary?"

"Of course. One moment, please." Duncan made the woman wait a full minute—even though he had the itinerary right in front of him—then read the number to her.

"Thank you, Mr. Alexander. And also, for security purposes, may I have the name and general description of the associate who will be flying in your place?"

Duncan smiled to himself. "Certainly. His name is Jeff Duncan. He's a handsome fellow if I do say so myself. Big beard, walks with a bit of a limp, carries one shoulder slightly lower than the other. His nose looks like he might have been Mike Tyson's sparring partner at one point. Will that do?"

"Of course, sir. What time should we expect Mr. Duncan?"

"He should be arriving any minute now, I'm sure."

"Very well. I'd like to thank you for your business, and I hope we have the pleasure of serving you personally in the future."

Duncan hung up on her, walked over to the cab line, and climbed into the back seat of the lead taxi. The driver touched eyes with him and said, "Where to?"

"Global-Air, please."

The driver half turned in his seat. "You're joking, right buddy? That's on the other side of the airport. I can make a better fare by waiting here another five minutes."

Duncan reached into his pocket and pulled out another one of Alberto's hundreds. "Will this cover it?" He pushed the bill through the slot in the plexiglass, then tipped his head to the side.

"Buckle up," the cabbie said. "It's the law."

KELLY SNOW WAS UP EARLY, CRANKED, AND READY TO leave for the airport. The morning news was playing on the TV, nothing more than background noise to keep her mind at bay. The thoughts of going out on more jobs—the fact that they were their final ones notwithstanding—made her nervous as hell. She had her bag packed and sitting by the front door, and was about to click the television off when she saw something that didn't make any sense at all. A news reporter was standing in front of Slips, or rather, what was left of Slips—half the building had sunk into the bay water, and the roof was gone—and there was a burned-out van sitting near the pier. She turned the volume up in time to hear the reporter say, "... and because of the accelerant in the van, both the police and fire department officials are saying they are all but certain arson was the cause of the fire. As I mentioned, the bodies found by divers have yet to be recovered, and officials at the scene don't know who they are, and haven't said when they will bring them up. For now, I'm Jennifer Chase, reporting. Back to you in the studio..."

Snow clicked the TV off. She couldn't believe it. Her bar had burned and ended up in the water. She'd always thought the damned place was going to slip into the drink, but not by burning. And what had the reporter said? Arson was suspected. And bodies. Not singular. What the hell had happened after she left last night?

She tried to call Bert, but his phone went straight to voicemail. She slid her phone into her pocket, then wiped the back of her neck with her hand, her Florida haircut failing to keep the sweat at bay in the heat of the moment.

Everyone knew Slips belonged to her. If the cops thought it was arson, that gave her two choices: Delay her departure—and the Indiana jobs—and cooperate with the authorities. She didn't burn the place down, after all. The other? Say to hell with it, do the jobs, and run. It's not like she was going to go back to the joint long-term anyway. But if she ran, they would immediately consider her their primary suspect. And it wouldn't be for arson alone. It'd be for murder.

She peeked out her apartment window looking for the cops but didn't see anyone. She quickly opened her laptop, got online, and changed her departure reservation from Tampa to Ft. Myers. With that done, she typed out a quick note to her landlord—a long-time friend and part-time lover, apologizing for the way she had to leave:

Billy:

Sorry to stiff you on the rent, among other things, but I'm running. They're going to say I did this, except I didn't. I hope you believe me. You can have anything you want out of my place, plus you've got the first and last, not to mention the security deposit, so let's call it square, huh? Find a good home for Skipper if you can, or keep him yourself. He's a good cat. Maybe I'll see you around sometime.

Take care,

Kelly

She hit the Print button, waited until the note popped out, then shut down her laptop and tossed it in her bag. She gave Skipper a goodbye squeeze, filled his food and water bowls to the brim, checked the window one more time, then hurried to her car. She was five miles away and merging onto I-75 South when the first Manatee County squad car turned into the apartment's parking lot.

SHE MADE THE FT. MYERS AIRPORT WITH AN HOUR TO spare. Once she was through security—a nerve-wracking event because she was now officially on the run—she settled in at the gate and waited for the boarding process to begin. When she looked out across the airport, she saw a large private jet lifting off to somewhere. *Must be nice,* she thought. Then, when she considered the amount of money she had set aside in crypto, she tried not to smile. *That'll be me in less than a month.*

Then her thoughts turned back to the bar and the news report she'd seen. She wasn't so much concerned for her own freedom as she was puzzled by the events that had unfolded after she'd left Bert alone to clean up Carver's blood. The new guy, Duncan, had already taken the body, so who were the *bodies* the newswoman spoke of? When she tried Bert's phone again, the result was no different than before. Straight to voicemail.

When she thought about it, she neither liked nor disliked Bert. He was a proper tool for a job...a hammer to a nail. He did his part well, and she handled the rest. Had he made her wealthy as promised? Almost. But the Indiana jobs would take care of that. So, money wasn't the problem.

Then another thought occurred to her: What if one of the bodies at Skips was Bert? In fact, the more she thought about it, the more likely it seemed. He was the last one there, and Duncan was already gone with Carver's body before she'd left. Had someone else come into the bar and had some sort of altercation with Bert, leaving both him and the assailant dead? That seemed unlikely, except for the fact that Bert had never been very forthcoming about the people he worked for. In fact, over the last five years, he never mentioned anything specific about them at all, whoever they were. Was all this somehow connected to the VA heist? Bert was plenty pissed about that. Had he mentioned it to the wrong people? If he did, were they covering their own tracks? She simply didn't know.

What she did know was this: If Bert was dead, then they had no intel on their upcoming jobs, which meant they'd have to make it from here on out with the money they already had. That would have been fine with Kelly Snow because she could have fed her share of previous jobs back through Skips, fixed the joint up some more, and gone on to live a pretty easy life...the taxes notwithstanding. Except the bar was gone, she was on the run and had no idea what waited for her when she arrived in Indiana. The whole thing left her feeling alone and unwanted somehow.

And that made her think of how she'd abandoned her cat, Skipper, and that made her cry.

DUNCAN ASKED THE FLIGHT CREW TO ARRANGE FOR A
rental car—nothing too flashy—and an hour after arriving
at the Million-Air FBO at the Indianapolis International
Airport, he was at a strip mall buying a new burner phone.
Once he had it set up, he broke his old one apart and
dropped the various pieces into four separate trash recep-
tacles. With that done, he found his way to the condo and
parked at the curb no more than twenty yards from the
building's main entrance. He'd have to sit and wait for
Snow to arrive before he went up. If he walked in on the
other men without her, he'd have a hard time convincing
them who he was. Plus, they'd want to know what
happened to Carver, and that was a story best told by
Snow...certainly not himself.

So he waited.

During the wait, he realized that he'd have to come up
with some sort of story to convince Snow that he had no
idea where Bert was. He'd play deaf, dumb, and don't
know. When it came to lies, the less said the better. The
real problem was how to explain the intel he'd taken from
Bert. The more he thought about it, he decided that the
'less said' method wasn't the way to go on this one. Maybe
a grand lie was in order...something big, but not so big
that he couldn't keep track of all the details.

He spent an hour concocting a tale, and when he was
sure he had all his bases covered, he took Bert's phone
out, found Snow's number, entered it into his burner, and

gave her a call. When she answered, he said, "It's Duncan. I'm at the condo. I'm not going up until you get here."

Snow, now in a rental of her own, said, "What the fuck happened at Slips?" She hissed it at him.

"Not over the phone, for Christ's sake. I'll be waiting when you get here." Then he hung up and smiled.

It felt good to be back home in Indy. He'd make a little money, have a little fun, and maybe even visit some old acquaintances. They'd be surprised to see him.

Very surprised.

CHAPTER SEVEN

Murton looked at Virgil. "What…you're going to reach into my dreams and put together a composite of the woman on the boat, a woman I've never seen before?"

"We'll see," Virgil said.

When Lawless was ready, he took Virgil through the same sequence he'd done with Murton, the singular exception being that instead of male features, he was working with predominantly female lineaments. They took their time with it, and Virgil wouldn't let Murton watch, or say anything about his dreams, mainly because he didn't want to be influenced by a source outside his own memory. He'd either be right or wrong, but one way or another, he'd get there on his own.

He let Lawless walk him through the process, but as it was happening, Virgil let his mind wander back to the days of his youth, and how they were spent much like any other Midwestern teenager. He and Murton would attend their high school's football games on Friday nights in the fall, the autumn air cool and thick with the aroma of smoldering maple leaves, and red and white striped boxes of salted corn popped over the heat of gas-fired oil pans from the concession stand.

At halftime, the marching band would perform and the sounds of the bass and snare drums would thunder off the outbuildings and reverberate through the grandstands like gunfire from a war not yet fought by young men... many of whom were only months away from sacrificing their lives for a cause some people thought was futile and unwarrantable.

The school football team's playing abilities were mediocre at best, their opponents often leaving Virgil and Murton's team scoreless and bloodied on their own battlefield, but Virgil remembered his school's marching band as one of the best he had ever encountered. During their halftime show, they would play songs that were popular from that era, many of them sounding like big brass band renditions of old-time rock and roll.

One song in particular they always played was Billy Joel's 'Only The Good Die Young.' Not only was it a popular song at the time, but it became the team's unofficial song of defiance. Every time at the end of the game after Virgil and Murton's team had been beaten—even sometimes humiliated at the hands of their opponents—

the band would strike up their rendition of that famous tune while the people in the grandstand stood and cheered for their defeated team like they'd just won the state championship. The opponents usually left the field scratching their heads as if they were the ones who had lost the battle, and in a way, Virgil thought, they had.

Virgil's grandfather would often accompany him to the games, then end up sitting by himself as Murton and Virgil walked the grandstand area visiting with their friends and classmates. Sometimes Virgil would look back at where his grandfather was sitting, only to discover he was watching him, not the game. It was during those times that Virgil would leave Murton to his teenage conquests and go back and sit with his grandfather and enjoy the game with him, their spoken words few, but their bond as strong as ever.

One evening as they swayed in the stands along with everyone else to Billy Joel's song at the end of the game, Virgil's grandfather turned to him. "That's a great song, isn't it, Virg?"

"You bet, Gramps," Virgil said, though, thinking back, he didn't remember looking at him when he spoke.

"It's true, you know, that only the good die young. That's what makes the song so meaningful."

"Yeah, I guess so," Virgil said, and when he did, his grandfather smiled and put his arm around him. They danced their way down the stands and out to the car for the ride home without a care in the world.

One year later, on the very night Murton was ripping open sterile gauze packs and pressing them into his brother's wounds, half a world away Virgil's grandfather died in his sleep of heart failure. He was only sixty-seven years old.

For months after Virgil returned from Iraq he carried an immeasurable sense of loss and anger over the events of the war, his injuries, and the loss of his grandfather while he was away. He was mad at himself for being gone when his grandfather died, mad at Murton for the loss of the men in their unit, and in truth, mad at his grandfather for abandoning him the way he did. He was even mad that Murton had saved him.

Those were the thoughts going through his head as he robotically answered Chip's questions, and the composite of the woman eventually came together. When they were finished, Virgil barely bothered to look at the picture. He handed it to Murton. "Is this the woman in your dreams? The one on the boat?"

Murton looked at the picture for a few seconds, then closed his eyes. When he finally opened them, he looked one more time, then said, "Yeah, that's her. I'm sure of it. Who is she? And who is the man with her?"

Virgil had long ago taken every single photograph that held any meaning to him and transferred them to both his computer and phone for safekeeping. He reached for his phone and brought up the photo app, then scrolled through the pictures until he found the one he was looking for. Once he had it, he set his phone on the table next to the composites. "It's these two people."

Becky came over and sat down between Virgil and Murton. "Who are they?" she said.

When Virgil answered, his voice held a mixture of both fondness and loss. "The woman's first name was Hana. Her maiden name was Abel. Hana Abel. She was a nurse who married the love of her life, a man who still lives in my heart and always will. She liked to call him Handsome Jack, but his full name was Jack Bellows."

This time it was Murton who turned pale after hearing the name. Becky looked at her husband and said, "Murt, what is it? What's wrong?"

Murton stood up so fast he almost fell over. "I don't know. This isn't happening. This can't be right. How are they in my dreams like this?"

Becky reached out and steadied her husband by grabbing his arm. At the same time, she turned and looked at Virgil. "Jonesy, who are Jack and Hana Bellows?"

Virgil looked up at Murton without moving his head. Then he turned to Becky and said, "Jack and Hana Bellows were my maternal grandparents."

DUE TO THE PERSONAL NATURE OF THE TOPIC AT HAND, Virgil thanked Chip, then sent him back to the MCU. After he was gone, Murton looked at the picture of Jack

Bellows. When he turned to Virgil, he said, "I should have recognized him. He was part of my life almost as long as yours."

Virgil flopped down on the sofa. "He was very young in that picture. It doesn't really surprise me that you didn't know who he was." Then he let out a breath, looked at Murton and said, "You know all those conversations I've had with my dad?"

Murton let his eyes go out of focus. "Uh, yeah, I think I recall you saying something about it from time to time."

Virgil wasn't trying to be difficult...he simply wanted Murton to know the truth. "The way you feel right now about the dreams, and more specifically the people in them? That's how I feel every time I speak with my dad. It's real. I know it's real, but there is always this part of my brain that tells me the whole thing is nothing more than my imagination."

Murton waved him off. "Get out of your own head, Jonesy. The conversations with Mason are real, not imaginary. In case you've forgotten, here are two reminders for you: You've got one of them on video...the night Jonas came into your life, and Small's. The other? I've heard him myself when Becky and I were moving out of his old house...you know, the one where Sarah and Ross are living right now."

"I know, Murt. I'm not saying the conversations aren't real. I'm simply saying that sometimes it *feels* like it could easily be my own brain chemistry running off the rails."

Becky interrupted the back and forth. She picked up the other composite and said, "Okay, this whole thing is weird enough. But what I want to know is this: In Murton's dreams, who's the guy in his head flying the plane...or whose head is Murton in as he's flying the plane? Wait, wait, wait, none of that sounds right. What I'm trying to say—"

Murton put his arm around his wife. "I know what you're saying, Becks. The problem is, we simply don't know."

"So how do we find out?" Becky said.

"More dreams, I guess," Virgil said.

"Easy for you to say," Murton said. "I already feel like the guys in white suits are going to show up any minute with giant butterfly nets. If that's not clear enough for you, try this: I'm not sure how much more I can take. I'm seeing myself commit suicide every night, or at the very least I'm inside someone else's head as they do. Either way, it doesn't make for what any reasonable person would call a restful slumber."

Virgil looked at his brother. "Maybe you should go see—"

"Stop right there, Jones-man. I've already told anyone who'll listen, I am not going to see a shrink."

Virgil gave Murton a look. "Well, if you'd let me finish my thought, you'd know that wasn't what I was going to say." When Murton didn't respond, Virgil said, "I was going to suggest you go talk to Bell and see if maybe he could give you something to take the edge off. A sleeping pill, or some tranquilizers, or something. It might help."

"Pills, huh? The answer to everything...at least for some people."

Virgil was getting irritated. He pointed his finger at Murton and said, "That's a rotten thing to say, especially to me."

Virgil was right, and Murton knew it. "Aw, c'mon, Jonesy, I'm sorry. I wasn't talking about you."

"It felt like you were," Virgil said, still a little upset.

"Well, I wasn't. I'm just having trouble keeping my thoughts straight because I'm running on about three hours of sleep a night. That sort of thing might have worked for Einstein, Steve Jobs, or that Tesla guy, but it sure doesn't work for me."

"So let's go talk to Bell," Virgil said. "What's the downside?"

"Other than having yet another person in my life think I'm losing my marbles? I can't think of anything. We might as well do it."

"We'd better hurry then," Virgil said.

"Why's that?" Becky said.

"Well, when it comes to marbles, Murt really only has the one."

CHAPTER EIGHT

Duncan saw Snow park her car not far from his own, and as she started toward the building, he gave the horn a couple of quick toots. When she turned toward the sound, Duncan stuck his head out the side window and waved her over.

Snow glanced at the condo, then headed over to Duncan. Once she was in the car, she turned to him and said "Answer my question right now, Cap. What happened at Slips? The place got torched and slid into the water. The news reports are saying it was arson."

Duncan nodded with what he hoped was a look of understanding and dismay. "I heard the report myself. I couldn't believe it."

"Was that your van?" Snow said.

Duncan nodded again. "It was. I did what Bert told me to do. I got rid of Carver's body, then—"

"How?"

"How what?"

"What did you do with the body?"

"Hey, take it easy, will you? I'm as confused about this as you are. To answer your question, I stuffed Carver into an old oil drum, then drove out to that marshy area...you know, the one to the north, then rolled him into the water. The barrel went under like it was a remake of the movie Titanic."

"Then what?"

"That's where it gets weird," Duncan said.

"Weird how?"

"I was driving back to my motel room—in fact, I was almost there—when Bert called me and said he needed my help with something, but he didn't want to talk about it over the phone. I told him I'd be there as soon as possible, so I got back in the van and headed for the bar."

Snow sat and listened, thinking back to the night before. When she walked out, Bert was alone in the bar, and Duncan had already left with Carver's body, so that all made sense. What didn't add up was the fire and the two bodies. "So, what did he need?"

"I don't know. I thought he probably wanted my help cleaning up the blood."

"How does cleaning up the blood lead to a case of arson, one that destroyed my bar? And more importantly, whose bodies were inside?"

Duncan looked down at his lap for a few seconds, then

looked Snow in the eye. "Listen, I know you're not going to like it, but here's what happened: When I got back to the bar, there was another vehicle there. Some hopped up greaser-mobile. I walked inside just in time to see two guys beating the hell out of Bert...they had him tied to a chair and were saying something about drugs and their cut of the money. They had accents like Bert, but heavier. I think they were Cubans. From what they were saying, it sounded like it might have had something to do with that VA job you guys pulled on your own."

Snow gave Duncan a suspicious look. "How do you know about that?"

"Bert told me all about it when he hired me to take over for Carver."

"Whatever. Forget about all that. What happened when you saw these guys with Bert? Did you do anything?"

"Of course I did. I shot one of them on the spot. Got him right between the eyes. When his partner saw me, he shot Bert in the back of the head, then started firing at me, so I ducked out the back door. I was going to circle around to the front, but he came out blasting away with some sort of automatic weapon. I was outgunned and alone. I hid behind the dumpster, hoping to get another shot off, but I never did."

"Why not?"

"Because the whole place was already soaked with gasoline. The other guy shot my tires out, then went back inside and started torching the place. I knew Bert was dead, so I said the hell with it and took off. Lucky for me, he'd left his keys in the ignition of his car. If he hadn't, I don't think I'd be alive right now. I did everything I could to save him."

Snow tipped her head back and let it rest against the seat, her eyes closed. Everything Duncan had told her made perfect sense. Bert had been angry about the VA job—in hindsight, angrier than Kelly thought he should have been—but he'd never told her why, other than to blame everything on Carver, who was now dead. But clearly Bert answered to someone, and whoever it was didn't like getting cut out of their share of the take. That presented two very big problems in Kelly's mind. Were the people Bert reported to the same people who provided the intel for the jobs they'd been doing the last five years, and more importantly, would they be coming for the rest of the crew—and their money? She didn't know. She looked at Duncan and said, "Well, we're screwed now. Burt had the intel on the jobs...which banks and credit unions, their security procedures, and when to make our moves."

"Maybe not as screwed as you think," Duncan said.

"Meaning?"

"When I got back to the motel, I started worrying about being seen. There was a lot of gunfire at the bar, not to mention the place went up like someone dropped a match at the refinery. I thought if anyone saw me driving away in Bert's car—you know, got the plate, or whatever —the cops could have been all over me. So I did a quick search of the car, put everything in my motel room, then drove the car to one of those all-night mega stores, locked it up, and walked away."

"How does that help us?" Snow said.

"Because when I got back to my motel room, I started going through Bert's stuff." He turned and reached into the back seat, then handed Snow the folder that contained all Bert's intel for the Indiana jobs. "It's all there. Dates, times, locations, security codes, passwords, details for the supplies and equipment, the works."

Kelly Snow felt like she didn't know what was real anymore and what wasn't. Bert had been right about one thing...they had been coasting along for five years, and not one single thing had gone wrong until they pulled that VA job. Now Carver and Bert were dead, she was on the hook for arson—which she had nothing to do with—and two murders. Three if you counted the VA guy...and she knew if she was ever caught, they'd count him for sure. So, arson, and three murders. All because of a dump like Slips, and her dumb-ass of a father.

She turned to Duncan and said, "I can't decide if we should go through with these last jobs or not. What if these Cuban guys know more than we think? What if they were the ones giving Bert the intel? If that's the case, they'll be waiting for us, and it won't be with a bouquet of flowers and a greeting card that says, 'Nice work.' It'll be with automatic weapons and lots of ammo."

There are no Cubans, you stupid bitch, Duncan thought. Time to change tactics. "You might be right. In fact, the whole thing is making me rethink my part in all of this. I don't have anything to lose by walking away, other than the money we might make on these jobs...if we survive."

Despite their immediate predicament, Snow actually laughed. "I guess I couldn't blame you. But where would you go, and what would you do?"

Duncan shook his head. "I don't know. I was counting on this gig to get me by for a couple of years. Something usually turns up, given the type of people I run with."

Snow looked out the window and watched the pedestrians walking by...moms with strollers, businessmen and their briefcases, delivery drivers dropping off packages, and as she did that, she thought about one thing: The money. She needed more. Even if she went deep into the heart of Mexico and disappeared—a gringo nobody living a relatively comfortable life—the money wouldn't last more than ten years. No, she needed these jobs, and if that was the case, she needed Duncan.

"What are you thinking?"

Snow brought her attention back inside the car. "I'm thinking it's worth the risk. I'm not sure how the others will feel."

Duncan was about to take a big risk, but he knew it

couldn't be avoided if they were going to move forward. "Who says we have to tell them the truth?"

Snow gave him a look, and for a split second, he thought he'd made a mistake. Then the look turned into a smile, and he knew he'd hit the mark.

"You're right. We don't actually have to say anything. We'll give them enough of the truth that they won't have any choice but to believe us. Then we'll tell them that we're handling Indiana on our own."

"Think they'll go along with that?"

"Why wouldn't they? We went out on our own with the VA job and nobody had any problem with that. Except for Bert...and Carver, of course, but that was after the fact."

Duncan shrugged. "Works for me. Listen, speaking of Carver—and I know you've got no reason to believe me, but I'm going to go ahead and say it anyway—Bert promised me that I'd get half of his previous take over the last five years, given that I'm coming into this whole thing blind and broke."

"Did he?"

Duncan wasn't sure if he'd heard the skepticism in her voice or not, but he played it as if he had. "I know, I know, it all sounds like bullshit. In fact, if I was in your shoes, I'd think the same thing if anyone tried to tell that to me. But that was the deal we made." Then he waved his hands like he was trying to erase his words from the air. "I wanted you to know, is all. I guess it doesn't matter because Bert is dead, so I don't know how I'd get the money anyway."

Snow couldn't quite understand the feelings of attraction she had for Duncan. There was something about him that made her want to please him, though she didn't know why. When she spoke, she didn't think...she simply said it. "I know how to get Carver's money."

Duncan slowly turned his head and looked at her. "You do?"

"Yeah. Why do you think I was keeping Skips going? We laundered all the money through there, all the boys were on the payroll, and I handled the transfers to the offshore accounts. You haven't met any of the other guys yet, but they're not the brightest bulbs in the chandelier. Don't get me wrong, they're good at what they do, but converting cash into crypto, then transferring it offshore isn't as easy as it sounds. I have access to Carver's account and everyone else's too. Other than their regular salaries from the bar, no one gets a dime until all the jobs are finished."

Now that's interesting, Duncan thought. "Well, whatever you can arrange on my behalf, I'd be grateful. I'm not even going to ask how much."

Snow was surprised. "Why not?"

Duncan brushed the fingertips of his right hand across the back of Snow's neck, then quickly pulled his hand away as if he was embarrassed. "Because I trust you. I could tell from the moment I met you we were going to be good together."

Snow tried to give him one of her hard-edged stares but failed. His fingers on the back of her neck had given her a little thrum, and she liked it. And, she had to agree because she'd thought the very same thing. They would be good together. The failed, hard-edged stare turned itself into a lopsided smile. The smile turned into a seductive look, and when Duncan saw that, he leaned over and kissed her, gently at first, then harder, his tongue exploring the slight gap between her two front teeth.

When he pulled away, Snow looked at him and said, "Let's get our story straight, then go up and meet the boys. Maybe later we can get some time to ourselves."

"Works for me," Duncan said.

CHAPTER NINE

Virgil gave Bell a quick call to see if he was home—
he was—so he and Murton headed that way. As
they drove, Virgil asked Murton if he ever spent much
time thinking about Grandpa Jack.

"Yeah, some, I guess. I always knew he was closer to
you than me, so maybe not as much time as you do. That
might be why I didn't recognize him in the composite. He
was so young."

"He was young." Then Virgil let out a little laugh.
"Hell, we all were at one point. Not so much anymore. In
that photo...the one on my phone...I think that was taken
right after they were married." Then, "Why did you say he
was closer to me? I don't remember it that way."

Murton shrugged. "I don't know. It's simply my recol-
lection of it. You were his blood. I wasn't."

"That's true, but I can tell you this, Murt: That man

loved you every bit as much as he did me. Just like Mom and Dad."

"Yeah, I guess you're probably right. It's weird, though. When you're a kid, you don't think much about those kinds of things, and if you do when you're an adult, your perspective is usually a little different."

They rode in silence for a while, Virgil's thoughts turning to Jonas, his own adopted son, hoping that his oldest boy never felt less loved than Wyatt.

Murton turned to Virgil and said, "Where you at, Jonesy?"

"I was thinking about the similarities between you and Jonas...the way you came into our lives so long ago, and then the way Jonas did. Even though the circumstances were different, in many ways they're the same." When Murton didn't respond, Virgil said, "I was also thinking about Gramps...how much I miss him, and how mad I was that he died while we were off fighting the war." Virgil shook his head. "We didn't even get to go to his funeral."

Murton gave his brother a pat on the shoulder. "I don't think he minded."

"I guess not. But I did. It feels like I never got to say goodbye. This is going to sound selfish—maybe even disrespectful to my dad—"

"You don't even have to say it, Jonesy, because I know what you're thinking. You'd like to visit with him the same way you do with Mason."

"Yeah, I sure would."

"I don't think it's disrespectful or selfish. It's simply a human desire."

"Did I ever tell you that the first time I saw Dad, I asked him to say hello to Gramps for me?"

"I don't know. I don't think so," Murton said.

"When I asked, he told me that Gramps spends most of his time with me. He also told me he hears me...that they all do...Mom, and everyone else."

Murton pushed his lower lip out slightly. "I can believe that. I mean, you've got to believe in something, right?"

"Yeah. And I know it's easier for me, given the fact that I'm able to speak with Dad sometimes, but what scares me isn't the fact that I can. It's what if the whole thing ends? I think about that more than anything."

"How many times are we going to have this conversation, Virgil? Count your blessings. He's still in your life, and that means you can't go around all the time worrying that one day he might not be."

"Easier said than done. You want to know something?"

"Sure," Murton said.

Virgil took his hand off the steering wheel and raised a finger to make his point. "I've never once dreamed about Gramps...not one single time since he died. I've dreamed about you, Sandy and the kids, Mom and Dad, Becky—"

Murton raised his eyebrows. "Tell me about the ones with Becky."

"I better not," Virgil said with an evil grin. "Sometimes they can be a little erotic. Hey, who are you calling?"

Murton looked at his brother. "Who else? Small. Someone has to get her up to speed on the fact that you're having erotic dreams about my—" Then he interrupted himself and said into the phone. "Hey, it's Murton. How's it going? Yeah? Well, that's good. Listen, the reason I'm calling is a little odd, but did you know that Virgil sometimes has these erotic dreams about you..."

Virgil grabbed the phone from his brother. "Hi, babydoll. Murt is just fooling around again. We didn't mean to bother you."

"Why are you calling me babydoll? Don't the two of you ever work?"

Even though he was driving, Virgil closed his eyes for a second. "Sorry, Betty. I thought Murton was calling someone else. I didn't know it was you."

"Uh-huh," Betty said. "He must have misdialed."

"I doubt it."

Betty hung up on him without saying anything else. When Virgil gave the phone back, Murton was laughing so hard he had tears running down his cheeks.

"You called her babydoll. Let's hope she doesn't file a complaint with HR. I don't think you're allowed to address someone who works for you in that manner. They have rules about those types of things."

Virgil stared straight out the front window, then shot Murton the bone without looking at him. Then a few seconds later he was laughing almost as hard as his brother.

BELL ANSWERED HIS FRONT DOOR WITH A SMILE, ONE that held both pleasure and a hint of concern. "Hello, Jonesy. Murt. C'mon inside." Once they were settled in Bell's office at the back of his house, he said, "What's going on? Is everyone okay?"

Virgil touched eyes with Bell and said, "Mostly." Then without moving his head, he let his eyes slide over to Murton.

Bell looked at Murton for a moment, and when no one said anything, Virgil cleared his throat and nudged his brother in the arm with his elbow.

Bell looked at Murton. "You know how this works, right? I'm a doctor, not a mind reader. If you have a problem that I can help you with, you first have to tell me what it is."

Murton shook his head. "This was a dumb idea. Let's get out of here."

"He can't sleep," Virgil said.

Bell looked at Murton. "You do look a little worn down. What's been going on lately?"

Murton took a deep breath, then said, "I've been having this recurring dream. It wakes me every night, and then I can't get back to sleep. Jonesy thought maybe you could set me up with some sleeping pills or something."

Bell nodded, then said, "I could give you some

sleeping pills, but they won't do anything about the dreams. In fact, they may make them more vivid."

"Maybe that's not a bad thing," Virgil said. "The vividness. It might help clarify things."

"Yeah, that's what I need," Murton said. "More clarity as I watch myself...or whoever's head I'm in commit murder and suicide all at the same time."

Bell removed his round John Lennon glasses and wiped them with his shirttail, then perched them back on his nose. "That sounds like quite the dream. Want to tell me about it?"

Murton said he did, then spent the next five minutes or so telling Bell everything he remembered. When he was finished, Bell looked at him and said, "Anything else?"

"I've hit the highlights, that's for sure."

"I have a suggestion, if you're willing to entertain it," Bell said.

"What's that?"

"Have you ever been hypnotized?"

Murton laughed. "C'mon, Bell, that's a bunch of hocus-pocus. What are you going to do, sit there and swing your pocket watch back and forth until I turn robotic? Forget it." Then he jerked his thumb at Virgil and said, "Plus, I don't want to end up walking around clucking like a chicken or something because this one here wanted to have a little fun."

"Well, it's a little more sophisticated than that these days," Bell said. "And it may give you a deeper insight into what the meaning behind the dreams are all about. It's really nothing more than an altered state of consciousness—one that you are in control of, by the way—that helps you recall certain details. And it does work. People have used it for years to help them with all sorts of maladies, from smoking cessation to the treatment of pain."

"I don't know, Bell. How about we just try the pills, huh?"

"Listen, Murton, I will write you a script for some sleeping pills. But I want you to try this. You're already here. What have you got to lose?"

Murton looked at Virgil and dropped some sarcasm in his voice. "My marble. According to Jonesy, I only have one."

Bell laughed kindly. "Don't worry, Murt. The process is simple, easy, and most people actually describe it as a pleasant experience."

"And you've done this before?" Murton said.

Bell bobbed his head around a bit, then said, "Well, I took some classes not long ago."

"Bell..."

"Relax, Murt. I'm only messing with you. I'm certified in hypnotic therapy by the American Psychological Association."

Murton tossed his hands in the air, then let them fall onto his lap. "Okay, what the hell. Let's give it a try. But I want the sleeping meds too."

"Don't worry," Bell said. "I'll get you what you need." Then to Virgil: "Jonesy, if you'd step out?"

Virgil pulled his chin in. "What? Why? I was hoping to watch."

"There's water and fresh juice in the fridge. Help yourself. We'll be about half an hour or so. Maybe forty-five minutes."

Virgil stood and moved to the door, a little disappointed. "Make him bark like a dog. Use a code word...you know, Huckleberry, or something like that."

ONCE VIRGIL WAS GONE, MURTON LOOKED AT BELL. "How does this work?"

"I'll tell you in a moment. First, I want you to sit up straight, put both feet flat on the floor, and rest your hands on your legs with your palms up, and close your eyes."

Murton did as he was told, and once he was in position, Bell, using a calm and ever-softer voice as he spoke, said, "To answer your question, basically, we're going to have a conversation, just like we are now. You'll be in a relaxed state, and I'll ask you some questions about your dream."

"What about what Jonesy said? Can you make me bark like a dog or any of that nonsense?"

Bell remained calm. "No, certainly not. This isn't

stagecraft. Contrary to some depictions of hypnosis in movies or television, people who are hypnotized do not lose control over their own behavior. Plus, you'll remain aware of who you are, where you are, and everything that transpired during our session."

Murton nodded. "Okay, let's get started."

Bell softened his voice even more and said, "We already have. You're safe, you're in control, and you've just realized you're flying the plane. You're upside down, and you see the people in the boat..."

———

THE SESSION WENT FASTER THAN VIRGIL THOUGHT IT would. When Bell opened the office door and came out with Murton, he said, "I'm going to give you ten days worth of sleeping pills to start. Since you've never had any trouble with sleep in the past, I don't want to mess with your brain chemistry any more than I have to. Agreed?"

"Yeah, Bell," Murton said. "That's fine. I appreciate it."

"How did it go?" Virgil said. "Any new insights?"

"I'm afraid not," Bell said.

Virgil looked at Murton, who simply shrugged. "It was worth a shot. I gotta tell you, even though we didn't discover anything new about the dreams, I do feel more relaxed."

Virgil looked at Bell. "So he was never really hypnotized?"

"I wouldn't say that. Not exactly. People differ in the degree to which they respond to hypnosis, and that includes Murton."

Virgil thought about that for a second, then looked at his brother and said, *"Huckleberry!"*

Murton put his arm around his brother's shoulders. "How many times are we going to go over this? Leave the jokes to the professionals, will you?"

Bell showed them to the door, then told Murton to let him know if the pills helped or not. "If they don't, there are a few different brands we can try. They each have their own unique way of helping the brain unwind, so to speak."

"Will do, Bell," Murton said. "Thanks again."

VIRGIL DROPPED MURTON BACK AT THE BAR, THEN TOLD him he was heading home for the day. "Little early for quitting time, isn't it?" Murton said.

"Maybe, but we really don't have much going on right now. I thought I'd spend some quality time with the boys."

"Afraid of Betty, huh?"

"No, I am not afraid of Betty. I just told you I feel like spending some time with the kids."

Murton raised his hands. "Hey, sell it to yourself anyway you have to."

"I'm not selling myself anything."

"Uh-huh. Whatever, I sort of like her. She starts to grow on you after a while."

"Right. Kind of like an ingrown toenail," Virgil said. "Get some sleep, brother. I'll catch you tomorrow."

CHAPTER TEN

At the same time Virgil and Murton were leaving Bell's place, Snow was introducing Duncan to the rest of the crew—Jimmy Bray, Bobby Stout, and Victor Potts.

"Where's Carver?" Stout said. He was lying on the sofa in a semi-reclined position, wearing nothing except a pair of loose-fitting boxer shorts. He scratched his left nut, and Snow gave him a look.

"Go put some clothes on, Stout," Snow said. "Where are the rest of the boys?"

Stout gave himself one more good scratch, then stood from the sofa. "Jimmy and Vic are in the other room playing some sort of online video game. I don't know where Carver is. No one has seen him." Then he gave Duncan a once-over and said, "Who's he?"

"We'll get to that in a minute," Snow said. "Get

dressed and get the others in here. We've got some things to talk about."

Stout scowled at her and said, "You're not answering my question. Did Carver show at the bar, or not?" Then he pointed at Duncan. "And who the hell is this goon?"

Duncan kept his cool, but it didn't stop him from taking a step forward. He got right in Stout's face, his voice calm, his arms hanging loose by his sides. "Do what the lady says, and do it now, or you'll find out exactly who I am."

Stout curled his lip, but decided it might be better to lose the battle rather than the entire war. "Whatever you say, chief." Then he turned and walked away.

Snow pulled Duncan aside and whispered in his ear. "Stout isn't someone you want to mess with. He doesn't trust anyone, and he's got a temper. Take it easy on him, will you?"

"We've got a story to tell, Kelly, and these guys have got to buy into every word of it. You said they have all done time. That means they know about respect. I can't come across as some sort of prison-yard bitch."

"I'm not asking you to be a wallflower. I'm simply saying let's not cause any trouble when it's not necessary. We're going to have a hard enough time getting these guys to accept you as Carver's replacement."

Duncan held his hands up in a peaceful gesture. "Okay, okay, I get it."

"And remember who runs the show around here," Snow said. "In case you've already forgotten, it's me."

Not for long, Duncan thought.

"What was that?"

"I said, you're not wrong." Then he put his hand on the back of her neck, pulled her close, and gave her a quick kiss. "C'mon, relax. It'll all work out. The varsity team has arrived."

Despite herself and the mess she was wrapped up in, Snow gave him a lopsided grin. "I hope you're right."

———

ONCE STOUT WAS DRESSED AND THE OTHER MEN WERE present, Snow told them the version of events she and Duncan had worked through earlier. "Has anyone been reading the news out of Florida?"

The three men all looked at each other, then back at Snow. "Not me," Potts said. "It's the same thing every damned day."

"Vic's right," Bray said. "It's pure disaster porn, with a little bit of weather thrown in every five minutes."

Stout laughed, a mean guttural grunt, then said, "And don't forget the uplifting story they always toss in for the last segment of the broadcast. If disaster porn is the theme, that's the media's version of a happy ending." The three men laughed, then Stout turned his attention to Snow. "How about it on the answers, sugar tits?"

"Call me that again and the only answer you'll get will come from the surgeon after he tries to reattach your arms."

"Think you can take me, huh, Snow?"

"I'll give it a go," Duncan said.

Stout was short, muscular, and solid, with a crew cut that made him look like he was part of the Arian Brotherhood. But when he turned his attention to Duncan and saw the look on his face, he knew he was serious. "Okay, Jesus. I was only kidding around." Then to Snow. "I meant it as a compliment."

Snow wasn't playing. "Fuck you. If you meant that as a compliment, it's no wonder you have to sit around and scratch your own nuts. Work on your game a little, and maybe someone would do it for you."

Potts decided to take the lead. He stood from his chair, walked over to Duncan, stuck out his hand to shake. "The bald guy is Jimmy Bray. I get the feeling you've already met Stout, our resident bully. I'm Victor Potts. Call me Vic."

Duncan shook his hand, then said, "Jeff Duncan. Most people call me Cap. You can call me anything you like... except sugar tits." That took the tension out of the room, and they all sat down and let Snow tell them her version of what happened.

"Since no one has been staying up on current events, let me fill you in. We had some trouble down at Slips after you guys left."

"What kind of trouble?" Bray said.

Snow shook her head. "The worst kind. And it all comes back to that VA job we pulled."

"Is Bert still whining about that?" Stout said.

"Not anymore," Duncan said.

"What's that supposed to mean?"

"It means Bert is dead," Snow said. "And so is Carver."

The three men took the news in silence, letting Snow's words worm their way into their collective brains. Finally, Potts looked up and said, "How did it go down?"

Snow shook her head and ran her fingers through her hair. "I'm not sure. It was about half an hour after you guys left Slips. Bert and I were waiting for Carver at the bar when a couple of Cuban guys came in like they held the mortgage on the joint."

"Cubans?" Stout said. The doubt in his voice was unmistakable.

"I'm pretty sure. They had the look. One of them spoke briefly with Bert, and the accent was the same as his, only heavier."

"What did he say?" Bray asked.

"I don't know. I couldn't hear much because I was at the other end of the bar. Then out of nowhere, one of the Cubans pulled a gun and blew the back of Bert's head off. When he turned the gun on me I got lucky, because that's when Carver walked through the door. He shot the guy who killed Bert, but the other guy pulled his gun and took Carver out. I ran for the door and barely got out alive."

"So you got lucky, but Bert and Carver didn't," Stout said.

"Yeah, I just said that. Thanks for the recap, Stout."

Potts was on his phone, looking at the news out of Florida. "They're reporting that Slips burned and slid into the water. The investigators are saying arson, and it looks like you're suspect numero uno."

"I'm aware," Snow said. "I got out of town before the cops showed up."

"And how does Mr. Duncan here fit into all of this?" Potts said.

"We're old friends," Snow said. "We've had a little thing going for the last five years or so. Sort of on and off, if you know what I mean."

Duncan snorted. "Yeah, more off than on, if you ask me."

"How is it that we've never heard of this relationship before?" Stout said.

Snow pointed a finger at him. "Because it's none of your business, you nut-scratching baboon."

Stout didn't care for the insult and started to stand. Duncan looked at him, and simply said, "Sit."

Stout sat, even though he didn't like it. He also didn't want to let it go. "What's your background, tough guy?"

"Heavy equipment, demolitions, and acquisitions."

"That's why I brought him in on this. With Carver gone, we're one man short, and we're going to need someone to drive the truck."

"How do we know he can be trusted?" Stout said.

"Because I trust him," Snow said. "And as the leader of this group, what I say goes. If any of you don't like it, I'll cash you out right now and you can be on your way." Nobody said anything for a few moments, then Bray looked at Snow, his face a question.

"What?" Snow said.

"Well, I was wondering...since Carver's dead, who's going to get his main cut when it's time to walk away?"

"We're going to split it five ways," Snow said. "That's the fair thing to do."

"Fair my ass," Stout said. "It should be a four-way split. Your on and off boyfriend here hasn't been risking his ass for five years with the rest of us. Why does he get a cut of Carver's take?"

"Two reasons," Snow said. "The most important being this: Because I said so. The other reason is we can't go forward with these last few jobs without him."

"Don't see how we can go forward anyway," Potts said. "Bert handled the intel. If he's dead, we've got nothing."

"That's not true, Vic," Snow said. "Bert and I were going over the intel right before the Cubans showed up. When the shooting started, I grabbed the files before I ran out the door."

"Why didn't the other Cuban come after you?" Stout said.

"Use your head, will you?" Snow said. "These guys had a job to do, and by my account they did it. Bert is dead because of our screw-up at the VA, and their job was to take him out and cover their tracks. Why do you think Slips got torched? The last Cuban guy didn't have to chase me all over the parking lot. All he had to do was burn the bar. When he did, it covered his ass—whoever he is—and put mine in the frying pan. I'm wanted for arson and three murders, none of which I did."

"So now what?" Bray said. "These Cubans can't possibly know where we are, can they?"

"I don't see how," Snow said. "Bert never once told me where he got his intel, and I never asked. But I'll tell you this: I don't think it was the Cubans. I think that was something else, something that didn't have anything to do with us. Why else would he be so upset about that VA job? He wanted a cut and never got one. I'm pretty sure it must have had something to do with an old debt he was still paying. "

"Why?" Stout said.

"Because my father used to run some coke through Slips back in the day. Bert was his main contact. When he approached me five years ago, he said he was out of the drug game."

"So he got out of drugs but still had some old debt to work off?" Bray said.

"I think that's the most likely scenario," Snow said.

"If Bert is dead, that breaks the link between him and us," Duncan said. "I don't think we're going to have to worry about any Cubans up here in the Midwest." He looked at Snow and said, "We're already getting short on time. The first job is tomorrow. You said Bert had everything lined up...the truck, the car, and the guns?"

"Yeah, I've got the intel in my bag. Everything is ready and waiting." She turned to Stout, Bray, and Potts. "The three of you wait here. Duncan and I will go get the vehicles and weapons. Tomorrow we start. By the end of the week, we'll be done and gone."

CHAPTER ELEVEN

When Virgil got home it was just past noon, the day was mild, and he thought about wetting a line and entertaining the fish for a while. Then his stomach rumbled at him, so he made a quick detour into the house and started poking around inside the fridge, looking for something to eat.

He had his head inside the door, trying to see what was at the back, when Huma Moon—Virgil and Sandy's live-in housekeeper and nanny to the boys—came around the corner and said, "I can make you a sandwich or something if you're hungry."

Virgil was so deep in the refrigerator he never heard her coming. At the sound of her voice, he jumped and knocked his head on the top shelf. "Jesus, Huma, you scared the hell out of me."

She smiled, then said, "I thought cops had some sort of super situational awareness or something."

Virgil rubbed the top of his head. "Usually we do, although we try to turn it off at home. How are you?"

"I'm well, Jonesy. I'm sort of surprised to see you here so early."

Virgil shrugged. "Slow day."

Huma's hair was shock-white, and she wore it in dreads. She tucked one of the dreads behind her ear, then said, "Hiding from Betty again, huh?"

Virgil put his hands on his hips, then immediately let them fall to his sides, mostly because he thought it made him look defensive...not to mention a little feminine. "I am not hiding from Betty. She's only been on the job for a month. I'm sure it will all work out. I haven't quite figured out how to mesh my management style with her, uh, unique personality."

"And you're planning on doing that from home?"

Virgil didn't want to talk about it, so he changed the subject. "I was going to do a little fishing. Where's Wyatt? I thought he'd like to join me."

"He just went down for his afternoon nap. He should be up in a couple of hours."

"In a couple of hours I'll be ready for my own afternoon nap. What about Jonas?"

"Still in school."

"I see. How are the girls?" Huma and Delroy had a baby girl named Aayla, and together they all lived in a separate wing of the house, one Virgil had built to keep Huma and Delroy close. Sarah Palmer, Ross's girlfriend also had a baby girl, Olivia, who everyone called Liv. Sarah worked with Huma at the house, an arrangement put in place after Sarah's former boyfriend had been beaten to death by Huma's ex-husband during one of Virgil's previous cases.

"The girls are fine, but I'm afraid they're napping as well. Boy, you are desperate for a fishing partner, aren't you? "

Virgil laughed. "No, not really. Just asking." Then, "What is it? Why are you looking at me like that?"

"Can we sit for a minute?"

"Sure," Virgil said.

They both took a seat at the kitchen table, and as was his habit, Virgil didn't speak. He simply waited. Finally, Huma looked him in the eye and said, "I've got some bad news."

Virgil put his face in his hands and spoke through his fingers. "Huma, please don't say it. Don't tell me you're leaving us. The boys would be devastated, and without you, this place would fall apart. We need you more than you could possibly imagine."

Huma reached out and pulled Virgil's hands from his face. "Jonesy, the way I came to be here was a combination of fate and planning. But no matter, I'm here, and I'll always be here until the boys are grown and gone...or as long as you'll have me."

Virgil was instantly relieved. "Thank God. I don't know why, but I was certain you were going to tell me that you're leaving us." Then, "So, uh, not to sound too happy about it, but since you're not leaving, what's the bad news?"

Virgil saw Huma glance behind him, but she didn't say anything. That's when Sarah came into the kitchen and put her hand on Virgil's shoulder. "Huma isn't leaving, Jonesy," she said. "I am."

———

HUMA EXCUSED HERSELF TO CHECK ON THE KIDS, AND to give Virgil and Sarah some privacy. They looked at each other for a few seconds without speaking, then Sarah let a sad smile form on her face. "I couldn't help but overhear that you were looking for someone to go fishing with. Will I do?"

Virgil had a lot of women in his life, and he loved them all dearly—Betty notwithstanding. Every single one of them had touched his heart in one way or another, and the beautiful young woman standing next to the table was like a daughter to him. When Sarah had lost her former boyfriend, Gary, Virgil had been there for her virtually every step of the way as she walked herself out of grief's relentless hold, ultimately ending up with Ross and a life she thought she'd never have.

"I didn't know you liked to fish," Virgil said.

"I don't. But I know you do."

Virgil grinned at her. "And that is why I love you, Sarah. It's why we all love you. Your heart is always in the right place...always looking out for everyone else."

"I love you too, Jonesy. I love everyone in this family. So, are you going to get the poles out, or do I have to do it for you?"

Virgil stood and gave Sarah a hug. "See you down at the pond."

VIRGIL WENT TO THE SHED, GRABBED HIS grandfather's cane pole, along with a more modern rod and reel, then pulled a small container of earthworms from the fridge. He set up a couple of chairs, baited the hooks, and had everything ready by the time Sarah came outside. He held the two poles—one in each hand—and said, "Do you want modern or old-fashioned?"

Sarah looked at the poles. "Isn't that your grandfather's cane pole? The one you always use?"

"That's right," Virgil said. "I had it repaired after a mishap a few years ago."

"Then I'll take the other."

"Know how to use it?"

"Jonesy, if I had to rely on my fishing skills to eat, the fish would die of boredom, and I'd die of starvation."

Virgil laughed, then said, "Okay, I'll get you started."

He cast into the pond, then handed her the pole. "If you feel it wiggle, give it a jerk and start reeling."

Sarah took the pole, but Virgil could tell her heart wasn't in it. Virgil threw his own line out, then they both sat down. As he'd done with Huma, he simply waited for Sarah to speak.

"When Gary died, I thought my life was over. The grief was so bad I couldn't see two feet in front of my own face. In fact, bad isn't even the right word. It was horrific. The entire ordeal was; Gary's murder, the cops beating me up, Hunter Moon running around like a madman, all of it. But through it all, you and Sandy were there for me and Liv. You took us in, gave me a place to live, a job working alongside Huma, and because of all that, I ended up meeting Ross. As tragic as everything was—and God forgive me for saying this—I can't believe how well my life has turned out and how happy I am."

"Look, Sarah, I'm not much on God…meaning I don't pretend to know what's what, but I do believe in *something*." Virgil glanced at his father's cross and said, "How could I not? But I'll tell you this: You don't need anyone's permission or forgiveness to be happy. Not God's, and if you'll pardon me for saying so, not Gary's either."

Sarah nodded. "I know, Jonesy. I know. But I meant what I said in the house. I love you and Sandy for everything you've done for me, but I can't do it any longer."

"Why not?"

Sarah let her head tip to the side. "Because I'm not selfish, that's why."

"I'm not sure I understand."

"How could you not?" Sarah said. "I've been taking advantage of you guys for far too long now. I show up here five days a week and I really don't do anything except help Huma, who, by the way, in case you haven't noticed, doesn't need it. Jonas is in school, and Wyatt is going to start kindergarten next year. If I stay, you'll basically be paying me a ridiculous salary to take care of my own child in your home. I can't do that to the people who brought me back from a place I thought I'd never escape."

"You brought yourself back, Sarah. Did we help? Yes. But you had to do the work. And, I pay you a ridiculous salary because you're worth every penny."

"You pay me what you do because you're a good and kindhearted man. I've abused your generosity, and that's not the way I was raised."

"Sarah, you are not abusing anything. You're here because we want you here."

"And that's the problem, isn't it? You want me here, but you don't need me, and we both know it. No wait, let me finish, please. If you had a waitress down at the bar who didn't really do anything except walk around and play with the napkin holders, you'd dump her, wouldn't you?"

Virgil smiled. "Well, I wouldn't, but Delroy probably would."

"I'm being serious, Jonesy."

"So am I. But don't do anything right away, okay? Take a little time and think about it."

Sarah shook her head. "I have thought about it. My mind is made up. I can't do this to you guys any longer. It's probably a lousy way to say thank you for everything you've ever done for me, but consider this conversation my two-week notice."

———

SARAH WIPED THE TEARS FROM HER CHEEKS, SET HER pole down in the grass, and walked away. Virgil turned and watched her all the way to the house, her red ponytail swishing back and forth as she climbed the steps to the back deck before disappearing inside.

"I thought you would have seen this coming," Mason said.

Virgil jumped at the sound of his father's voice. When he turned toward the cross, he saw Mason standing there —shirtless as always—the scar where the bullet had entered his chest still pink and fresh. He had a bar towel thrown over his shoulder, and a fishing pole in one hand. When Virgil glanced down at the ground where Sarah had set her pole, he discovered it wasn't there. He looked at his father and said, "Is it necessary to always sneak up on me like that?"

Mason laughed, and the sound made Virgil's heart ache. "No, it's not necessary, but a guy's gotta get his fun where he can. Like Murton. That stunt he pulled on you with Betty? It was a thing of beauty."

"Yeah, it was so funny I almost wet myself," Virgil said. "How are you, Dad?"

"I'm well, Son. But I am concerned about something."

"Yeah, so am I. I'm not sure what to do, Dad."

"You hired her, not me," Mason said.

"I hired her because it was the right thing...not only for her, but for me too. She was grieving, out of work, and she needed someone who could help her get her life back on track."

Mason cast into the pond—a beautiful, sidearm swing —and the bobber settled on the surface water as gently as a fallen feather. Then he looked at Virgil and said, "As usual, we're reading the same book, but I think we might be on different pages."

"What do you mean?"

"I wasn't speaking of Sarah, Son. I was referring to Betty."

"Why does everyone want to keep talking about Betty?"

"I don't think anyone is talking about Betty. The word I used was referring. As in, I was referring to the situation you find yourself in as it relates to your current staffing headaches."

Virgil set his pole down in the grass next to his chair. He shook his head and let out a little chuckle. "Almost everything I just said applies to her too, doesn't it? She was grieving, needed a job, and a little help getting her life back together."

"That's true," Mason said. "The upshot is this: You jumped the gun."

"In what way?"

"Isn't it obvious?" Mason said. "If you'd have waited a little longer, you could have hired Sarah as the departmental secretary instead of Betty."

Virgil rubbed his face with his hand, the realization of what his father said landing on him like a wet blanket. "Waiting, huh? This from the guy who's always saying that time isn't real."

"It's all about perspective, Son. Maybe you should think about getting some."

"Look, Dad, you're right about Sarah. With her prior job history, she'd be a perfect fit for the MCU. But what's done is done. No matter how I feel, I can't fire Betty so I can hire Sarah."

"Who says you have to fire her? It certainly wasn't me. Work the situation, Virg. You're very good at making things happen. The solution is practically staring you in the face. All you have to do is put the pieces together."

Virgil knew he wouldn't get anywhere regarding Betty or Sarah by speaking with his father, so he changed the subject. "You said you were concerned about something, and I'm pretty sure it isn't my staffing problems at work... or home, for that matter. So, what is it?"

Mason reeled his line in, then leaned the pole against

the cross. "The fish aren't biting today. It's almost like they don't want to take the bait, if you catch my meaning."

"I do. And I'm all ears. How about you come out with it already?"

"Murton is in trouble, Virg. He's having these dreams for a reason. If the two of you don't figure out why, he's going to come to no good end."

"What? How is that possible? They're only dreams."

"And I'm just in your imagination, right?"

"Of course not," Virgil said. "But I don't understand how a dream could hurt him."

Mason shook his head. "It's not the dream that's going to hurt him, Son. It's what's behind the dream that matters."

Virgil felt his anxiety growing. "What's behind the dreams, Dad?"

Mason looked away from Virgil and stared at Murton's house on the other side of the pond for a few moments. When he turned back, he said, "Did you ever hear the story about Grandpa Jack's brother, Joe Bellows?"

Virgil looked down in thought, then nodded. "Yeah, bits and pieces of it, anyway. He fell off the roof and died when he was a teenager, right?"

Mason nodded. "That's the gist of it, yes. But everything that happened as a result of that awful event is still at play in one way or another, and Murton is at the center of it."

"What? How can that be? Grandpa Jack was a kid when Uncle Joe died. You and mom weren't even born yet."

"Yet Murton is dreaming about your maternal grandparents. You'd better start connecting the dots before it's too late, Son."

"How?" Virgil said. "I don't even know where to start. There's no common denominator."

"Yes, there is. You're simply not seeing it. Your grandfather lost his entire family when he was only sixteen years old. He did what he had to do to survive."

"Like what?" Virgil said.

Mason seemed to consider his response before he spoke. "Suffice it to say he got mixed up with some wayward strangers—both before the war and after."

"And that's what Murton's dreams are about?"

"I don't know how many times I have to say it, Virg: It's all connected."

CHAPTER TWELVE

Snow and Duncan got turned around a few times, the nav system in their rental taking them on a circuitous route to where they wanted to go. Eventually, they found their way to the storage facility where one of Alberto's contacts had stashed the car...a chocolate brown Mini Cooper Countryman, along with four fully automatic M-10X rifles—the modern version of the Russian AK-47—and five Heckler & Koch HK45's, each complete with a Dead Air Ghost tactical suppressor.

Duncan inventoried the guns, then looked at Snow and said, "Pretty impressive."

Snow nodded. "Yeah, Bert never scrimped on the hardware."

"I don't see any ammo."

"Should be in the back of the Coop," Snow said.

Duncan went to the back of the car and opened the

rear hatch. When he was sure Snow wasn't looking, he bent down and attached a magnetic key holder to the underside of the Mini's bumper. Then he did a quick inventory of the ammunition and said, "Yep. Looks like enough to take down half the cops in the city."

"Let's hope it doesn't come to that," Snow said. "We've been doing this for five years and never once had to fire a shot or kill anyone."

"Except for the guy that Carver killed during the VA heist."

Snow drew her mouth into a thin line, then shook her head in a sad way. "That idiot...I don't know what he was thinking. It wasn't necessary. We were getting out clean."

"So why did he do it?"

"The guard said something to him he didn't like. I'm not sure what because I wasn't in the building. I was in the car acting as the lookout and driver."

"Carver never told you what the guard said?"

"I just told you I don't know."

Duncan held his hands up. "Okay, Jesus, relax, will you? I was only asking."

Snow gave him a tight nod. "Yeah, yeah. I'm sort of getting a little amped up. These jobs...we are so close to being done. I don't want to get caught."

"We're not going to get caught," Duncan said. "I promise."

"Don't make promises you can't keep."

"I'm not. We've got excellent intel, a decent crew, and a plan that is practically foolproof."

"I'd feel a lot better about your last statement if you would have left the word 'practically' out."

Duncan gave her a squeeze, then said, "We can't worry about things we have no control over." When Snow didn't respond, he said, "So, how about we go check the truck and trailer?"

"Yeah, sounds good. I'll take the Coop and follow you. Take it slow, and don't lose me either. I've got a carload of guns and ammo. The last thing I need right now is a traffic stop."

"You're right." Duncan took one of the HK45's, attached the Dead Air Ghost suppressor to the end of the barrel, then loaded one of the magazines.

When he was finished, Snow looked at him and said, "What are you doing?"

"Taking this with me. If we do get stopped, it'll be a bad day for the men in blue."

THEY DROVE CAREFULLY, DUNCAN LETTING THE NAV unit lead the way, with Snow right behind him. The truck and trailer were parked in a Walmart lot in Greenfield, just east of the city, essentially hidden in plain sight. They wouldn't take it now for two reasons: It was perfectly safe where it was, and there would be no place to park the rig at the condo. They'd swing by and pick it up in the morning on their way to do the job. Once they were done, they'd bring it back and leave it again until they were ready to hit their next target.

They checked the inside of the trailer—a custom car hauler—then made sure the keys worked on the truck, a powerful Dodge dually with enough room for six people. "Nice setup," Duncan said.

"Like I said, Bert never scrimped."

That's when Duncan had a thought. "Something's bothering me."

"What's that?" Snow said.

"You told me Bert never said where he got his intel, right?"

"Yeah, that's right. But it's always been good. We've never had one single problem."

"But that's not entirely true, is it?"

"What are you talking about?"

"I'm talking about Slips and everything that happened there."

Snow thought about it for a few seconds, then said, "I'm not making the connection."

Duncan leaned against the side of the truck and crossed his arms. "Think about it for a minute. If we don't know where Bert got his intel, that means we don't know who he had on this end to place the Mini Cooper and guns in the storage facility."

Snow immediately saw the connection. She tipped a

finger at him and said, "And that means we don't know who put the truck and trailer here either."

"You're right. It was probably the same people, but that's beside the point. This lot is packed with all sorts of vehicles. For all we know, they could be watching us right now."

Snow looked around without being too obvious about it. "What do you think?"

"I think this is the perfect spot to keep the truck and trailer, except now we can't do that. If Bert was still alive, I'd say we don't have a problem. But he isn't, so we might have to do something."

"Maybe we're being a little paranoid," Snow said.

Duncan nodded at her. "Maybe, but the thing is, it's not paranoia if you're right. So I have to ask, why risk it?"

Snow thought about it, then said, "Okay, I think that makes sense. But where do we take it?"

"To another Walmart." Duncan took out his phone and brought up the map function. When he found what he needed, he moved closer to Snow and said, "Look at this."

Snow looked at the map. "Eaton, Ohio?"

"I think it's the best choice. It's practically right across the state line, and it's less than seventy miles from where we are right now."

"What about the guns?" Snow said.

"We leave them where they are. We'll load the Coop into the trailer right here and take the whole thing with us. I'll drive the truck, you follow me in the rental, and we'll be back in time for dinner."

"I guess that works," Snow said. "But it also means we're going to have to get an earlier start tomorrow."

Duncan shrugged. "What's that old saying? Something about an early bird and a worm? C'mon, let's get going. Watch for a tail. I'll probably double back once or twice off the highway to be sure, but we should be okay."

"I hope you're right," Snow said. Then she gave Duncan a quick kiss. After that, they loaded the Mini into the trailer and headed out, east on I-70 going from one Walmart to another, Snow fighting her paranoia the entire time.

And Duncan's plan coming together, piece by piece.

IT TOOK A LITTLE OVER TWO HOURS TO GET TO EATON, mainly because they stuck to the speed limit, and also doubled back twice to make sure they didn't have a tail. By the time they arrived, they were as confident as they could be that no one was following them.

Once they had the rig in place, Snow walked over to Duncan, lowered her voice a bit—even though it really wasn't necessary—and said, "I thought of something on the way over here."

"What's that?"

"If we're concerned that someone might be following

us—and we are—don't you think we should look for a tracking device?"

Duncan thought the woman might be smarter than he originally thought, but he didn't want her to know it, and he certainly didn't want her to know she was playing right into his hands. When he spoke, he chose his words with care. "I hadn't thought of that. You might be right, but I think we have to ask ourselves how likely that might be."

"I've been asking myself that all the way here. Look at this truck and trailer...not to mention the car and the guns. It's all top-of-the-line stuff. A tracking device would be nothing to whoever supplied everything else."

"I guess it's worth a look," Duncan said. "We've come this far and it'd all be for nothing if they've got a tracker on us." He looked up at the sky as he spoke. "We're running out of daylight. We better get started. Let's try not to be too obvious about it. You take the inside of the truck. I'll check the exterior."

"Okay."

They spent almost an hour looking but didn't find anything. "You're sure the exterior is clean?" Snow said.

"Yeah, I'm positive. I checked every inch. Waste of time, huh?"

"Not really," Snow said. "At least we know there's nothing else to worry—"

Duncan looked at Snow and said, "What?"

Snow tipped her head at the trailer. "The Coop. What if they planted it there?"

Duncan made a show of slapping his forehead. "Geez, I never even thought of that. We'd better take a look."

They opened the back of the hauler and went inside. Duncan pulled the ramp closed, then flipped on the interior lights. "I'll check the inside this time if you don't mind. It's sort of a tight fit in here. You'll be able to get a better look at the exterior."

Snow nodded, and they got to work again. Duncan made a show of checking under the seats, in the glove compartment, and under the dash. He'd only been at it for a few minutes when he heard Snow call out to him.

"Hey, Duncan?"

"Yeah?"

"You better get out here."

Duncan had to make a concerted effort not to smile. When he backed out of the car, he had a frown on his face. "What?"

"Take a look at this." Snow handed him the magnetic key holder. "I found it under the rear bumper."

"You open it yet?"

Snow shook her head.

Duncan looked at the key holder like he'd never seen it before. When he turned to Snow, he said, "Did Bert ever do this...leave an extra key or anything like that?"

"Not that I know of. He never said anything, and you've seen the level of detail he gives us with the intel. If there was an extra key, I think Bert would have said something." When Duncan didn't respond, Snow said, "We better open it up. If it's a key, we're in the clear. If it's a tracker, we're in big trouble."

Duncan forced his hands to tremble a bit as he slid the top of the key holder back. When he saw what was inside, he visibly swallowed. "Christ."

Snow looked inside the container and saw a little round disc that looked like a watch battery, only bigger and fatter. It was all black and had a two-inch wire attached to the bottom. She ran her fingers through her short hair, then said, "Well, fuck me."

Duncan closed the lid on the holder. "I intend to, but I'm afraid it will have to wait for now."

Snow was starting to panic. "What are we going to do?"

"Plan B. C'mon, let's go outside. It's getting stuffy in here."

They stepped out of the trailer, locked it up, and once that was done, Snow looked at Duncan and said, "I thought coming here was plan B."

Duncan tipped his head to the side. "Okay, plan C, then."

"Which is what?"

"Give me a minute, will you?" Duncan said. "I'm thinking, here."

"Well, you better think fast because I'm feeling a little vulnerable right about now."

Duncan took a few steps away as if he was deep in

thought. That's when he heard an engine from one of the semi delivery trucks start up. He walked back over to Snow and said, "I've got an idea."

"What is it?" Snow said.

"We're going to triple bluff whoever is behind all this."

"How?"

"We're going to put the truck, the trailer, and the Mini back where we found them...in Greenfield."

"How is that a triple bluff?"

"Bluff one was coming here, right?"

"Yeah."

"So bluff three would be to take it back."

"Look Duncan, I'm not exactly what anyone would call a math whiz, but you left out bluff two."

"Because that's the best part. Did you catch the sign along I-70 right before we turned off?"

"What sign?"

"The one that said there was a rest stop two miles further east."

"So what?"

Duncan smiled at her. "That's where we're going. You take the rental, and I'll take the rig. We'll pull into the rest stop, find a long-haul truck, and attach the tracker to the semi's trailer. It doesn't matter which one because the interstate is a divided highway, which means the truck that's going to carry our little bug will be going further east. When the truck leaves, we'll follow, then take the next exit and double back to Indiana."

"You think that will work?"

"It's either that or scrap the last three jobs."

Snow looked down at the pavement. "I can't believe we drove all the way out here for nothing."

"But we didn't," Duncan said. "Don't you see? If we hadn't, we wouldn't have thought to check for a tracker. That means at some point tomorrow, we'd have a bunch of Cubans waiting for us...and the money."

Snow suddenly reached out and grabbed Duncan's arm. "If these guys knew about the Mini and the storage facility, that must mean they know everything...which jobs, when we're doing them, and where. It's not too much of a stretch to think the condo might be compromised as well."

Duncan tipped his head to the side. "I think you're partially right. The condo is probably safe. The tracker means these guys don't have all the intel...only some of it."

"What makes you so sure?"

Duncan thought, *Hmm, maybe not so smart after all.* "Because if they knew when and where the jobs were, they wouldn't need the tracker to follow us, would they?"

"No, I guess not."

Duncan wrapped her up in a hug. "C'mon, let's head on down the highway to the rest stop. We'll ditch these guys and head back. Call one of the boys at the condo and fill them in. Tell them we'll be there in a few hours."

Snow made the call, and once she was in the rental, Duncan got into the Dodge and they made their way out to the highway. Twenty minutes later the tracker—which was nothing more than a piece of black plastic that couldn't track anything—was headed east, and Duncan, in the truck was smiling like he'd just hit the jackpot... because in a way, he had. The crew's leader was off-balance and paranoid, and that's all he really needed.

For now, anyway.

CHAPTER THIRTEEN

Sarah had left for the day, Sandy was at a political function with Mac, Delroy and Huma were having a quiet evening to themselves with their little girl, Aayla, so Virgil invited himself and the boys to dinner at Murton and Becky's house. Once everyone was fed, Murton found a TV program suitable for the boys, helped Becky and Virgil clear the dishes, then they all sat back down at the kitchen table.

Virgil looked at Murton. "So you're going to give the sleeping pills a try tonight?"

Murton let his eyelid droop. "No...I thought I'd wait until tomorrow morning."

Virgil chuckled. "Who knows, Murt? They might help."

"He's not what you would call overly optimistic," Becky said.

Murton yawned. "I'll tell you what I am...I'm exhausted. I'm also a little nervous."

"Why?" Virgil said.

"Because this dream keeps waking me up, and once it does, I can't go back to sleep."

Virgil nodded. "Thus, the sleeping pills."

"That's the part that makes me nervous. What if instead of waking up, I keep having the dream over and over again? I feel like I'm losing my goddamned mind." Then Murton sighed, reached into his pocket, took out a dollar bill, and held it over his shoulder.

Jonas walked by and snatched the bill. "Thanks, Uncle Murt."

Becky looked at Virgil. "That kid is either going to grow up to be a banker or a loan shark."

Virgil shrugged. "Same job, different suit." Then to Murton: "Let me ask you something."

"What's that?" Murton said.

"Who are the people in the boat?"

"We've already been through this, Jones-man. It's your maternal grandparents."

Virgil shook his head. "No, no, that's not what I meant. Who are the people in the other boat? The one you...uh...take out with the plane."

"I have no idea."

"But you've seen their faces," Virgil said.

Murton shook his head. "No, I haven't. The plane is going too fast, and by the time I'm close enough, they all have their backs to me because they know what's coming. And the truth is I can't see that well because for some reason I'm wearing an eye patch." Then, "Listen, I really don't want to talk about this anymore. Let's change the subject, okay?"

Virgil shrugged. "Okay. Well, here's some news for you: Sarah quit today."

Becky punched Virgil in the shoulder. "Shut up."

Virgil rubbed his shoulder. "I really wish you wouldn't do that. Anyway, she gave me her two-week notice. Said she felt like she was taking advantage of me and Sandy."

"What'd you tell her?" Murton said.

"I asked her to think about it...not to do anything rash, but based on the way the conversation went, it looks like she's made up her mind."

Becky gave Virgil a look.

"What?"

"Nothing," Becky said. "It's none of my business, I'm sure."

Virgil let out a breath and said, "That's never stopped you before, Becks."

"Well, I was simply thinking that if you'd have waited to hire a secretary a little longer, you could have given the job to Sarah instead of Betty."

Virgil gave her the brow. "No kidding. My dad told me the same thing today right after she told me she was leaving."

"Drop the brow, will you?" Becky said.

"I will if you quit punching me."

"What else did he say?" Murton said.

"You don't want to know," Virgil said.

"Why not?"

"Because you told me and your lovely wife that you don't want to talk about it anymore."

Murton smiled. "She is lovely, isn't she?" Then he turned to Becky. "Did you know that Jonesy sometimes has erotic dreams about you?"

Becky made a rude noise with her lips. "Yeah, him and every other red-blooded American male." Then to Virgil: "C'mon, Jonesy, let's hear it."

"Becky, I was just fooling around. I don't have erotic dreams about you."

Becky held up her hand and ticked a couple of points off her fingers. "One, I don't believe you, and two, that's not what I'm talking about. I want to hear what Mason said."

Virgil looked at his brother. "Murt?"

Murton shrugged. "It seems to be the topic du jour. Be my guest."

Virgil looked at nothing for a few seconds, gathering his thoughts. "He said that you were in trouble and that you're having these dreams for a reason."

Murton chuffed like a dog. "That's not really a news-flash, Jonesy."

"Maybe not," Virgil said. "But he also told me that if we don't figure out why, you're going to come to no good end."

"At the risk of repeating myself, that's not newsworthy either, because if we don't figure it all out and stop these dreams, I'm going to end up at the funny farm."

"It's not the dream that's going to hurt you, Murt. I mean, I get it. You're tired, or exhausted, or whatever, but it's only a dream. According to Dad, it's what's behind the dream that matters. He was as serious as I've ever seen him. It sort of scared me."

Murton tapped the kitchen table with the tip of his index finger. "How am I supposed to figure out what's behind the dream?"

"I'm not sure," Virgil said. "But after he told me that, he asked me if I'd ever heard the story about Uncle Joe."

"Who's that?" Becky said.

"Grandpa Jack's brother," Murton said. Then he quickly told Becky the meat of the story.

"So Jack lost his brother and his parents almost all at once?" Becky said.

Virgil nodded. "Yeah. It must have been a hell of a thing. But what bothers me is this: Dad said everything that happened as a result of that event is still in play, and Murt is at the center of it."

"How can that be?" Becky said.

"That's what I asked," Virgil said.

"Did you get an answer?" Murton said.

"Yeah, and it was—as usual—cryptic enough to make me want to pull my hair out. He said that Grandpa Jack got mixed up with some wayward strangers and that it's all connected."

Murton yawned, and waved it all away. "Look, I'm not a cultural anthropologist, so the two of you can stay up all night and talk about it if you want, but I'm going to hit the hay." He kissed Becky, then ruffled the top of Virgil's head like he was a kid. "See you in the morning."

"Sweet dreams," Virgil said.

That got him another punch from Becky.

After Murton had gone to bed, Virgil and Becky talked it around for a while, then the boys started getting tired, so Virgil gathered them up, thanked Becky for dinner, and walked back home. After he was gone, Becky sat alone in the kitchen, thinking about the statement her husband had made before he went to bed.

And that gave her an idea.

———

WHEN DUNCAN AND SNOW GOT BACK TO THE CONDO, Potts was already asleep, and Bray was watching ESPN with the volume muted. "Where's Stout?"

"He got hungry," Bray said.

Snow was instantly mad. "You mean thirsty, don't you?"

Bray turned his palms up and gave her a what-can-you-do sort of look. "You know how he gets before a job. The booze helps him keep his nerves in check."

"Where did he go?"

Bray rubbed his face with his hands, then looked at Duncan. "How do you grow a beard like that? It must itch like crazy. If I don't shave every day it drives me nuts."

Duncan ignored him, but Snow didn't. "Answer my question, Jimmy. Where did Stout go?"

"He said something about walking over to that bar a couple of blocks away. The one next to the sporting goods store."

Snow took out her phone and tried to call Stout, but it went straight to voicemail. "That idiot. If he gets drunk and starts shooting his mouth with some local broad, it could seriously mess us up. Why didn't he go to the liquor store like he always does?"

"Beats me," Bray said. "He probably wanted to get some fresh air. Don't sweat it."

"Sweating it...and everything else is my job." She shook her head, grabbed her purse. "I'll be right back."

Duncan followed her outside, then gently grabbed her arm. "Let me go. I'll bring him back."

Snow pulled her arm free and said, "I've got this."

Duncan looked her in the eye. "You're too angry. The last thing we need right now is a confrontation in public. I'll go to the bar, sit down and have a beer with him, then suggest we head back. Believe me, this is the right play."

"You don't know Stout. He doesn't like to be pushed around."

"And that's why you need to let me handle this for you.

If you show up and start handing out marching orders, how well do you think that will go over...in public, no less. Let me do this. I know the city, and I know the place where he is. Besides, if I have a beer with the guy, maybe he'll lighten up on me a little bit."

Snow thought it over for a few seconds, then decided Duncan was probably right. She was mad enough that if she saw Stout right now, she'd probably take a swing at him, and that wouldn't be good for anyone. "Okay. One beer, then get his ass back here."

Duncan smiled and said, "Yes, ma'am."

That took a little steam out of her engine. She placed her hand on Duncan's chest. "You know, if I had three guys as smart as you, we'd be done with all this by now."

Duncan kissed her, then said, "One step at a time, boss. Like you said, we're almost done anyway. I'll be back in an hour. Got the keys?"

"You're not walking?"

Duncan tapped his thigh. "With this leg? You're kidding, right?"

Snow dropped her head, her face and neck turning red. "You move around so well on that thing, I forgot all about it."

"I've had a lot of practice. But it does start to wear on me if I do too much walking."

Snow handed him the keys, then said, "Be careful. Stout can be...erratic."

"Don't worry, I've dealt with worse. Stout will be like a

walk in the park. Or I guess I should say a limp through the park." Then he laughed like he didn't have a care in the world...mostly because he didn't.

DUNCAN STOPPED AT THE SPORTING GOODS STORE AND caught them right as they were closing. "I'll only be a minute," he said. "I need a plastic tarp if you've got one."

The clerk, a freckle-faced kid with an unfortunate haircut shook his head and whined at him. "C'mon, mister. I've already cashed out."

"Then this is your lucky day," Duncan said. He reached into his pocket and pulled out a hundred dollar bill. "Get me the tarp, and keep the change."

The kid took off like Duncan had him on the clock and was back in less than a minute. "Will this work?"

Duncan told him it would, then grabbed the plastic tarp and walked out the door.

When he got to the bar, he parked the rental at the back of the establishment—a place called Ricky's—and spread the tarp out in the trunk before going inside. He found Stout sitting at the far end of the bar, a bottle of Bud and an empty shot glass in front of him. His head was hanging down slightly, and when he picked up his bottle of beer, he almost knocked it over.

Duncan stayed near the front and got the bartender's

attention. When he walked over, he said, "What can I get you?"

"Nothing for me," Duncan said. "But I'd like to take care of my buddy's tab and get him out of here."

The bartender turned and looked at Stout. "If your buddy is that guy sitting down there at the end, I'm about to consider you my new best friend."

"Been giving you trouble?"

"Nothing I can't handle," the bartender said. "I just don't want to. I've had the cops in here three times this month so far. If they show up again, I'm in danger of losing my liquor license."

Duncan gave him a friendly grin. "Well, we can't have that, can we? What's the damage?"

"Forty-two on the nose."

Duncan reached into his pocket and peeled off another one of Bert's hundreds. "Keep the change. He won't be back."

"Man, thanks. That's a hell of a tip."

"I wouldn't thank me yet."

The bartender gave him a one-eyed squint. "Why not?"

"There might be a little damage. Don't worry, I'll cover it. Just stay off the phone. Anyone else in here going to give me any trouble?"

"Naw, they're all a bunch of drunks. I doubt if any of them could find themselves in a mirror, let alone take a swing at someone like you."

Duncan was mildly intrigued. "If they're all a bunch of drunks, why do they get a pass and my buddy down there doesn't?"

"Because they're regulars, and none of them are assholes like your friend."

Duncan nodded. "Fair enough. Back door unlocked?"

"Yep. Right down the hall past the can. Not to sound ungrateful, but don't let it hit you in the ass on the way out."

"Don't worry, you won't see me or my friend ever again."

The bartender shrugged. "Well, you're welcome back anytime. First drink is on me."

"You might change your mind about that in a minute. Got a mop and bucket?" Then Duncan headed toward Stout.

The bartender shook his head and thought, *Oh boy.*

DUNCAN SAT DOWN NEXT TO STOUT, WHO BARELY registered his presence. He leaned close and said, "Your intemperate habits are going to get you hurt."

Stout swung his head in an exaggerated manner and looked at Duncan. "Hey, man. What are you doing here? Want a beer?"

"No thanks. I've paid your tab. It's time to go."

When Stout didn't respond or move, Duncan stood

and said, "Suit yourself." Then he grabbed the back of Stout's neck and smashed his face against the bar railing. When he pulled his head back up, Stout's nose was bent at an awkward angle, and one of his front teeth fell on the floor. The combination of the alcohol and the blow to the face had knocked him out cold. Duncan gave the bartender another hundred, then dragged Stout through the back door. When it closed behind him, he heard the lock click into place.

Works for me, he thought. He opened the trunk, tossed the still-unconscious Stout inside, then carefully looked around for any security cameras. When he didn't see any, he took out the gun he'd stolen from Alberto, with the suppressor still attached, and shot Stout twice in the chest and once in the forehead. Then he closed the lid, got in the driver's seat and took off.

One down, two to go.

CHAPTER FOURTEEN

Duncan took his time looking for the right spot to dump Stout's body. He wanted him found, but not right away. After cruising the city for an hour, he decided that maybe he was overthinking things, which, he knew from experience, never really worked out. But then he had a thought, one that made him smile. He was so caught up in the back and forth of the idea he had to pull over for a minute to weigh the pros and cons of it all. Ultimately, he thought, *what the hell,* and decided to do it. Why not make a little trouble where trouble was due?

Twenty minutes later he found the dumpster he was looking for in a back alley, heaved Stout from the trunk, and shoved him behind the dumpster, tarp and all. He dropped the gun on top of Stout's body, then headed back to the condo, where he found Snow, Bray, and Potts waiting for him.

Snow was practically out of her mind with fear and anger. "Where the hell have you been? I've tried your phone about twenty times."

Duncan let a look of shame and embarrassment form on his face. "My battery died. But that's the least of our problems."

"Where's Stout?" Snow said. She tried not to hiss it at him, but wasn't quite sure if she pulled it off or not.

Duncan shook his head. "He wasn't at the tavern. When I described him and asked the bartender if he'd been in, he told me he was there for about fifteen minutes. Said he had one beer and left. Didn't know where he went after that. I checked every bar within a six-block radius...twice, and never found him. I'm not sure what happened, but he's gone."

Snow pulled at her hair with both hands. "No, no, no. He can't be gone. He wouldn't walk away from us. There's too much money waiting for him in the account."

"He doesn't have access to the account, does he?" Duncan said.

"Of course not," Snow said. "Even if he did, he wouldn't know how to get the money out. It's not as easy as making a withdrawal from an ATM."

"Maybe the cops have him," Bray said. "What if he got good and tanked, and they picked him up on a drunk and disorderly?"

"What if he got hit by a car or injured some other way?" Potts said.

"There's no way to tell," Snow said. "It's not like we can go to the cops and start asking questions. Same with the hospitals. If he got himself arrested, then he's done. If he's hurt bad enough to be in the hospital, we can't use him. Either way, we're screwed now." She walked to the front door and pulled it open. "I gotta get some air and think about this."

"Let me go with you," Duncan said. "You shouldn't be out alone."

Snow turned to Bray and Potts. "Forget what I said a second ago. Start calling the hospitals. See if you can find him."

Both men said they would, and Duncan followed Snow outside. Once they were clear of the building, Duncan stopped her. "Listen, maybe he'll turn up. For all we know he's passed out in an alley somewhere."

Snow thought about that for a second. "He does have a hell of a problem with the booze, but he's never let it interfere with the jobs."

Duncan let a little skepticism slide across his tongue. "Never?"

Snow dipped her head in defeat. "Well, not like this."

"So maybe he'll turn up later tonight, or first thing in the morning. If he does, you can chew his ass out, and we can get on with it."

"And if he doesn't?" Snow said.

Duncan looked away for a moment. When he turned back, he said, "I think we can still make it work."

"How?"

"We simply shuffle the responsibilities a little."

"How about you spell it out for me?"

"You can drive the truck, right?"

"Of course I can drive the truck. It's nothing more than a big pickup with a trailer."

"Ever done it before?" Duncan said.

"Yeah, I used to haul my boat back and forth to the marina all the time."

"So there you go. You handle the rig, I'll take the inside with Vic and Jimmy, and it'll be business as usual."

Snow shook her head. "But it won't. Don't you see? We won't have anyone on the outside."

Duncan tried very hard not to belittle her. "It doesn't matter, Kelly. The person on the outside serves no real purpose. They can't do anything if the cops show up, except maybe get away...and even that is a big maybe. Not having a driver waiting in the Mini is going to add about five seconds to the whole thing because that's how long it takes to open the door and start the car."

"I don't know..."

Duncan pressed her. "Look, if nothing else, it takes the heat off of you. Now, instead of waiting outside the bank like a sitting duck, you'll be a block or two away with the trailer. I can make this work. All you have to do is have some faith in me. I didn't let you down at Slips when the Cubans showed up, I didn't let you down earlier tonight when we found the tracker, and I won't let you down tomorrow."

Snow looked at Duncan, his bright eyes, his big bushy beard, and his never-quit attitude, and knew that he was right. "I guess I don't have a choice."

"Atta girl. Now, let's figure out how to sell it to Bray and Potts."

"There's nothing to sell. They'll do whatever I tell them to do. I'm the boss."

Yeah, Duncan thought. *Keep thinking that, sweetheart.*

THE NEXT MORNING THE CREW WAS READY. DUNCAN and Snow didn't say anything to Bray or Potts about what they'd done the night before with the truck and trailer... Duncan for his own personal reasons, and Snow because she wanted them focused on the job at hand. If she would have told them about the tracker on the Mini, one or both of them might have thought it too risky, especially with Stout having gone MIA. So the secret—her's and Duncan's would remain between them.

They rolled out of the Walmart lot in Greenfield at six, a little tired and a little grumpy. Coffee helped with the tiredness, but the grumpy part was simply something to deal with, each in their own way.

Snow drove the Dodge dually, with Duncan riding

shotgun, and Bray and Potts in the back seat. Potts leaned forward. "How long until we get there?"

Snow checked her watch. "About two hours. That'll give us enough time to find a place to park the rig."

They were headed north to Warren, Indiana, which sat at the southern edge of Huntington County. Warren was perfect because it had a large banking footprint in the county, but within the town itself, the police force was small enough that it wouldn't be a problem. In fact, the entire town's population was just over a thousand residents, and those were the types of places they liked to hit.

The target was Bippus State Bank, a small branch that handled the town's financial affairs, including most of its residents as well. According to the intel they had from Bert and their own research on Google Earth, it would be an easy in and out job. They'd park the truck and trailer a block away, take the Mini Cooper into the lot, go in hard, and come out fast. They never stayed inside longer than three minutes, and they'd never failed. Gloves took care of any fingerprints, and watch caps that rolled down into face masks took care of any security cameras.

Snow cruised down the town's main drag, went past the bank, then continued north out of town all the way past I-69 and turned into the Warren travel plaza. She parked at the far edge of the lot, killed the engine, and Duncan stepped out to get the Mini from the trailer.

She turned and spoke to the two men in the back seat.

"Okay, this is really no different from before, except Duncan is going to drive the Mini instead of me. I know you'll be going in one man short, but the three of you shouldn't have any trouble. Skip the tellers, hit the vault, and get out. Try not to hurt anyone."

Bray looked at Snow and said, "Is he up for this? Duncan?"

Snow didn't hesitate. "I'm sure he is. He has a military background, he knows his guns, and his morals seem to be right where we like them."

"You mean non-existent, right?" Potts said, his voice a little snarky.

"Don't start with me, Vic. I'm doing the best I can here."

They felt the Mini bump out of the trailer, and when they did, Bray gave Snow one last look. "Be ready when we get back. Ten minutes, tops."

"Don't worry. I'll be waiting in the Dollar General lot with the trailer open."

"You sure Duncan's good?"

"I'm positive," Snow said. "But keep an eye on him anyway. I want to know how he does."

"You got it, boss. See you in ten."

———

POTTS CLIMBED INTO THE PASSENGER SEAT OF THE Mini, and Bray took the back. They followed Snow back into town and watched her park behind the Dollar General. Thirty seconds later they were turning into the bank's parking lot. Bray leaned forward and tapped Duncan on the shoulder as he put the car in park. "Keep it running, and follow my lead. Got it?"

"I'm ready," Duncan said. "Let's do this."

The three men checked their guns one final time, rolled their caps down into face masks, jumped out of the Mini and ran for the front door.

They were only two steps into the lobby when it all went sideways, which was exactly the direction Duncan wanted it to go.

THE BANK DIDN'T HAVE A SECURITY GUARD, BUT IT DID have a pretty young teller, one whose husband happened to be the second-in-command at the Warren Police Department. Since the town was small and they both worked almost the exact same hours, the cop always dropped his wife off at the bank before going on duty. Sometimes, like this morning, he'd stay and chat her up a little before heading down to the station.

And that's what he was doing when Potts, Bray, and Duncan burst through the door, masks down, and guns up. They came in so fast and hard that everyone in the bank turned and looked. The cop's wife said, "On your six, baby," even though it wasn't necessary. The branch manager screamed like a little girl, two of the other tellers and a loan officer all froze, and the cop almost had his gun free of his holster when Duncan opened up on him.

The cop went down, someone else screamed, and Bray shouted, "Back out, back out."

But Duncan wasn't done yet. He had a job, and a plan, and he was sticking to it. He turned toward Bray and Potts, said, "So long, boys." Then he mowed them down with his M-10X automatic. The suppressors were good but he'd still made a hell of a racket. He dropped the rifle, pulled his HK45, and put one round in the Warren police officer's head to make sure he was gone, then jumped over the counter and took out the tellers and the branch manager.

Then he ran. Once he was outside, he climbed into the Mini and took off around the block, keeping an eye on the rearview mirror. When he turned into the lot, the trailer gate was down, and Snow was sitting in the driver's seat of the Dodge. He hit the ramp—maybe a bit too fast — but got the Mini out of sight. Then he jumped from the car, closed the trailer's ramp, and ran to the driver's side of the truck. He yanked the door open and shouted at Snow. "Move over, I'm driving."

Snow didn't know what the hell was going on, but when she saw the look on Duncan's face, she didn't argue. Duncan had the rig rolling before she was settled in her own seat. "What happened? Where are Potts and Bray?"

Duncan stayed calm because he knew it was the only

way to keep Snow in check. "Dead. The bank was full of cops. They cut them down like dogs. I took out the cops and anyone else I could see, then backed out and took off. I didn't have a choice."

Snow was leaning forward like she was about to vomit. "Oh no. Oh, Christ." When she sat back up, tears were running down her cheeks. "How did you make it out? Wait...never mind that. Why are you taking us back through town?"

Duncan pulled over to the curb to let a town cop car go by, its lights flashing, the siren screaming. A few seconds later two Huntington County squad cars went racing past as well. Duncan watched them in his rearview mirror until they were all out of sight. "That's why. Bank robbers don't usually run back into town after a job. They try to take a back road through the country to make their escape. The problem is, it never works. This is safer."

"Safer? Are you out of your mind?"

Of course I am, Duncan thought. "Trust me. I know what I'm doing." He went around the block, then pulled up next to the curb and parked the truck and trailer.

"Why are we stopping? We've got to get out of here."

Duncan put his hand on Snow's forearm. "Kelly, listen to me. I know what I'm doing. Let's go across the street to that bakery and get a cup of coffee. If anyone saw the Mini, that's what the cops will be looking for...not a big Dodge pickup with a trailer. We couldn't be any safer if we were sitting down at Slips right now. This is the best play, believe me."

Snow was trying to catch her breath, think straight, and keep her cool all at the same time. "Okay, okay, listen: You're probably right. We'll wait here for a bit and see what happens."

"Not quite, love. We're going to spend the day in town. They'll have the roads blocked off by now. Our best bet is to find a nice little bed and breakfast and spend the night."

Snow didn't really like the idea, but she went along with it. "Okay, I get it. Now, tell me how you got out, but Vic and Jimmy didn't."

Duncan puffed his cheeks and let out a breath. "It was like a war zone in there. Potts took the door, with Bray on his heels. I was right behind both of them. When the cops started shooting, they dropped right at my feet. It all happened so fast. I started to return fire before Potts and Bray ever hit the ground. Neither of them ever got a single shot off. But the M-10 was no match for the cops. I killed all of them. There may have been some civilian collateral damage."

Snow beat the dashboard of the truck with her fists. "We're finished. Do you hear me? We're done."

"Not as finished as Bray and Potts. We're still alive, Kelly. And I plan on keeping it that way. Don't worry, I've got an idea. We'll talk about it once we're settled in someplace safe. Then tomorrow we'll get rid of this truck and trailer."

"Where?" Snow said.

Duncan grinned at her. "Well, Eaton, Ohio comes to mind."

CHAPTER FIFTEEN

Virgil sat at his desk with his feet up, his fingers laced behind his head, and his eyes closed. In the background he heard the sound of someone running a jackhammer on the sidewalk outside his office window, and when the air-powered spike hit the pavement the sound reverberated through the double-paned glass behind him in a muffled fashion, as if the worker's tool of choice for concrete removal might have been a rubber mallet instead of a steel bit.

Virgil was dressed for the day in his usual attire, tan Timberland boots, blue jeans with a hole in one knee, and a brand new white T-shirt. When his boss, Cora LaRue walked in the door, he made no move to get up, put his feet down, or even open his eyes. Cora closed the door and sat down on the other side of Virgil's desk.

"Wake up, Jonesy," Cora said. "We've got something going."

Virgil left his eyes closed but arched an eyebrow. He didn't want his boss to think he was being disrespectful. "I'm not sleeping," Virgil said. "I'm working on something."

"I can see that," Cora said. She sat still for a moment, then stood and tapped the tip of Virgil's boot. "Conference room, two minutes. The governor is on the way over." She stood and moved to the door. "And we need to have a little chat about your new secretary."

That got Virgil's eyes open. When he glanced at the clock, he saw it was a little past ten in the morning.

VIRGIL TOOK THE STAIRS DOWN ONE FLOOR TO THE corner conference room, but before he went in, he stopped to get a cup of coffee from the machine in the hall. When he turned, he found Betty standing behind him, her arms folded defensively across her chest.

"What's the matter?" Betty said. "Don't you like the way I make the coffee? Ben never had a problem with it."

Virgil tried to suppress a sigh but failed miserably. "Look, Betty, I'm not Ben, okay? I never will be."

"You won't get any argument from me on that account."

Virgil didn't want to argue or debate anything, especially with Betty, so he changed the subject. "I understand you've met Cora."

"Who?" Betty said.

"Cora LaRue. She's the governor's chief of staff."

"If you're talking about the overweight black woman with a crew cut, then yes, we've met. She walked in here like she owns the place. Quite frankly, I'm not sure I care for her. Seems to have a bit of an attitude problem, if you ask me."

She does? "Betty, as I said, Cora is the governor's chief, and, as a point of fact, my direct boss. I expect you to give her the respect she's due."

"Respect is a two-way street. That means you get what you give."

Virgil looked over Betty's shoulder and saw the governor headed his way. "Betty, go back to your desk and do some secretarial things will you, please?"

"That's what I was doing before I came to the conference room. There are some reports in there you're going to want to see. Detectives Ross and Rosencrantz are already inside. I have no idea where your so-called partner is."

"It's nothing for you to worry about," Virgil said. "Please, go now."

But it was too late. The governor walked up, said hello to Virgil, then turned to Betty. "I don't believe I've had the pleasure." He stuck out his hand to shake. "Governor

McConnell. You must be the MCU's new departmental secretary."

Betty shook hands with the governor and said, "I am." Then she raised her nose in Virgil's direction. "Although I'm not sure my efforts are appreciated by everyone in this department."

The governor gave Betty his best political smile. "Well, don't be too hard on Virgil, here." Then he lowered his voice in a conspiratorial way and said, "We're still breaking him in."

Betty shook her head in a sad way. "Your charm is lost on me, sir. I think in the interest of full disclosure I should let you know that I voted for your opponent. He didn't seem quite as...slick, if you take my meaning." Then she turned and walked away.

The governor watched her for a few seconds, then turned to Virgil, his smile still in place, except for the look in his eyes. "I wouldn't let that one get away. She seems like a wonderful addition to the MCU."

Virgil dropped his head in shame. "I'm sorry about all that, Mac. She's a little, uh, brassy."

The governor waved him off. "Everyone present and accounted for?"

Virgil nodded. "Except for Murt. He's running a little late this morning. He should be here in a bit."

"How's he doing? The dreams and all that?"

"He's working his way through it. I don't have any

doubts about his ability to function as a member of this unit though, if that's what you're really asking."

The governor shook his head. "Nor do I, Jonesy. Simple concern for a friend."

"I appreciate it, Mac. So, what brings you down?"

"These days? Almost everything. Ah, but you're speaking of in the moment, aren't you?" Then, without waiting for an answer, he said, "Let's step into the conference room. Everyone should hear this at once."

THE GOVERNOR TOOK A SEAT AT THE HEAD OF THE table, said hello to everyone, then lifted his chin at Cora.

"We've been asked to assist a number of federal three-letter agencies, effective immediately," Cora said. "Does anyone know where Warren, Indiana is?"

"No idea," Virgil said.

Ross, who was something of a state history buff, said, "You should. It was founded a couple hundred years ago by a guy named Samuel Jones. Maybe you're related. Anyway, the town is on the southern edge of Huntington County. Sits just northeast of the Salamonie River."

Ross's partner, Tom Rosencrantz, nudged him in the ribs. "Easy there, Rain Man."

"What?" Ross said. "The lady asked a question and I answered it."

Virgil cleared his throat, then looked at Cora. "What's

happening in Warren, and why are we being asked to assist the feds?"

"Not more than two hours ago one of the town's banks was hit by three masked men with fully automatic weapons. The branch manager was killed, along with everyone else in the bank at the time, including one of the town's police officers. The town marshal immediately called the state police for assistance. We've got troopers on the scene now, along with several Huntington County deputies."

"How many dead?" Rosencrantz said.

"Four bank employees, the Warren cop, and two of the three robbers," Cora said. "If you're keeping count, that makes seven."

"Did the Warren officer take out—"

Virgil didn't even get to finish his question. "No," Cora said. "The town marshal has seen the security footage and says that his man was one of the first to die."

"Then who killed the other two crooks?" Ross said.

"The third one. For some reason he turned on his own men, then killed everyone else in the bank."

"What was the take?" Rosencrantz said.

"Zero. The shooter ran for the door and drove off in a Mini Cooper, of all things. Half the state is looking for the car, but so far there's been nothing."

"Do we know if the feds are on the scene yet?" Mac asked.

"The FBI field office out of Ft. Wayne has two agents on the way. They've probably already arrived." Cora turned to Virgil. "I want everyone on this. Cool is at the airport and waiting as we speak. This is more than a simple bank robbery gone bad. This is a mass shooting in our state, and the MCU will be focusing on that aspect of the case. Let the feds worry about whatever it is they want to worry about, but I want this killer caught, Jonesy."

Virgil looked at Ross and Rosencrantz, then stood from the table. "We're on it, Cora." Then to Mac: "Anything sensitive we need to know about?"

Then something happened that gave Virgil pause. The governor tipped his head to the side and said, "Why would you ask me that?"

Virgil opened his mouth to answer, then closed it. After a few seconds, he said, "Just wondering. Is everything okay?"

The governor stood and shot his cuffs. "Get to work, and keep Cora in the loop." Then he walked out the door without saying another word.

Virgil looked at Cora, and when he did, she gave him a very subtle head shake. The message was clear: Not now. Then she stood as well and said, "Get up there, cooperate, and figure out what's happening, Jones-man. I'll take updates day or night. Clear?"

"Sure," Virgil said. "But what—"

"That will be all, Detective," Cora said. "Get to it."

After the governor and Cora had left, Rosencrantz looked at Virgil. "Boy, she's as wound up as Betty."

Virgil gave him a dry look. "Yeah, except she's the boss, and Betty isn't."

Ross laughed, then said, "Right. Keep telling yourself that."

As soon as Virgil was in his truck, he called Murton. "How are you feeling?"

"Like I'm running on empty."

"The sleeping pills didn't help?" Virgil said.

"No. If anything, they made it worse."

"In what way?"

"I'm not sure how to explain it," Murton said. "I had the dream again, but because of the pills, I didn't fully wake up. Thanks to that, the dream kept replaying, except this time I was more aware of it...if that makes any sense."

"Yeah, I get it," Virgil said. "But remember, Bell said the pills might make the dream more vivid."

Murton laughed without humor. "He was right about that." Then, "Listen, I know I'm late, but I'll be there in about five minutes."

"Don't bother," Virgil said. "Head for the airport. I'm on my way right now. So are Ross and Rosencrantz. Cool's waiting for us."

"What's going on?"

Virgil gave Murton the basics, then said, "When was the last time you spoke with Mac?"

"I'm not sure...about a week or so, I guess. Why?"

Virgil didn't answer his brother right away. Instead, he asked another question. "How did he seem to you?"

"In what regard?"

"I don't know...did he seem uptight or evasive?"

"Not that I recall," Murton said. "He tried to give me grief about my wardrobe, but when I mentioned he was missing a button on the sleeve of his suit coat, that ended that. Anyway, it was a regular conversation...you know, how's Becky, everything okay at the house and bar, that sort of thing."

Virgil trusted his brother's intuition as much as his own. "Did it feel like he was fishing for something?"

"No, not at all. What's going on, Jonesy?"

"I'm not sure, but after the briefing was finished—this was right before he left—I asked him if there was anything sensitive we needed to know about. I was simply asking because the feds are involved."

"Seems like a reasonable question," Murton said.

"That's what I thought. But his response was a little out of character. He was pretty abrupt. Defensive, even. He said, 'Why would you ask me that?' When I asked him if he was okay, he simply told us to get to work, and then he left."

Murton was quiet for so long Virgil thought the connection had dropped. "You still there, Murt?"

"Yeah. I don't know what to tell you, Jonesy. He gets a lot of pressure from any number of sources. Maybe it's nothing more than this attempted heist we're going to look at. Seven dead, and one of them a cop…that kind of thing tends to rattle the political big shots."

"I hope that's all it is. Anyway, how soon before you get to the airport? We're about twenty minutes out."

"I'm already there," Murton said. "I wanted to ask Cool about something. As usual, I'm waiting on you."

CHAPTER SIXTEEN

Murton ended the call with Virgil as Cool walked back into the FBO building. "I spoke with the guy," Cool said. "His hangar is two down from here. He'd be happy to let you have a look."

Murton clapped him on the back. "Thanks, Rich. We've only got about twenty minutes before Virgil and the other guys show up. We better hurry, huh?"

"You go ahead, Murt. I told him who you were and what you wanted. The guy's name is Gene Walker. I have to get the chopper ready and file the flight plan."

Murton gave Cool a nod, then jogged down to the hangar. When he arrived, he opened the side door, then stopped dead in his tracks. For a moment, the sight of the plane made him wonder if he was dreaming again.

A stocky man in a pilot's jumpsuit walked over, wiped

his hands with a red shop rag, then said, "You must be Detective Wheeler."

Murton nodded, then stuck out his hand. "I am. Thanks for this, Mr. Walker. I needed to see one in person."

"My pleasure. And call me Gene. She's a beauty, isn't she?"

Murton looked at the Hellcat fighter and had to admit that not only was it an impressive sight, but the plane also looked bigger than he'd imagined. It was painted in tricolor camouflage, with a large white star near the aft end of the fuselage. He turned to Walker. "You did the restoration yourself?"

"Everything except the paint. Only took me about seven years. Say, are you all right? You look a little pale."

Murton nodded. "I don't doubt it, but I'm fine. If you don't mind me asking, is it a museum piece, or is it airworthy?"

Walker turned the corners of his mouth down. "A bit of both, I suppose. Don't get me wrong, it's as airworthy as it was the day it rolled off the assembly line, but it doesn't see the sky all that much anymore. If I take it up, it costs more to insure than it does to operate. I do a few airshows a year...that sort of thing. As a matter of fact, I've got one coming up pretty soon down in Evansville."

"I'll bet that's quite a show," Murton said. "Listen, I don't have a lot of time, but is there any chance I could sit in the cockpit for a minute or two?"

Walker didn't hesitate. "I was a Marion County deputy back in the day. So was my dad, although he died about twenty years ago."

"Worked for Mason Jones?"

Walker nodded. "Best boss we ever had. Did you know Mason?"

"He was my adoptive father," Murton said.

Walker opened his mouth to speak, but no words came out.

Murton looked at him and said, "I know the feeling. Sometimes there aren't any words."

Walker turned and moved a wheeled ladder over to the plane. "You want to have a seat, it'd be my honor. Watch your step going up."

Murton climbed the wheeled stand next to the plane, then looked at Walker, his face a question.

"It's okay," Walker said. "Step right up on the wing. You can't hurt it."

Murton did as he was told, then slid into the seat. Everything in the cockpit was the same as in his dream... the leather harness, the instrumentation, the sliding canopy, all of it. He put one hand on the stick and the other on the throttle, then closed his eyes.

After a few minutes, Walker climbed up on the wing and said, "Are you okay?"

Murton opened his eyes. "I'm not sure. If you'll excuse me, I have to get back to work." He climbed out of the cockpit and made his way down the ladder. "Thanks. I really appreciate it. Fly safe, and enjoy the airshow." He shook Walker's hand. "Sorry about your old man."

"Long time ago," Walker said.

Murton tipped his head and said, "Was it?"

The question caused Walker to give him an odd look. Murton scratched his cheek with the back of his thumbnail, then walked away without another word.

———

MURTON MADE IT BACK TO COOL AND THE HELICOPTER just as Virgil, Ross, and Rosencrantz arrived. Virgil looked at his brother. "Everything okay, Murt?"

Murton glanced back at the building where the Hellcat was hangared. "I really wish everyone would stop asking me that. Let's go, huh?"

Virgil looked at Cool. "We all set, Rich?"

"Ready when you are. Nice short flight up to Warren. There aren't any airports nearby, but the fire department is right across the street from the bank. I told them that we were coming, and they've given us permission to use their lot. We'll have plenty of room."

"Good enough," Virgil said. They all climbed on board, and five minutes later they were headed north to Warren. Rosencrantz brought everyone up to speed on his girlfriend, Carla Martin, who was the new sheriff of Shelby County. Ross and Virgil gave him all kinds of grief for dating a county sheriff.

Murton sat up front next to Cool and stared out the window. He didn't say a word during the entire trip.

———

DUNCAN AND SNOW GOT A ROOM AT THE COMFORT INN on the north side of town. Once they were settled, Duncan wanted to have a little fun, but Snow wasn't in the mood after everything that had happened. She sat on the edge of the bed and looked at Duncan. "Earlier you said you had an idea. I want to know what it is."

Duncan sensed that Snow needed more than an answer...she needed some personal space. He pulled the chair out from under the small desk—the only other seat available in the room—and moved it up against the wall. He sat down, then said, "Look, you and I both know that we can't do the remaining two jobs by ourselves."

Snow rolled her eyes at him. "Really? That hadn't occurred to me."

Duncan ignored the sarcasm. "Yes. But here's the thing: I'm beginning to think that the cops at the bank might have been expecting us."

"What makes you say that?"

"Look, Kelly, you've got to remember that everything happened really fast, so I'll be the first to admit that my impression of events might be skewed a bit."

"But?"

"Those cops weren't there by accident. I think they might have been tipped off by someone."

"Who?"

Duncan turned his palms up. "No way to tell. Probably the Cubans, or whoever they have working for them. The tracker we found on the Mini all but proves it."

Snow wasn't convinced. "If they tipped off the cops, don't you think they would have been ready for you?"

Duncan nodded. "I see where you're going, except in a town this size they've got what...four or five full-time cops? Plus, this isn't the big city. They probably thought it was a hoax or something."

"If they thought it was a hoax, why bother sending anyone?"

"To cover their asses. That's what I meant by my impression being skewed. The cops were there, but they weren't ready. If we hadn't fired first, they might have been able to take us all down."

Snow waved him off. "Whatever. None of it matters now. And, you still haven't told me about your idea."

Duncan gave her a friendly grin. "Well, it's more of a safety check than an idea."

"I'm all ears," Snow said.

Duncan put some teeth into his next statement without really meaning to. "How about you can the sarcasm and get in the game, sweetheart."

"I am in the goddamned game, but in case you haven't noticed, the final score has been posted. We lost."

Duncan forced himself to remain calm. He had to keep Snow's thinking on track, or his entire plan would fail. "I have noticed, but I'm more worried about the future than the past. That's why we need to do a little safety check."

"I'm not sure what you're talking about."

"Let's look at the facts," Duncan said. "Bert and Carver were killed. Skips got torched. Stout is gone...most likely dead, and we found the tracker on the Mini. Whoever these guys are, they are not fucking around. And that creates a problem for both of us."

"What are you suggesting?"

Duncan stood from his chair, then walked over and sat down on the bed at a respectful distance. "All the account information is on your laptop, right?"

"Yeah, back at the condo. What about it?"

Duncan thought, *Jesus, this broad has been the leader?* "I'm hoping it's encrypted."

"It is. No one could ever get to the account without me and my passwords, which, by the way, are all in my head."

"And that's the problem," Duncan said. "If these guys get their hands on you, how far do you think they'll go to get those passwords out of that pretty little head of yours? I've seen people like this before, Kelly. They have no boundaries and no mercy whatsoever. I'm not trying to scare you, but they'll start taking your fingers off one knuckle at a time until you either give them what they want or bleed out. Neither of those options work for me."

Snow visibly swallowed, and when she did, Duncan knew he had her. "What do we do?"

"Not we. Me. I'm guessing the condo has been compromised. There's a very good chance that the Cubans are waiting there for you and your crew."

Snow swallowed again and said, "I hadn't thought of that."

Duncan nodded at her. "I have. That's why I'm going to unhook the trailer and take the truck back. I'm the new guy, which means they don't have much, if any intel on me. I'll grab the laptop, get out, and bring it back here to you."

"For a price, I assume," Snow said, the cynicism in her tone almost as nasty as the bedspread they were currently sitting on.

Duncan waved his hands in the air. "This isn't about the money for me. It's about getting out alive. I don't know how much you've got in that account, but with the others all dead and gone, I'm guessing if you combine their shares with your own, you'll have enough to walk away and go someplace where no one can ever find you. Don't get me wrong...if you want to break me off a piece for helping you out, I'll take it because now I'm on the run too."

"And if I don't?" Snow said.

Duncan turned the corners of his mouth down. "I took this job from Bert as a favor. I've got about five other Berts in my hip pocket. I won't starve, but I won't be able to hide."

Snow thought about it for a few minutes, and Duncan let her. She'd already promised him a cut of Carver's take, and now with everyone else dead, even if she gave up all of Carver's cut, she'd still be able to do everything Duncan said. She'd be able to get out of the country and live a nice quiet life of luxury. But in order to do that she needed her laptop, and the only way to get it was to send Duncan.

She pinched one eye shut and looked at the man sitting next to her. "If you do this for me, I'll give you all of Carver's cut. That's a little over two mil and change, depending on the price of crypto and a few other variables."

"Like I said, I'd be grateful." Then, with a wry smile, "Boy, you will be all set, won't you? If my math is right, you'll be walking away with somewhere between seven and eight."

"Something like that...if we survive."

Duncan stood, looked at her and said, "Don't worry. You'll be safe." Then he took out the HK45 with the suppressor still attached and handed it to her. "Know how to use it?"

"Yeah. Point, pull the trigger, and it goes bang."

Duncan laughed. "That's the gist of it. Stay in the room, and if anyone comes through that door other than me, don't hesitate because I promise you they won't. I should be back in six hours or so."

"What if you're not?"

"I'll have to do a little surveillance at the condo. If I'm running late, I'll call and let you know. If you haven't heard from me in six hours, that means I'm probably dead. It also means that you call a cab or an Uber, or whatever, get to the nearest car rental agency and get the hell out of the state."

Snow looked away for a few seconds, then said, "I don't want to sound insensitive, but if you're dead, what about the laptop?"

Duncan shrugged. "Like you said, it's encrypted. Go to BestBuy or whatever and get a new one. I assume you can access the accounts that way."

Snow nodded. "Yeah, it'd take some doing, but I could get a new rig set up. It'd be a major pain in the ass, though."

Duncan smiled, then gave her a quick kiss. "Don't worry, I'm all but certain it won't come to that. Lock the door behind me, and keep that gun close. I'll see you in six hours."

Duncan put a baseball hat on, pulled it down low, stepped outside the room and waited until he heard the door being locked from the inside. Then he went out, unhooked the trailer, jumped into the pickup, and headed south through town, thinking about what was coming and what he was going to do. In truth, he was having a good time.

And the real fun hadn't even started yet.

CHAPTER SEVENTEEN

Cool let the helicopter settle gently in the back corner of the Warren fire department lot, all the firemen standing outside to watch the landing. Everyone climbed out and began walking toward the street. Virgil turned to Cool. "You coming, or are you going to stay here?"

Cool looked across the street and saw all the squad cars, along with a bunch of cops doing absolutely nothing. "I think I'll hang here if you don't mind."

"Not at all," Virgil said. "I'll let you know how long we'll be in a little while."

"No problem."

One of the firemen walked over. "Coffee's hot if you want some. Got extra bunks too if you'd rather take a nap."

"Thanks," Cool said. "I appreciate it."

The fireman tipped his chin at the state's helicopter. "Is that thing hard to fly?"

Cool shook his head and grinned. "Nope. It does take big balls though."

The fireman shook his head. "You might have the balls, but we've got the hose if you know what I mean."

Ross stopped when he heard that. He looked at the fireman and said, "Speaking of hoses, what size line do you usually use on an average fire?" He made his question sound so sincere the fireman didn't hesitate.

"Depends," he said, not realizing he'd walked right into Ross's trap. "Usually a three inch—" Then he interrupted himself and said, "Aw, fuck me."

Everyone had a good laugh at that, then Virgil and the rest of the MCU walked out of the lot to cross the street. Just as Murton stepped off the sidewalk, a pickup truck drove by. The driver gave Murton a casual glance and went past like he didn't have a care in the world.

Murton looked at the man behind the wheel. He had a ball cap pulled low across his brow and a big bushy mountain man beard. When Murton saw him he felt something click in his brain. He couldn't quite put his finger on it, but the man looked familiar somehow. But given his state of mind over the past week or so...the recurring dream, the lack of sleep, and his mental exhaustion, he let the thought go. He had work to do, and by the looks of the building across the street, plenty of it.

A JUNIOR FBI AGENT NAMED HARRISON TRIED TO STOP them from accessing the scene. "Stop right there, guys. Orders from the top brass. No one else gets in without prior approval."

Virgil sighed. "We do have prior approval. We're here at the behest of the governor of the state." Virgil took out his phone. "Would you like to speak with him? I've got his number on speed dial."

"That won't be necessary," Agent Franklin said to Harrison. Franklin Franklin was the lead agent for the state's arm of the Department of Homeland Security. "These men are with me and Agent Parr, and we expect you and your people to give them access to everything and anything they want. Have I made myself clear?" Then, without waiting for an answer, Franklin turned to Virgil. "How's it going, Jonesy?"

"Other than what's going on here, I'd say it's going well. Want to run it for me?"

Franklin looked at Harrison and said, "That'll be all, son." Then he lifted the crime scene tape so Virgil and the rest of the MCU could make their way into the blocked-off area.

"Bank robberies are handled by the FBI," Harrison said, not quite ready to let it go.

Franklin gave him a thoughtful nod. "Yes, they are. But in case you've forgotten, here are a couple of noteworthy facts: The F in FBI stands for federal. That's number one. Two, these gentlemen are with the state. They are here to cover the murders that occurred earlier this morning because no money was actually stolen, and murder is a state crime."

"Murder in the commission of a bank robbery is a federal offense," Harrison said.

Franklin clapped him on the back...maybe a little harder than necessary. "Right you are, young man. But since DHS is at the top of the federal food chain, that means I'm the senior agent on scene. Run along now. I'll get in touch if we need anything. You know...coffee, doughnuts...that sort of thing."

Harrison turned about three different shades of red before he turned and walked away.

"Little hard on the guy, weren't you?" Ross said.

Franklin had been involved with the MCU on any number of cases in the past, so he not only knew Ross, he knew about his direct, matter-of-fact attitude. "This from you?" Then to Virgil: "I hope you're not letting him go soft on you."

Virgil stuck his tongue in his cheek, then said, "How about we hear what went down?"

"Fair enough," Franklin said. "No witnesses to the actual crime, but the security footage caught it all. We're looking for a chocolate brown Mini Cooper Countryman. The tags come back to a sixty-seven year old woman out of Florida who says she had no idea her plates had been stolen."

"Who made contact with her?" Virgil said. "The woman in Florida." He was taking notes as Franklin spoke.

"A Manatee County sheriff's deputy. The sheriff is a guy named Greg Laun. Not like the yard. It's spelled L-a-u-n."

"No sign of the vehicle, I take it," Murton said.

"None," Franklin said. "Though I have to admit, I'm not surprised. There were no witnesses left, the shooters used suppressed automatic weapons, and by the time anyone figured out what was happening and made the call, that car could have been fifty miles down the highway."

"Who called it in?" Rosencrantz said.

"One of the firemen across the street. He served in the army and recognized the sound of automatic weapons. Never saw the car though. He was in his bunk, and by the time he got dressed and made it outside, the vehicle was gone."

Virgil turned to Rosencrantz and tipped his head at the fire station. "I'm on it," Rosencrantz said. He ducked under the tape and headed back across the street.

"What else?" Virgil said.

Franklin gave him a half shrug. "The troopers have put out the description of the car across the state, and have notified every county to be on the lookout. They also made contact with Illinois, Michigan, Ohio, and Kentucky, though it's probably a waste of time. The car is either well-hidden or at the bottom of a lake by now. The rest I can tell you about, but it would be quicker and easier if you simply watch the video."

Virgil turned toward Murton. "Have Becky get in touch with the Manatee County guys and get the scoop on this woman and her plates."

"You got it, Jonesy." Murton took out his phone and made the call.

Virgil turned back to Franklin and said, "I take it your involvement with this has to do with the crew that's been hitting the banks and credit unions all over the country."

"That's why I'm here," Franklin said. "Otherwise, I'd probably be on the golf course losing my pension to Parr."

Virgil laughed through his nose. "Let's go take a look, huh?"

EVERYONE STOPPED AT THE ENTRANCE OF THE BANK and looked through the front door. The inside of the building looked like it might have been used for automatic weapons training. Bullet holes and shell casings were everywhere, half the ceiling tiles were either hanging awkwardly from their support brackets or ripped to shreds and resting on the floor. Wires hung down from above where the ceiling tiles used to be, and the overhead light fixtures dangled three to four feet off the ground. Most of the windows were shattered, the glass partition between the lobby and the teller area was broken and jagged, the edges razor sharp. The dead Warren police officer was near one of the teller windows, his body bloodied and resting at unnatural angles.

Murton puffed his cheeks and said, "These guys weren't messing around."

At the sound of his voice, one of the Huntington County crime scene techs looked their way. "If you guys are going to come in, I'd appreciate it if you'd let me guide you through."

"Like to get a look at the security footage, if we could," Virgil said.

The tech nodded. "Agent Franklin has already seen it. I've got one of my guys making a copy right now. He should be finished in a—"

Another tech appeared out of a back office and said, "I uploaded it to our system. If you give me your number, you'll be able to see it all on your phone in about thirty seconds."

Virgil recited his number to the tech, who wrote it down, then said, "Hang on a second." Then he disappeared back into the office. True to his word, Virgil's phone buzzed at him thirty seconds later. When the tech came back out, he said, "Do you guys need to come in?"

Virgil shook his head. "No, go ahead and do your

thing. Us coming in and contaminating your scene won't accomplish anything."

"Appreciate it," the tech said.

"You've got my number," Virgil said. "If you come up with anything—I don't care how small, let me know, will you?"

The tech said he would and went back to work. Virgil and everyone else backed out of the entryway.

Once they were clear of the building, Murton looked back over his shoulder. "If it weren't for all the bullet holes and shell casings, I'd say it looked like someone tossed a couple of grenades in there."

Virgil saw Rosencrantz jogging back across the street, so he waited to bring the video up on his phone.

"What'd I miss?" Rosencrantz said.

"Death and destruction at its worst," Murton said. "Jonesy has the footage."

Franklin looked at everyone and said, "I have to make a few calls." Then he turned to walk away.

"You don't want to see this?" Ross said.

Franklin shook his head. "I already have. Once was enough, believe me."

———

VIRGIL BROUGHT THE FOOTAGE UP, AND EVERYONE crowded around him to watch. The entire clip was only about ninety seconds long, but there was enough death and destruction visible from multiple camera angles it took them almost ten minutes to watch everything that had unfolded.

"The shooter who got away took out his own guys," Murton said.

"Looks that way," Virgil said.

"Greed?" Rosencrantz asked.

"I don't think so," Virgil said. "What's the point in taking out your own guys during the actual robbery? If it was simple greed, they'd have done the job first. Murt?"

Murton nodded. "I tend to agree. They took the cop out first, and once that was done, the guy who got away opened up on his partners before killing everyone else. Doesn't make much sense, but these types usually aren't the brightest bulbs in the lamp."

"I'll tell you what I don't understand," Rosencrantz said. "Why kill everyone in the building? The cop? I get it. That would be a pure panic move. But everyone was masked up and wearing gloves. If it goes bad right out of the gate, why not back out and go? This guy not only took out his own guys, he took the time to murder all the other employees."

Virgil got Franklin's attention and waved him over. Franklin ended his call, then said, "Quite a show, wasn't it?"

Virgil didn't answer because he knew Franklin's question was rhetorical in nature. Instead, he asked a question of his own. "This crew...they've been pulling these jobs all over the country. Do I have that right?"

"You do," Franklin said.

"And they've been at it for how long?"

"At least five years based on the intelligence we've gathered."

"How many jobs?"

"I have to admit it's hard to say with any certainty, but based on the data that's been collected, and the similarities between the—"

"Franklin?" Virgil said.

"Yes?"

"This isn't a deposition. How many?"

"We believe at least twenty. Possibly more."

"So, one job every three months, give or take," Murton said.

"That would be a fair assumption, outside the lines of demonstrable proof," Franklin said.

"And out of all those jobs, how many times was anyone hurt or killed?" Virgil said.

"You're saying this is a different crew?"

Virgil shook his head. "No, I'm simply asking a question."

Franklin wrinkled his nose. "The answer is none. No one has ever been hurt or killed by the crew everyone is searching for. Scarred for life, or psychologically affected in some way? Certainly. But other than that, no killings. In fact, no shots ever fired."

Murton looked at his brother. "What are you think-ing, Jones-man?"

"It's one of two scenarios. We've either got a crew that is unraveling, or this was a different group who didn't know what they were doing and panicked when they saw the cop."

"What say your gut?" Franklin said.

Virgil looked at nothing for a few seconds, then said, "Too soon to tell."

CHAPTER EIGHTEEN

R osencrantz looked at Virgil. "Now what, boss?"

"Did you get anything useful out of the fireman?"

Rosencrantz shook his head. "Nothing at all. Said he recognized the sound of automatic weapons but didn't see a thing."

"Okay...it was worth a shot." Virgil turned to Murton and said, "Let's watch that security footage again."

Murton shrugged. "Okay, but I think I've had my fill of video murder and mayhem for the day. It's not even noon yet."

"Part of the job, brother."

They spent twenty minutes going through the footage, stopping and restarting at different sections to make sure they weren't missing anything. At one point, Murton said, "Pause it right there."

Virgil was a little slow on the button, so he had to back the video up a few seconds. "Here?"

"Yeah. Right there."

"What is it?"

"That's the only full-on face shot of the guy. It looks like he's got a beard." He took the phone from Virgil and zoomed in on the paused shot. "See that? It's sticking out from under his mask a little at the bottom."

Virgil called Ross and Rosencrantz over. "Rosie, go find Franklin and ask him to come over here, would you?"

"Sure."

"Ross, tell the crime scene techs that the guy who got away had a beard. See if they've found any facial hair on the floor."

Ross took off, then Murton looked at Virgil and said, "You're thinking DNA?"

Virgil rolled his head around. "It's a long shot, but it's not nothing."

"So what now?" Murton said.

"I'm probably going to make your wife mad at me."

Murton chuffed. "That'd be a first."

Franklin walked over and said, rather dryly, "You beckoned, my lord?"

Virgil winced a little. "Sorry. I didn't know where you were."

"Standing right here and ready to assist the state in any way possible. Despite what you may have heard, it's what I live for."

"All the jobs this crew has pulled...you said, what? Twenty?"

"Yes. We—and we collectively being the DHS, FBI, ATF, and other various federal and state agencies—believe they have done at least twenty. Personally, I think it may be more."

"Can you get me all the security footage from the known jobs? The ones where you're positive it's the same crew."

Franklin gave Virgil a fake smile. "When do you need it?"

"Quicker the sooner, Franklin."

"I believe that might be the sloppiest grammatical sentence I've ever heard you utter," Franklin said. "I assume you'd want it to go to Mr. Taylor's wife here?"

Virgil barked out a laugh. "Yeah, that'd be great."

"That stopped being funny shortly after our honeymoon," Murton said.

Then at the exact same time—as if they could read each other's minds—Virgil and Franklin said, "That's what she said."

Murton gave it his best effort but couldn't resist and ended up laughing right along with them.

VIRGIL CALLED BECKY AT THE BAR AND ASKED ABOUT the Manatee County sheriff. "Did Sheriff Laun have any useful information on the stolen plates?"

"Yes," Becky said. "I was getting ready to call you. It seems the reason this woman didn't know her plates had been stolen is because they were swapped out. The Manatee guys followed the swap back through five different vehicles."

"That sounds like someone was trying very hard to cover their tracks."

"Clearly," Becky said. "Anyway, you might want to give the sheriff down there a call."

Virgil thought that odd and said so. "Why?"

"It wasn't his request...it's my suggestion. He seems like a good guy, and he's a bit of a talker."

"What'd he want to talk about?"

"At first, nothing. At least nothing important. Then he told me that they were working an arson case out of a town called Cortez. I guess it's somewhere down between Tampa and Sarasota, along the Gulf Coast."

Virgil was getting impatient. "Good for him. And this affects us how?"

"That's what I'm trying to tell you, if you'd give a girl a minute. It seems the arson case is marginally connected to the stolen plates."

"In what way?"

"Manatee County had one of their crime scene people go out with the detective who was tracking the plates. They printed all four of them and got partial matches on two. The prints came back almost immediately because they belonged to a guy named Alex Carver."

"Who the hell is he?" Virgil said.

"An ex-con who did a little state time down in Louisiana about ten years ago. He did the full bit, then dropped off the map."

Virgil's mind was racing. "And the sheriff thinks this Carver guy is the one behind his arson case?"

"No, not unless he's the worst arsonist in the world. They found his body...Carver's, along with an unidentified male inside the building that got torched."

"And the Manatee guys are sure it was arson?"

"They're positive, Jonesy. Said the place smelled like a refinery."

"Well, it happens," Virgil said. "I've heard of it before. The arsonist tries to burn a place to the ground but gets caught up in the fire and doesn't make it out."

"Yeah, except that's not what happened here. The Manatee medical examiner says Carver had been shot twice in the chest and once in the head."

"So, they've got two dead inside a torched building, and one of them is the guy who swapped out all the plates that connects to our bank robbery up here."

"Yep. Like I said, you might want to give the sheriff a call."

"You're the best, Becks. I'll do that right now. When was the last time I told you I loved you?"

Becky snorted. "I don't remember, but I'll settle for the erotic dreams." Then she hung up.

VIRGIL CALLED HER RIGHT BACK. "YOU HUNG UP on me."

"I thought the conversation was over," Becky said.

"Right. It almost was. I want to send you some video security footage, courtesy of our friend, Franklin."

"What is it, and how much?"

"It's footage of every bank job this crew has pulled over the last five years. I'd like you to go through it and compare it to the footage of the attempted robbery we're looking at now."

"What am I looking for?" Becky said.

"To be honest, I'm not sure. These guys are masked up, but I'd like to get your eyes on it and see if you notice any similarities. Height, weight, the way they move...that sort of thing."

"It sounds like a lot of video."

"Well, I won't kid you...it probably is a lot, but this crew goes in quick, and they don't stay long. I don't need a frame-by-frame comparison or any of that nonsense, but if you see anything that connects all the past jobs to this one, I'll take it."

Becky sighed and said, "Okay, tell Franklin to send it."

"I already did. Love you, Becks." And this time it was Virgil who hung up.

Ross walked up to Virgil as he finished his call with Becky. "The crime scene techs made a note of your request regarding facial hair, but they didn't seem overly optimistic."

"Why not?" Virgil said.

Ross shrugged. "They said with all the destruction and debris...not to mention the blood and other bodily fluids already present, it would be quite a while before they find anything."

Virgil nodded. "That's okay as long as we've got them looking."

"What now?" Ross said.

"Get with Rosie and find out who's doing point on canvass. Everybody keeps saying there weren't any witnesses, but I'm hoping someone saw something. Tell whoever is in charge to keep pushing and widen the area if they have to."

"You got it, boss."

Virgil's phone buzzed at him, and when he checked the screen he saw a text from Becky with the Manatee County sheriff's phone number. He punched the number in, and ten seconds later the sheriff was on the line.

"Sheriff Laun."

"Sheriff, Detective Virgil Jones with the Indiana State Police Major Crimes Unit. How are you, sir?"

"I'm well, Detective. You?"

"I've been better if I'm being honest with you. Call me Jonesy, please."

"You got it. Sounds like you're as busy and baffled as we are."

"That might be an understatement," Virgil said. "I've received a verbal report from our researcher, Becky Wheeler, regarding your investigation. I'd like to hear a few of the particulars from you."

"Your researcher sounds like quite a gal. Doesn't seem to miss much."

"She certainly doesn't," Virgil said. Then he filled the sheriff in on everything Becky had already told him. He finished by saying, "So, what I'd like to know is this: If the license plate swaps connect Carver to the crew that's doing the bank jobs, and Carver is dead, how does the arson fit into the equation?"

"That's what we're still trying to figure out," the sheriff said. "The arson happened at a bar called Slips. It was mostly a dive joint, but one of those places that tourists like to visit when they come down here. Makes them feel like they've been someplace authentic."

"Yeah, I get it," Virgil said. "Who owns Slips?"

"Owned would probably be a better word. The place was reduced to damned near nothing. It lived up to its name though because the fire caused it to slip from its foundation. What's left—which isn't much, by the way—is sitting in the water next to the docks."

"Was it insurance fraud?"

"Nope. Even if it was, the check might have amounted to about fifty bucks."

"Geez, the place must have been very authentic," Virgil said.

The sheriff let out a little chuckle. "Yeah, well, not so much anymore."

"So...the owner?" Virgil said, trying to keep the sheriff on point.

"A woman named Kelly Snow, who, coincidentally, can't be found."

"Is there any chance she was a victim herself?"

"None whatsoever."

"Why not?" Virgil said.

"A couple of reasons," the sheriff said. "One, the divers didn't find anyone besides this Carver fellow, along with another unidentified male victim. And our divers are very good. If she was in the water, they would have found her."

"Okay, good enough. What's the other reason?"

"She was one of the first people we tried to contact once the fire was out and we knew it was arson. When one of my men went to her residence, she was nowhere to be found. I authorized entry for a safety check, and my deputy found a note to her landlord telling him she was running. She denies the arson...it's all in the note, but you have to ask yourself, if she didn't do it, why run?"

Virgil thought about it for a few moments. "With two dead at the scene and Snow listed as the owner, I'm wondering if she witnessed the killings. She might not be running because of the arson...she might be running because she's a target."

"That's a possibility, and one we're looking into."

"Did your people talk to her landlord?"

"Yeah, we brought him in and sweated him a little, but my gut says he didn't know or have anything to do with it. He was as clueless as we are."

"How'd you get the ID on Carver so fast?" Virgil said.

"We simply followed the chain. The medical examiner matched Carver's dental records from the prison, and since his prints were on the swapped-out plates, that one was a bit of a no-brainer."

"What about the other victim? Any chance of making an ID?"

"I'd put those chances at zero unless we can find Miss Snow. She probably knows who he was, but unless that happens, we might never know. His teeth were smashed out, and the fire took care of his fingerprints."

"Let me ask you something, Sheriff: Assume for a minute that Snow is telling the truth, and the reason she's running is because she is in fear for her life. If that's the case, do you have any leads that might indicate who set the fire?"

"Not yet."

"The way you said that...did I catch something in your tone there?"

"You did," the sheriff said. "There was a van at the scene of the fire that was torched as well, and it wasn't accidental. It was mostly reduced to scrap metal, but my crime scene people are trying to recover the VIN stamps from the engine and frame. If they can get those, it's one more piece of the puzzle."

"Sounds like you're doing everything you can," Virgil said.

"We are. Hope it does some good."

"Well, you know how it works. Every little bit helps." Then, "Before I let you go, could you send us all your reports?"

"That spunky little researcher of yours already asked for them. I'm sure she has everything by now. My secretary sent them almost an hour ago."

Virgil nodded to himself. Becky was on the ball, as usual. "Listen, about your secretary..."

"What about her?"

Virgil shook his head. "Aw, nothing. Forget I mentioned it. If you come up with anything else, I'd appreciate a call. You've got my number."

The sheriff told Virgil he'd keep him in the loop, then ended the call.

Virgil saw Murton, Ross, and Rosencrantz coming around the back side of the bank. He walked toward them and said, "What have we got?"

"Nothing," Murton said. "Thought I'd help look for witnesses, but nobody has found anyone who saw a damn thing. I'm running out of ideas here, Jonesy."

"Where's Franklin? Have you seen him?"

"He's staying close to the crime scene people, hoping for a miracle," Rosencrantz said. "I don't think he's going to get one."

"Let's all go talk to him," Virgil said. "I got some partial information from a Florida sheriff who knows more than he knows. I'll fill everyone in at once."

Franklin was indeed staying close to the crime scene people. He was practically hovering inside the door. Virgil and the rest of the MCU walked up and when Franklin turned around, he said, "Speaking on behalf of the United States federal government, I really do hope your time here has been more productive than mine."

Virgil gave him a toothless grin. "I do have some information to share. I spoke with—" Virgil's phone buzzed, so he held up a wait-a-minute finger, then answered without bothering to look at the screen. "Jonesy." Just as he answered, Murton's phone rang as well.

"Virgil, it Delroy. I need you at the bar right now, me. *Right now.*" Virgil could hear the fear and panic in Delroy's voice.

"What is it, Delroy? Delroy, are you there? What's going on?"

Murton shoved his phone in his pocket and grabbed Virgil's arm. "Time to go, brother." Then he looked at

Ross and Rosencrantz. "Go get Cool moving. We're going back to Indy right now."

Virgil was being dragged along by his brother, trying to hear what Delroy was saying. Franklin followed the whole group.

"Delroy?" Virgil said. "Talk to me." Then Virgil heard two quick beeps that told him the call had been dropped.

Cool, who was sitting in the back of the helicopter with his feet up, saw the entire squad running his way. He didn't know what was happening, but he knew they were leaving, and quick. He jumped up front and began flipping switches.

Murton looked at Virgil as they ran. "That was Becky who called me."

"What's going on?" Virgil said.

"It's Robert. He's been arrested. According to Becky, Metro homicide is tearing the bar apart."

The words that came out of Murton's mouth were so surprising that Virgil stopped in his tracks. "What? Robert? What the hell is going on?"

Murton pulled at Virgil's arm again. "Let's go, Virgil. They're charging Robert with murder."

CHAPTER NINETEEN

The drive from the airport in Indianapolis to Jonesy's bar took longer than the flight back from Warren. When the entire MCU, along with Franklin arrived, they found the bar surrounded by city squad cars, along with a host of gawkers standing outside the taped-off crime scene area. Virgil ignored the city cop who tried to stop him from entering his own bar, and when he did, the cop grabbed his arm and spun him around.

Murton was right behind Virgil and grabbed the cop and pushed him to the ground. Then he and Virgil pulled open the front door and ran inside. What they saw stopped them in their tracks...for about a half second. Becky, Delroy, and Robert were handcuffed to the bar rail. Robert had a black eye, and Brent Williams, the former lead detective of the Indianapolis Metro Homicide Unit had his finger in Robert's face.

"Tell me right now," Williams said. "This is your last chance before you get hauled down to central booking and charged with murder. Why'd you kill him?"

Virgil hurried over to Williams, with Murton right on his heels. When Williams saw them coming, he looked back at Robert and said, "Better make it quick."

Murton glanced at Becky, gave her a wink, then pulled Virgil back before the situation became worse than it already was. He walked right up to Williams and whispered in his ear. "If you don't get your finger out of my chef's face, Williams, I promise you I'll show you the other end of it. You're an embarrassment to the unit you used to run. Now step back."

Williams lowered his finger and turned to Virgil. "I see your hound dog hasn't lost his touch."

"You don't know the half of it, Brent." Virgil knew if he didn't somehow manage to keep his cool, the situation would go from bad to worse. "You mind telling me what's going on? Before you start, why do you have both my bar managers—not to mention my researcher—cuffed to the bar?"

Murton clapped Virgil on the back. "Get Williams out of here. They won't be cuffed for long." Murton took out his handcuff keys and started to unhook his wife and friends.

When Williams saw what Murton was doing, he tried to get past Virgil, who got right in his face. "I don't know what's going on here, Brent, but whatever it is, cuffing my people inside their own establishment is way over the top. Where are all your men?"

That's when Virgil heard the slide on a semi-automatic handgun. "One of them is right behind you," said the cop Murton had pushed to the ground. "Everybody freeze and set your weapons on the floor, or we're going to have a big problem here."

What the cop didn't realize was that Ross and Rosencrantz were right behind him. Ross took the gun from the cop with such expertise that the officer didn't know he'd been disarmed until it was too late. "I'll keep this for now," Ross said. "My partner will show you out."

Rosencrantz hustled the city cop back outside, then mentioned in a matter-of-fact way that if he wanted his gun back without a report being filed, he should not reenter the bar.

Virgil turned back to Williams. "Brent?"

Williams was so mad his jaw was quivering. "Let's step out back."

Murton got Becky, Delroy, and Robert unhooked, then told them to wait where they were. He wanted to hear their story, but he wanted to hear Williams's version first. He followed Virgil through the kitchen and out the back door.

Once they were outside, Williams led them around to the alley, where the bar's dumpster was located. He pointed at the body on the ground. "That's why your chef, Robert Whyte, is under arrest. A routine patrol car passed the alleyway and spotted Robert standing over the body, holding a gun. The officer indicated that the weapon was pointed at the deceased. He turned into the alley, told Robert to drop the gun, and then called it in."

The area around the body had already been taped off, and Virgil knew better than to try to get past the tape. That'd only make matters worse. He looked at Williams and said, "Wait here. I'll be right back."

Virgil ran back into the bar and looked at Becky. "Lock the front door, Becks. Do it right now."

Becky gave him a tight nod, then did as she was asked. Virgil looked at Robert, then raised his eyebrows. "Chef?" The meaning behind the question wasn't lost on anyone.

"You know better than that, you," Robert said. "I prayed over him."

Virgil nodded. "I know. I just needed to hear you say it. Nobody talks to anyone without me or Murton present, got it?"

Becky, Delroy, and Robert all said they understood. Virgil told Ross and Rosencrantz that the bar was off-limits to everyone, including the cops, until he had the situation under control.

"We got the inside covered, Boss-man," Rosencrantz said. "Keep us up."

Virgil said he would, then looked at Becky. "Get upstairs and start pulling the security tapes. The last twenty-four hours should do it."

"You got it, Jonesy."

As Becky ran up the stairs, Virgil looked around his bar. All the tables had been overturned, the liquor bottles behind the bar had been smashed on the floor, and the kitchen was an absolute mess with pots and pans scattered everywhere. Virgil took a breath, forced himself to calm down, then went back outside.

WILLIAMS WAS INSIDE THE TAPED-OFF AREA SPEAKING with a city crime scene technician, so Virgil walked over to Murton. "Did he say anything?"

"Williams? No. He's doing his best to pretend we don't exist."

Virgil lowered his voice. "That's because he's still pissed about what went down with Ross and Brenner."

Murton bobbed his head. "Yeah, I've sort of deduced that all on my own. You see the condition of the kitchen?"

Virgil nodded. "Yeah. I'm not worried about it. Insurance will cover the damage, and by the time I'm done with Williams, the city will cover the deductible, I guarantee it."

Murton tipped his head toward the front of the alley. "See that uniformed guy sitting in his squad?"

Virgil turned and looked. "Yeah, what about him?"

"He's been trying to get my attention. I'm pretty sure he's the one who rolled up on...whatever this is."

"I'll go speak with him. Becky's pulling the video. Ross

and Rosencrantz have the inside locked down. Let me know when she's got the footage."

"No problem, Jonesy."

Virgil walked over to the city squad car, and when he did, the uniformed cop got out. Virgil knew him as one of the regulars at the bar, and had seen him inside any number of times with his wife. "Jake? You caught this?"

"Hey, Jonesy. Yeah, this is part of my sector. Man, my wife and I love this place so much I make it a part of my regular patrol."

Virgil shook hands with him. "I appreciate it. Murt said you were trying to get his attention?"

Jake Abrams nodded. "I've been trying to get someone to listen to me ever since Metro rolled up."

"Tell me what happened," Virgil said.

Abrams turned a little red in the face, then said, "I have to tell you, some of it might be on me."

"How's that?"

"I could have handled it better. Slower maybe. When I saw Robert with the gun, I didn't know it was him. All I could see was a black guy standing over a body next to the dumpster with a weapon in his hand. He was sort of standing there like he wasn't sure what to do. I immediately called it in. I mean, you see a man with a gun standing over a body? I had to."

Virgil nodded. "Following proper procedure is never a bad thing, Jake. What happened next?"

"I burped the siren, then got out, drew my weapon, and told Robert to drop the gun."

"Did he comply?"

"Yes, he absolutely did. He set it on the lid of the dumpster and backed away with his hands up."

"Did you cuff him?"

Abrams looked surprised at the question. "Of course not. Once I saw who it was, I secured my weapon, told Robert everything would be okay, and to step back and wait. He did everything I asked. I checked the victim to make sure he was dead, then called it in as a homicide. You can probably put the rest together yourself, but I'll tell you this, Robert didn't kill anyone. I'd bet my badge on that. I wish I could have done something more."

"Jake, you did everything right and nothing wrong. Williams got wind of this, and that's when it all went sideways."

"You're telling me," Jake said. "He wouldn't hardly listen to a word I said."

"I'm not surprised. We've had some bad blood over the past couple of years. That's part of the reason he got demoted. Don't worry about it. Head back to the station and write your report. Copy me and Murton on it, and we'll take it from there."

"Williams told me to wait here."

"I don't think Williams will be giving too many more orders after all this."

Jake nodded, then said, "I hope you're right. Listen, I

saw Robert's black eye and the bruise on Delroy's arm. Are they okay? Williams was knocking them around pretty hard."

"We'll have the medics check them out, but I'm sure they'll be fine."

"I also saw the inside of the bar...and the kitchen. How long do you think you'll be shut down?"

Virgil shrugged. "I'm not sure. Maybe a week or so." Then Virgil's phone buzzed at him. When he checked the screen, he saw it was a message from Becky. She'd attached the security footage. Virgil took a minute to watch, and let Abrams do so as well. There were three sections, the first showing an unidentified man pulling a body from the trunk of a late model sedan and placing it behind the dumpster. The video was captured at night, so Virgil couldn't tell who it was.

The second section showed Williams punching Robert in the face, and manhandling Becky and Delroy as he handcuffed them, then started trashing the bar. He took Robert's baseball bat from the kitchen and swung at the liquor bottles on the shelves by the mirror, upended all the tables, smashed most of the chairs, and did as much damage as possible in a very short amount of time.

The third section showed Robert carrying a box of trash out to the dumpster and tossing it in. It also showed him doing everything Jake had just described. Robert dragged the body out, then quickly freed it from the tarp, and rested his ear over the victim's chest. Then he noticed the weapon and picked it up. That's when the sound of Jake's siren could be heard.

"Like I said."

Virgil nodded. "Tell you what...hang around for a minute, will you?"

"Sure. How come?"

"I'm going to need you to transport someone over to central booking for me."

VIRGIL WALKED BACK OVER TO MURTON AND SAID, "Becky send you the footage?"

"Yep." Then, in his best Ricky Ricardo accent, Murton said, "Somebody's got some splainin' to do."

"Make sure everything is okay inside, then have Ross and Rosencrantz come out here. We might need the backup."

Murton raised his eyebrows. "You sure you want to handle it this way?"

"No, but I'm going to anyway. Don't forget, he had your wife cuffed to the bar as well."

"Oh, not to worry, Jones-man. If you weren't going to do it, I would." He gave his brother a wink. "I'll be right back."

Thirty seconds later Murton, Ross, and Rosencrantz all walked back outside and stood behind their boss. Virgil whistled at Williams to get his attention. "Hey,

Brent. Need a quick word."

Williams made a show of pointing one or two things out to the crime scene tech, then took off his gloves and walked over to Virgil. "What is it? In case you haven't noticed, I'm a little busy. In fact, I'm starting to lose count of how many bodies have turned up around this bar of yours."

Virgil moved his jaw back and forth, then said, "Uh-huh. Anyway, I wanted to ask why you trashed my place and assaulted my people."

Williams gave him a wicked smile. "We were looking for evidence and not getting much cooperation. We've already got the gun with your cook's fingerprints all over it. We wanted to make sure there weren't more weapons we needed to know about."

"There are," Murton said. "Given all the damage you've done, I'm surprised you didn't find them."

"Don't worry, hotshot, we will."

"No, you won't, Brent," Virgil said. "In fact, you'll never set foot in this bar again, I promise you."

Williams actually laughed. "I'll set foot in there right now if I want to, and any other time during the course of this investigation."

"I doubt it," Murton said. "You don't have a warrant."

"We didn't need a warrant, asshole. We had probable cause. Your man was standing over a dead body holding the murder weapon."

Murton turned to Virgil. "Did he just refer to me as a rectum?"

Virgil ignored Murton and said, "No, you didn't have probable cause, Brent. As a point of fact, the only thing you've ever had over the last two years is a hard-on for the MCU and the way we operate. You're out of control and a disgrace to the badge."

"I'm a disgrace? Why don't you tell me what really happened with Roje Brenner? Then we'll see who's the disgrace around here."

Virgil shook his head. "Yesterday's box score, Brent, and quite frankly, above your pay grade, not to mention your level of intelligence. But never mind all that. You've got bigger things to worry about right now."

"Like what?"

"Well, your pension comes to mind," Murton said. Then he reached inside his jacket and pulled out his weapon. "Turn around and put your hands on the wall, Williams. You're under arrest."

"Fuck you, Wheeler. Under arrest for what?"

Virgil got right up next to Williams and pushed him face-first against the wall and cuffed his wrists behind his back. Then he took his gun and badge, and stuck them in his pocket. "You are under arrest for unlawful entry, destruction of public and private property, false arrest, dereliction of duty, obstruction of justice in an ongoing state and federal investigation, and assault on innocent civilians."

"You know," Murton said, "since Robert and Delroy are both black, that might be considered a hate crime."

Virgil yanked him off the wall, then he and Murton walked him down to Jake's squad car, and read him his rights.

"I'm not done with you, Jones," Williams said. "You either, Wheeler. I'll take this to my boss, to the union, to the mayor, and my lawyer."

"Take it to the Pope for all I care," Virgil said with a smile. "Just don't take it personally. Look how far that's gotten you." Then he bent him over and stuffed him in the back of the squad. "Watch your head, now."

CHAPTER TWENTY

A few of the city officers tried to intervene on behalf of Williams but Virgil could tell their hearts really weren't into it. Besides, most of the cops present were at the scene because they either knew Jonesy and Murton as friends, or they frequented the bar on a regular basis. Once everyone agreed that Williams had been acting out for personal reasons, the situation turned away from him and toward the investigation.

Virgil asked Rosencrantz to take charge of the scene because it wouldn't be proper procedure to investigate a homicide that occurred on his own property.

"No problem, Jonesy," Rosencrantz said. "I'd like to get Chip or Mimi down here to finish the crime scene stuff."

"I'd tend to agree," Virgil said. "But like I said, you're in charge. Use Ross as well. Murt and I will stay on the bank jobs. When you get this mess taken care of the two of you will be back with us."

"Sounds good," Rosencrantz said.

Virgil turned to walk away, then stopped and said, "Make sure Chip gets pictures of the inside of the bar, including Robert's black eye and Delroy's bruise."

Rosencrantz said he would and made the call.

VIRGIL TOOK A CALL FROM THE CENTRAL BOOKING watch commander, a no-nonsense lieutenant named Don Hammond. "Jones, would you care to explain to me why I've got a senior detective—one who used to be in charge of Metro Homicide, no less—sitting in a holding cell like a common thug?"

"I'd have no problem explaining it at all, Lieutenant. He rolled on a homicide call at my bar. The body was found outside, behind a dumpster by one of my—"

"Abrams already gave me the verbal. He's typing up the report right now. Do you know how bad this looks for my department? I don't need this kind of grief. I want you to kick this guy loose. Am I making myself clear?"

"Tell you what, Lou...give me your personal cell number and I'll send you some security footage."

"What kind of footage?"

Virgil didn't like to be pushed around, city brass or

not. "I already told you. Security footage from the scene. How about it on the number?"

Hammond gave him the number then said, "Whatever you're sending better be worthy of an Academy Award, or I'm kicking Williams loose and we'll see how it all plays out." Then he hung up.

Virgil sent the footage that showed Williams trashing the bar, getting rough with Becky, and punching Robert in the eye.

Five minutes later Hammond called back. "I'm turning the whole thing over to IA. It's their beef now. Do you have his badge and gun?"

"I do," Virgil said.

"I'll have one of the patrol guys get it from you. It'll save you a trip downtown. Get me your report as soon as you can."

"I will. Thanks, Lieutenant."

"Yeah, yeah, you're fucking welcome. Do you know how much grief and paperwork you've dropped on me?" Then, before Virgil could answer: "Your people okay?"

"Looks like it."

"What's the story with Williams, anyway? He used to be a solid cop."

"I have no idea," Virgil lied. "Maybe he doesn't like the way I dress."

Hammond actually laughed. "Nobody likes the way you dress. And get a haircut next time you happen to pass by a barbershop." Then he hung up.

Virgil smiled to himself, then he got back to work. He went back into the bar and pulled Robert away from everyone else. "Are you okay?"

"Yeah, mon. I'm fine, me. Da bar, not so much. I tink we probably be closed for a while. A week at least."

Virgil nodded. "You and Delroy tell the entire staff that their salaries will be covered for however long it takes. I don't want to lose anybody."

"You a good man, Virgil Jones."

"So are you, Robert. But listen, next time you find a body, it might be better for everyone—especially you—if you didn't touch it or move it in any way."

"Yeah, mon. I already put dat together, me. Da only reason I did was to make sure he didn't need help, him."

"I understand. But let me ask you this: Why did you pick up the gun?"

"It was sitting right on top of da tarp. I didn't have no choice, me. Am I in any trouble?"

Virgil put his arm around Robert's shoulders. "Not at all, my friend. In fact, you could probably press charges against Detective Williams for assault if you want to."

Robert shook his head. "Dat not my way, Virgil."

Virgil nodded. "I figured as much. Listen, you'll have to give a statement to Rosie. Keep your story simple and tell the truth. Everything will be okay. I promise."

"Da truth the only ting I know how to tell, Virgil."

"No one knows that better than me, Robert. And

listen, I want you to go see an eye doctor. I'm going to call Bell and see who he recommends."

"I really don't tink dat necessary."

Virgil clapped him on the back. "It's not a request, my friend. Don't worry, insurance will cover it. Get with Rosie, give him your statement, and I'll let you know what Bell says, okay?"

"Yeah, mon. Waste of time, though. I've been hit harder by Jamaican mosquitos." Then he laughed at his own joke and walked away.

Murton was going around surveying the damage to the bar. Virgil found him in the kitchen. When he took a closer look, the destruction was worse than he'd originally thought. "I'm surprised he didn't try to burn the place down."

"Well, he's still probably down in holding," Murton said. "Give him time. I'm guessing this won't be the last of it."

"It'd better be," Virgil said.

Just then, Franklin walked in through the back. "I see the remodeling project is coming along nicely. What the hell happened?"

"Remember Williams, from Metro Homicide?"

Franklin tucked his chin slightly. "He did this?"

Virgil nodded. "Go take a look out front."

Franklin walked into the bar right as Chip Lawless, one of the MCU crime scene technicians came through the door. "Mimi is working the victim with the city. Becky said you wanted pictures in here?"

"Hey, Chip," Virgil said. "I do. Kitchen and bar area. I don't think Williams made it upstairs."

"He didn't," Murton said. "I already checked. Becky is up there right now going through the footage Franklin sent."

Lawless looked around. "Williams tore the place up?"

Franklin walked back into the kitchen. "That's the same thing I asked. Apparently, the answer is yes." Then to Virgil: "Did Becky get the videos?"

"She did," Virgil said. "Is Parr in Louisiana yet?"

Franklin checked his watch. "He should be landing any minute. Said he'd call once he had anything from Carver's residence."

"Why don't we all go take a look at the security footage with Becky?" Murton said. "It'll get us out of Chip's way."

Virgil made a quick call to Bell and got the information for an eye doctor. Bell told him he'd set the appointment for Robert. "The guy owes me a few favors," Bell said. "I'll be able to get him in today, I'm sure of it."

Virgil thanked him, then, as they were heading up the stairs, he told Robert to expect a call from Bell.

"I'll drive him over, me," Delroy said. "Nothing to do here until all da Red Stripes leave, no?"

"That'll work," Virgil said. "Thanks, Delroy."

AT THE SAME TIME VIRGIL, MURTON, AND FRANKLIN were reviewing the video footage and comparing them to the Warren robbery, Kelly Snow was sitting on the bed in her room at the Comfort Inn watching the local news.

At first she was surprised that a TV crew would come all the way from Ft. Wayne to cover a small-town bank robbery. But the reporter made it clear that a mass shooting in a town with a little over a thousand residents was big news.

And as it happened, the news was bigger than Snow thought...not because of the attempted robbery, or even the killings. It was because of the interview with the Warren town marshal. The reporter asked about the victims, and even though the marshal knew it went outside the lines of proper protocol, he answered the one question that made Snow want to scream.

"I've seen the security footage from the bank," the marshal said. "Of the seven dead, one was a town police officer, four were bank employees, and the other two were the robbers. We're still not sure why the third robber turned on his own men, but it's clear from the video that he wasn't going to leave anyone alive. He mowed everyone down with an illegal automatic weapon."

"Were any other officers hurt or killed in the attack?"

"No, just my man," the marshal said. "He was the only officer present. And the only reason he was there was because he liked to drop his wife at work before starting his shift."

"Who's running the investigation, Marshal? Is the town handling it, or are you calling on outside resources?"

"The town will definitely be involved, but we are already receiving assistance at the federal level, and it's my understanding that the state's Major Crimes Unit is working alongside the various federal agencies."

Snow listened to the report and couldn't believe what she was hearing. Duncan had told her the bank had been full of cops. Not only that, he'd said that the cops started shooting and that was how Bray and Potts had been killed. Why did he lie? And if he lied about that, what else had he been lying about?

Kelly Snow's life was unraveling right before her eyes, and she didn't know what to do about it. She grabbed a pillow from the bed, covered her face, and screamed.

After she'd screamed herself out, she looked at the gun Duncan had left her. Then she came up with a plan. She went to the bathroom, got a hand towel, and began wiping the room. Needed to get rid of the prints.

BECKY HAD TWO COMPUTER MONITORS RUNNING AT THE same time. One showed a repeating loop of the Warren robbers, with the other playing different shots of all the various heists that had taken place across the country. She paused the videos when the upstairs office door popped open. "We've got an ID on the victim out back," Rosencrantz said.

Virgil was impressed. "You got his prints back that fast?"

Rosencrantz stuck his tongue in his cheek. "Uh, no. But we did get his wallet out of his back pocket." Rosencrantz opened his notebook and said, "Guy's name is Robert Stout. No middle initial. Driver's license photo matches his face...at least as best as we can tell. He's pretty smashed up. Anyway, Mimi says she's ninety percent it's him, and I'd take Mimi's ninety percent any day of the week."

"Me too," Virgil said. "What's his address?"

Rosencrantz went back to his notebook. "Havana."

"Cuba?" Becky said.

Rosencrantz smiled at her. "No. I looked it up. It's a town down near the panhandle of Florida, north of Tallahassee."

Virgil and Murton looked at each other. "Florida seems to be popping up in the equation a little too often if you ask me," Franklin said.

"I agree," Virgil said. "Do you think Parr could head that way when he finishes up in Louisiana?"

Franklin looked down in thought. "He could, but I don't know how long he'll be."

"Too bad there aren't any other federal agents just sitting around," Murton said. "You know, one of those types of guys who'd like to break a five-year case wide open."

Franklin gave Murton a dry look. "Your subtlety is not lost on me, sir." Then he stood, smiled and said, "Time to spend some federal funds."

Virgil cleared his throat. "Uh, couldn't you call someone from down there and let them handle it?"

"Of course I could," Franklin said. "But why give credit to someone else when it's mine for the taking? I'll be in touch. Let me know if you figure anything out on those tapes." And then he was gone.

After Franklin left, they went back to the videos. They were fifteen minutes into it when Virgil's phone buzzed at him. It was sitting right there on Becky's desk, and when Murton glanced at the screen, he said, "That right there is exactly why I don't want to be the boss."

Virgil hit the answer button. "Cora, I can explain."

"Explain what?"

"Uh, I may have misspoke. I meant to say I can explain why I haven't given you any updates on what we've learned so far about the bank job in Warren."

"I was beginning to think you'd forgotten all about me."

"No, it's just been a very busy day."

"I can imagine," Cora said. "Whenever you're ready."

Virgil gave Cora all the facts regarding the robbery and what they'd learned so far. He finished with: "We're currently in the process of comparing security footage that Franklin provided with what was captured today."

"Anything solid yet?"

"I'm afraid not," Virgil said. "Franklin and Parr are working on a few things out of state. Florida seems to be wiggling its way into the scheme of things."

"I'm aware," Cora said. "Franklin has brought me up to speed on his end."

"I see," Virgil said. "So, listen, I'm sorry I didn't get with you sooner. Like I said, we've been pretty busy. Anything else?"

"No, that about covers it. Let me know what else turns up."

"I will. Say, before you go, is everything okay with Mac?"

"Not now, Jonesy."

"That's not really the answer I was looking for."

"Well, that's the answer you've got. Deal with it. Oh, and before I forget, next time you decide to arrest one of the city's veteran detectives, make sure you run it up the flag pole first, will you?" Then she hung up.

Murton looked at Virgil and said, "All in all, that went pretty well."

"Yeah," Virgil said. "Like clockwork."

CHAPTER TWENTY-ONE

Snow checked the clock and saw that it was almost six in the evening. Duncan had left shortly after noon, so she still had a little time. She needed to figure out a way to get rid of Duncan without getting herself killed. The problem was, she didn't know how to do that. She was a former bar owner and crew manager...not a killer.

She took out her phone and called her former landlord, Billy. When he answered, he wasn't happy.

"Thanks a pant load for taking off on me like that, Kelly. What the hell were you thinking?"

"Look, Billy, I can't get into all that right now. How's Skipper? Are you taking care of him?"

"Skipper? Christ, woman, half the cops in the state are looking for you, and you're worried about your cat?"

"You've got to make sure he has plenty of food and

water. Even if his bowl has some food in it, he'll only eat if it's completely filled. And his water dish has to be cleaned out every day because he's always sticking his paws in there."

"Kelly, he's a cat. If he's hungry, he'll eat. If he's thirsty, he'll drink. Forget about Skipper. He's fine. What happened at Slips, and if you didn't burn the place, why'd you run?"

"I ran because I didn't have a choice, Billy. Did the cops come by my place?"

"Did they come by? That's a little like asking if it's humid down here in August. The cops came by in force, Kelly. They tore the place apart. They interrogated me like I had something to do with this Carver guy they found at the bar. The other dead guy too. What have you gotten yourself into?"

"Carver? They said that name? You're sure?"

"Not the first time they came by. But once they had an ID, they came back. I don't know any Carver. Who is he?"

"I can't tell you that, Billy. And believe me, you don't want to know." She bit at the end of a fingernail and ripped it off, right down to the quick. "I gotta go. I gotta think. Take care, Billy, and take care of Skipper, okay?"

"Yeah, yeah, I'll take care of everything."

"And Billy?"

"What?"

"If you want to stay out of this, the best way is to play dumb with the cops."

"I am out of this, Kelly. And I don't have to play dumb because I don't know anything, other than the fact that you skipped out on your lease. I hope I never see you again."

———

DUNCAN WALKED IN THE DOOR THIRTY MINUTES LATER with the laptop. He looked at Snow and said, "What'd I miss?"

Snow did her best to remain calm. "Nothing. The news didn't have anything on the bank. Small town bull-shit doesn't make it in the city." She walked over and took the laptop, then set it on the bed. "What about the condo?"

Duncan shrugged. "I think we're good. I spent half the time just watching the place. There's nothing going on. If the Cubans thought we were there, they didn't show. I don't think they have any idea where we are."

That's because there are no Cubans, Snow thought. "You're sure?"

"As sure as I can be," Duncan said.

"Good, let's hook up the trailer and get the hell out of here. I want to get back to Indy and figure out where I'm going to go from there. This place feels like a prison cell."

Duncan put a little toe-in-the-dirt look on his face. "That's fine with me, but I was sort of hoping we could take care of business first. You know...Carver's cut?"

"Do you have your banking info?"

Duncan pulled a piece of paper from his pocket and handed it to her. "Will this do?"

"It's your money," Snow said.

"Is something wrong?"

"No, nothing is wrong, other than the fact that my entire crew is dead, my bar is a pile of ash, and every cop in the country is looking for us."

"Don't worry so much, Kelly. In a few days, this will all be over. You'll be sitting on a beach somewhere without a care in the world."

Snow was in the process of transferring Carver's money from the offshore account to Duncan's bank. "And where will you be?"

"Is that an invitation?" Duncan said.

"Hardly. Look, I know we've got a little chemistry thing going on between us, but when I split, I'm going alone. No hard feelings."

"Works for me," Duncan said. "Besides, I still have some unfinished personal business to take care of."

"What kind of business?"

"I already said. Personal."

Snow didn't care. The sooner she could get away from this nut job, the better. "Okay, whatever. Check your account. The money should be there by now."

"I thought it might take longer."

"I know how to move money around. I've only been

doing it for five years now. Are you going to check or not?"

"Yeah, Jesus, don't get yourself in a twist." Duncan took out his phone and checked his bank. When he saw a little over two million dollars in his account, he smiled and put the phone back in his pocket. He looked at Snow and said, "Thanks."

"I'd tell you to thank Carver if you could, but he's dead."

"Are you sure you're okay? You seem pretty wound up."

"Stop asking me that, will you?"

Duncan turned his palms up. "I'm only trying to show some concern."

"If you want to show some concern, how about you go and get us something to eat before we hit the road. I'm starving."

"We could get some snacks from the travel plaza."

"I want real food. There must be something around here."

"Okay, I'll go get us a couple of burgers and fries. That okay?"

Snow nodded. "Yeah, but make sure they're from someplace good."

"Listen, I don't want to sound too paranoid, but how do I know that you won't pull that money back out of my account once we split up?"

Snow rolled her eyes at him. "Change your password."

Duncan laughed at himself. "Yeah, I guess that'd do it, huh?"

"How about it on the grub?"

Duncan shrugged. "Okay, back in a half-hour or so."

As soon as he was out the door, Snow opened her laptop, reversed the money transfer, then found the number for the MCU. Once she had it, she picked up her burner and made the call. "I need to speak to the lead detective. I don't know his name."

"Regarding?" Betty said.

"The bank robbery today in Warren. I have information, but I don't have a lot of time."

"I'm afraid the detective isn't here at the moment."

"Then give me his cell number," Snow said. "And hurry."

"Please hold," Betty said.

Snow heard the click and it made her want to scream again.

———

DUNCAN KNEW SOMETHING WAS WRONG WITH THE way Snow had been acting, but he couldn't quite put his finger on it. Had she somehow figured out that he'd been lying to her the entire time? One of the first things she'd said when he returned was that she wanted to leave, but then she sent him out for something to eat. It didn't make sense. He tried to think his way through it, but he couldn't come up with any meaningful answers.

Then something occurred to him. If she had discovered his deceptions, did that mean she was going to try to turn him in? But that didn't really add up either, because if he got caught, he could simply tell the cops everything he knew about what she'd done over the past five years. She wouldn't be safe anywhere in the world. Plus, if she was going to turn him in, wouldn't she have done that already? Why give up over two mil only to have the feds come crashing down on her head? He pulled over and decided no matter what was happening, he still needed to change the password on his account. When he took out his phone and logged in, he saw the money was gone. He beat the steering wheel with his fists, then turned the truck around and headed back to the hotel.

THE VIDEO FOOTAGE WAS CIRCUMSTANTIAL AT BEST, AND Murton said so. "Anyone could watch these tapes and say, yeah, these guys are the same ones. I mean, you can tell by the way they move, their height and weight and all that, but no jury in the world would ever convict today's shooter on the footage alone. He's only in one of the videos...the one from today."

"A new guy," Becky said.

"That's probably true," Virgil said. "Let's look at the

facts we have. In every job this crew has ever pulled, they used five people. A driver waits outside and four guys go in. Except that didn't happen today. They showed up with only three guys, and no driver, but two of the guys look like part of the same crew. That means for some reason, they're short on manpower and had to bring in someone from the outside. And it's the outsider who took out the other two robbers."

"What are you getting at, Jonesy?" Becky said.

"We know that Carver—who was killed at Slips—was part of the crew. The new guy replaced Carver, and for some reason is taking out the rest of the gang as well. I'd be willing to bet that the body found out in our alley is part of the same crew. We'll have a better idea about all that once we hear from Franklin and Parr, but for now, let's say he is."

"Don't forget that Kelly Snow, the owner of Slips, claims innocence but is running anyway," Murton said. "If you watch those tapes long enough, it's not hard to convince yourself that she's the driver. Either that, or it's a very small man."

Virgil nodded. "I agree. So we've got Snow, Carver, the two dead guys at the bank in Warren, and Stout. There's your crew."

"And there's your problem," Murton said. "If you're right, four of the original five are dead, Snow is on the run, we don't know who the new guy is, and no actual proof that would hold up in court."

Virgil's phone buzzed, and when he saw who was calling, he dropped his head before answering. He put the phone on speaker. "Yes, Betty? What is it?"

"Hello to you too. You know, back in my day, when someone answered a phone, they used a proper greeting."

"I'll try to keep that in mind. How can I help you?"

"You can't."

Virgil clenched his jaw. "Then why are you calling?"

"Because I've got a woman on hold who asked to speak with you...although she didn't know your name. Something to do with the bank robbery today. She wanted your phone number, but I told her that was against policy."

"Betty, give her my number right now. Tell her to call me."

Betty said, "Yes, Commander," then hung up.

Murton looked at Virgil and said, "What are the chances?"

"They're not zero," Virgil said. Then to Becky: "Get a trace set up."

"I'm already on it, Jonesy."

Her fingers were flying across her keyboard when Virgil's phone rang. Virgil decided to take a chance. "Miss Snow, this is detective Virgil Jones with the state's Major Crimes Unit. Before you say anything, I have to ask...are you in imminent danger right now?"

The use of her name caught Snow off guard. "How did

you know it was me? I never told the woman who answered my name."

"I didn't," Virgil said. "I took a chance is all. Are you safe?"

"I don't know. I think he's coming for me."

"Who? Who is coming for you?"

"His name is Jeff Duncan. He killed one of my customers...a guy named Alex Carver, and then burned down my bar. All the cops think I did it, but I had nothing to do with any of it. I think he's mixed up in that bank robbery business. I saw the news about that today. These guys are like some kind of gang or something. They were always in my bar, hanging around with a guy named Alberto something. I don't know his last name. But I saw Duncan kill Bert and Carver."

"Do you know the names of the two men killed today?"

"Yes, Jimmy Bray and Victor Potts. They were usually there with Carver and Bert. Duncan killed them at the bank."

"What about a guy named Stout?"

"Yes, him too. Duncan has been looking for him. I think he's trying to kill him as well."

"How is it that you ended up with Duncan?"

"He's my boyfriend, but he's out of his mind. I have to get away from him."

"Tell me where you are and I'll have the police there as fast as I can."

"I didn't have anything to do with any of this," Snow said. "I'm the victim."

"I believe you," Virgil lied. "Let me help you."

"No, I think you'll arrest me. Everyone is going to say that I was a part of all these bank robberies, but I wasn't. Check my bank account. I've got about two hundred bucks to my name."

"We'll do that, Kelly, I promise, but right now, your safety is our main concern. Please tell me where you are, and I'll do everything in my power to protect you."

"We're in Warren, at the Comfort Inn. He's driving a—"

Murton grabbed his phone and ran from the bar office.

"We've got someone on the way right now. What room? Kelly? Miss Snow?" Then Virgil heard a door slam, and Snow made a yelping noise. It sounded like the phone had fallen to the floor, and it was clear that a struggle was taking place. Then Virgil and Becky both heard two muffled gunshots.

Even though he knew it was pointless, Virgil tried again. "Miss Snow? Are you there? Hello?"

CHAPTER TWENTY-TWO

Duncan had his key card out and was about to stick it in the slot to unlock the door when he heard Snow speaking to someone. He carefully put his ear to the door and listened. Even though the sound was muffled, he could hear what she was saying.

"We're in Warren, at the Comfort Inn. He's driving a—"

When Duncan heard that, he knew he'd been right. He rushed the room, walked right up to Snow and slapped the phone from her hand, then grabbed the gun from the table. Snow tried to fight back, but Duncan was too big and too fast. He pushed her back on the bed, then fired two quick shots into her chest.

He knew he didn't have any time at all, but he couldn't resist. He grabbed a tissue from the nightstand and used it to pick up the phone and listen.

"Miss Snow? Are you there? Hello?"

Duncan laughed into the phone, then said, "So long, Asshole."

Then he tossed the phone and ran.

———

VIRGIL TOLD BECKY TO GET COOL ON THE PHONE. "Tell him we're coming quick. I want that chopper running and ready for liftoff as soon as we're there."

"You got it, Jonesy. She was telling the truth. The call pinged off a tower right outside of Warren."

"See what you can find out about Jeff Duncan. I'll take everything and anything you've got. Might want to start in Florida."

"Pretty common name, Jonesy."

Virgil didn't bother to respond. He just ran. Murton was at the bottom of the steps, and when Virgil passed him, Murton fell right in line. "The Warren cops are sending a unit over to the Comfort Inn. Huntington County is backing them up. Truck or car?"

"Car," Virgil said.

Murton tossed him the keys and took the passenger seat. Virgil lit everything up and turned out into the street, almost hitting a bicyclist. The biker had to swerve and ended up crashing into a parked car.

"There's some paperwork for you," Murton said.

Then, "If I call Cool, he could meet us at Central Book-ing. It's closer for us and faster for him."

Virgil said, "Do it," checked his mirror, then hit the parking brake and put the Charger into a power slide, letting the car drift around until they'd made a complete 180-degree turn. Then he released the brake and stood on the gas. As they raced back past the bar, the biker gave them the finger.

Murton smiled and waved at the biker, then got to work. "Cross traffic on the right...watch the light, watch the light...there you go. Pedestrian crossing at the corner... slide into the left lane, then cut back. Good, good, clear on the right now, your turn is three blocks ahead..."

THEY TURNED INTO THE LOT RIGHT AS COOL WAS touching down. Virgil dumped the car in an open spot and thirty seconds later they were airborne.

Virgil tapped Cool on the shoulder. "Comfort Inn, north of Warren, at the I-69 interchange. Keep us as low as you can. I don't want to lose my cell signal."

"Got it," Cool said. "The flight will be about sixty seconds longer than last time."

Virgil looked at Murton and shook his head. "Doesn't really matter at this point. Kelly Snow is dead."

Except she wasn't. By the time Virgil and Murton

made the scene, the EMTs had already taken her to the nearest hospital. The Warren town marshal told Virgil and Murton that she'd taken two in the chest. "The medical guys didn't think she was going to make it, but she was still pumping when we got here."

"What about Duncan?"

The town marshal looked at Virgil and Murton. "Who is Becky Wheeler?"

"My wife, and researcher for the MCU," Murton said.

"Well, she sure seems like she's on the ball. She called, told me you guys were on your way and brought me up to speed on the conversation Miss Snow had with you before she was shot. To answer your question, we have no actionable intelligence or evidence on Duncan. He's in the wind."

"Who's handling the crime scene? We'd like to get prints if we can. We have reason to believe that Duncan must have spent enough time in this room to leave a print somewhere."

"Huntington County is going to handle it. Their people are up there right now."

"Let's go look at the room," Virgil said. "We won't go in, but I want to take a quick peek."

They all walked down the hall to the room where Duncan had shot Snow, and once there, they saw three Huntington County crime scene technicians already at work. The bed and part of the floor were covered in blood, and yellow evidence markers were set up next to the shell casings left behind after the shooting.

Virgil saw the laptop on the nightstand, then caught the eye of one of the techs. "Detective Virgil Jones, MCU."

The tech tipped his head. "Busy day."

"That's something of an understatement. Listen, we have a dying declaration from the victim—this was prior to the shooting—that whoever shot her was part of the bank robbery. I know you guys have a certain way of doing things, but I need to ask a favor."

Another one of the techs said, "A detective who needs a favor from crime scene. Man, that, like, never happens." He didn't even bother to look up when he said it.

Virgil and the other tech ignored him. "What do you need?"

"Two things," Virgil said. "The first is easy. As soon as you get any prints out of this room, I need them sent back to my researcher."

He gave the tech Becky's information, and once he'd written it down, the tech looked at Virgil. "What's the other thing? You said there were two."

Virgil nodded. "I need that laptop printed right now. I need to take it back with me. I'll wait right here until you're done."

The tech tipped his head from side to side, getting the kinks out of his neck. "We're not done with the pictures yet. It'll be about an hour or so before we can get you the laptop. If you don't mind waiting, we'll do that first."

Virgil nodded. "No problem. We'll wait." Virgil started to move away from the door, but the tech called out and stopped him.

"Detective?"

Virgil stopped and turned back. "Yeah?"

"I wouldn't get my hopes up on the prints, I were you. I took a quick look the minute we walked in. I'm pretty sure the place has been wiped already. We might get something, but don't hold your breath."

Virgil nodded. "I understand. Let me know, and get me that laptop as soon as you can."

THE WARREN TOWN MARSHAL'S NAME WAS TIM Williams. When Virgil finally took note of his name tag, he looked at Murton, lowered his voice and said, "Did you catch the marshal's last name?"

Murton took a casual glance at the marshal who was speaking with one of his officers. "That might be a fly in the ointment."

"Only one way to find out," Virgil said. He walked over to the marshal and said, "Your last name is almost as common as mine."

The marshal gave him a polite grin, then said, "Well, almost."

"Are you by any chance related to an Indianapolis City detective by the name of Brent Williams?"

The marshal shook his head. "Nope. Never heard of him. Why?"

Virgil was instantly relieved. "No reason. I know the guy and wondered if he was part of your clan." Then, before the marshal could respond, Virgil said, "The crime scene tech said we've got about an hour to kill. My partner and I would like to make a quick run over to the hospital and check on Miss Snow. We might be able to get a description of her attacker or the vehicle he's driving. Hoping one of your men might be able to give us a ride. I don't think we'll be gone very long."

"Won't do you any good," the marshal said. "One of my guys got the call. She died on the table."

Virgil and Murton walked down the hall and away from the room. "Well, at least something is going our way," Virgil said.

Murton gave his brother an odd look, and when he spoke, the tone of his voice was less than polite. "Crook or not, I'd hardly call Kelly Snow's death something that's going our way."

"Ease up, Murt. I was talking about the marshal's last name."

Murton dropped his head. "Ah, geez, sorry Jones-man. My thinking is a little off. If I don't figure out how to get rid of these damned dreams, I'm going to die of exhaustion. Either that or someone is going to pop me for saying the wrong thing."

Virgil put his arm around his brother's shoulders. "Don't worry. I get it. Let's go see what we can find out from the hotel manager, huh?"

They walked down to the lobby of the Comfort Inn, and what they found was a line of irritated people all trying to make a mass exit at once.

Murton turned to Virgil. "It looks like a hotel shooting is bad for business. I'll bet that guy would do anything right about now to get out from behind that counter."

Virgil looked at the panicked people, all trying to either get their money back, or simply check out and leave. "Let's go find out."

Murton badged the hotel manager, then tipped his head to the side. The manager met him at the end of the counter. "I'll cooperate in any way I can, but in case you haven't noticed, I'm a little busy here. In fact, if I don't get all these people taken care of, I might be the victim in your next murder investigation."

Murton shook his head. "They can wait. The shooter is long gone. Get some of your other people out here to help. We need to look at your security footage."

"I'd love to, believe me, but as the manager, I'm the only one who has the authorization codes to issue full and complete refunds. I can't leave the desk."

Virgil was losing patience and stepped in. "Then find

someone who knows the security system and get us access...right now. Otherwise, you're going to have a much bigger problem than a group of travelers, and the reviews they're going to leave you on Trip Advisor."

The manager knew he didn't have a choice. He walked over to one of the other clerks, pointed at Virgil and Murton, said a few words, then went back to his departing guests.

The clerk walked over—a middle-aged woman with yellowish teeth and nicotine-stained fingers—and said, "Follow me, gentlemen. The security monitors are in the back office."

Once they were in the room, Virgil turned to the woman, introduced himself and Murton, then said, "We need two things: The first is the date that either Jeff Duncan or Kelly Snow checked into the hotel. The other is any footage your security cameras might have caught that shows their faces. Mr. Duncan's in particular."

The clerk put her hand to her chest. "Is he the one who did the shooting?"

Murton, a former federal agent, knew how to play the part. "That's classified information, ma'am. I'm afraid we're not at liberty to say."

The clerk gave Murton a dull look, then sat down at the computer. She clacked away at the keyboard for a few minutes, then said, "I've got a Kelly Snow who checked in here late this morning."

"Is Mr. Duncan listed?" Virgil said.

The clerk shook her head. "No. If he was with Miss Snow, she didn't tell anyone. The room was booked as a single. But that sort of thing happens all the time anyway."

"Do your cameras show the front lobby and check-in area?" Murton said.

"Of course."

Murton tipped his head, opened his eyes as wide as possible, then gave the clerk a slow blink. "Care to show us the video?"

"I'll pull it up, and you can watch it yourself. I need a smoke."

She brought the video up. "Have at it." Then she walked out.

"I think you might have irritated her," Virgil said.

"She'll survive, I'm sure. It amazes me how easy it is to ruin someone's day anymore."

Virgil pointed at the monitor. "Here we go."

They watched as Snow and Duncan entered the lobby. Snow walked up to the counter and got the room, while Duncan hung back, close to the entrance. They were both dressed casually, but Duncan wore a billed hat pulled low across his brow, along with sunglasses. Murton paused the video, then looked at Virgil. "I saw that guy. I'm sure of it."

"When?"

Murton pulled out his phone and snapped a picture of Duncan. "It was when we were crossing the street from the fire station. He drove past and looked right at me. I don't think I would have recognized him if it weren't for that big beard. It's pretty distinctive."

"What was he driving? Do you remember?"

Murton closed his eyes in thought and let the events of earlier replay in his mind. "A pickup truck. White. I think it might have been a Dodge. Dual wheels on the rear. Didn't catch the plate. Didn't even bother to look."

Virgil clapped him on the back. "That's okay, partner. It's a start, and a good one at that. Listen, keep watching. I'm going to go find that clerk and have her make a copy of this for us. Hey, Murt? Are you okay?"

Murton nodded. "Yeah...mostly. I'm probably just tired, but there's something about this guy that looks familiar somehow."

"Well, you said you saw him earlier," Virgil said.

"Yeah, but there's something else. I can't quite describe it. It's more of a feeling than anything."

"Keep watching," Virgil said. "Maybe it'll come to you. I'll be right back."

CHAPTER TWENTY-THREE

The clerk made them a copy of the video footage, sent it to both their phones, then went back to the front counter to help her manager deal with the departing guests. Virgil sent the footage to Becky, then called and asked her to use it in her search for anything they could come up with regarding Duncan's history.

"I'm on it, Jonesy," Becky said.

"Anything yet?"

"No. I'm in every database in the state I can think of, but so far there hasn't been anything."

"Keep at it, Becks. If we can round this guy up, we'll have the whole crew."

Becky said she would, and with that done, Virgil and Murton went back up to the room where Duncan had killed Snow. The crime scene tech saw them hovering right outside the doorway.

"I need about another half hour or so on the laptop, and then it's all yours," the tech said.

Virgil told him that was fine. "Getting anything else?"

The tech nodded. "We found a phone on the floor on the far side of the bed. Looks like a burner."

Virgil and Murton looked at each other, and the tech caught the look. "Okay, let me revise my last statement. I can tell by the look you gave each other that you're going to want the phone as well. That means we're back to a full hour."

Virgil and Murton understood, but they were pushing. "Man, we really need that phone."

"Go get a bite to eat," the tech said. "I'll have it for you as quick as I can. By the way...what I said before? The room had been wiped, but not all that well. Looks like whoever did it was in a hurry. But we've got prints on the computer, and we'll probably have something from the phone."

Virgil thanked the tech, then looked at Murton. "You hungry?"

Murton nodded. "It is well past my usual dinner hour. I could eat."

"Me too," Virgil said. "Let's go find Cool and get a sandwich or something."

When they arrived earlier, Cool had landed in an empty field behind the hotel. They found him sitting in the back of the helicopter, his arms crossed, and his chin resting on his chest. Murton looked at Virgil and said, "Wake him, or leave him?"

"I'm awake," Cool said. "Just resting my eyes."

"Murt and I are going to go get a sandwich. Are you a cool motherfucker, or a hungry motherfucker?"

Cool lifted his head and rolled the kinks out of his neck. "As it turns out, I'm both." He hopped out and said, "What sounds good?"

"I think I saw a Subway across the street when we were coming in," Virgil said.

"You did," Cool said. "I saw it as well. Let's go. You're buying."

"That would be an absolute first, wouldn't it?" Then, as Cool started to walk away, Virgil said, "Uh, Rich?"

Cool stopped and turned back. "Yeah?"

"You're going the wrong way. The Subway shop is on the other side of the hotel."

Cool nodded. "I know it is. But if we go around this way, it's shorter. Trust me. I know how to navigate."

Virgil looked at Murton, who simply gave him a shrug, and turned to follow Cool.

And it changed their entire night.

THEY ROUNDED THE CORNER OF THE HOTEL, WHICH PUT them in the spare lot used for oversized vehicles. The lot was mostly empty, but there were a few semi trucks, and pickups with trailers. They were walking along with Virgil and Murton flanking Cool on either side of him. All of a sudden Cool put both arms out across Virgil's and Murton's chests and stopped dead in his tracks.

"What is it?" Murton said.

Cool turned to Virgil. "Remember that time when we were looking for that crop duster, and I sort of busted the whole case wide open?"

Virgil let his eyelids droop. "You did identify the murder weapon used against the pilot, I'll give you that. But I wouldn't really say that you busted the case wide open."

"Think what you want, but answer this: Didn't you guys say that the car used in the bank job a few miles from here was a Mini Cooper with Florida tags?"

"Yeah," Virgil said as he looked around the lot. "But since there aren't any Mini's out here, what I'm trying to understand is why we're talking and not walking?"

"No one ever saw the car after it left the scene, right?"

"That's right," Murton said.

"Follow me," Cool said. "I think we walked past the Mini without realizing it."

He turned around and started walking back the way they came. When they got to the end of the lot, he pointed at one of the trailers. "And that right there is my superior intellect at work...once again busting your case wide open. Check the tags on that car hauler...the one without a truck hooked up to it."

Virgil and Murton looked at the license plate on the trailer and saw that it had a Florida tag.

"It's locked up tight," Murton said. "Double padlocks on the door handles."

"Wait here," Virgil said. "I'm going to go get the town marshal...and a pair of bolt cutters."

VIRGIL AND THE TOWN MARSHAL WERE BACK IN LESS than ten minutes. The marshal held a pair of bolt cutters he'd taken from the trunk of his squad car but was reluctant to open the trailer. He looked at Virgil and Murton. "I don't know how you boys do things in the big city, but we don't have a warrant. I could lose my job over this."

Virgil took a pair of gloves out of his pocket, put them on, then said, "We don't need a warrant. I think I hear someone inside calling for help."

"That's a load of crap, and you know it," the marshal said.

Virgil didn't want to waste any more time. "Look, Marshal, I know this isn't the right way to do this, but one way or another, this trailer is getting opened in about thirty seconds. So either hand over the cutter, or stand back and I'll shoot the locks off. If I'm wrong, I'll apologize to the owner and personally cover any damage to the trailer."

The marshal shook his head. "Good God almighty."

Then he said something that surprised Virgil. He held out his free hand and said, "Give me forty dollars."

Virgil squinted at the marshal. "Why?"

"Because these bolt cutters belong to my department. If the state wants to buy them, I'm having what you might call an on-the-spot Warren town fundraiser. In case you don't quite get my drift, the sale will make them your equipment and your responsibility."

Virgil took out his wallet, looked inside, then turned to Murton. "I need fifteen bucks."

Murton let his shoulders slump. "You know, for a rich guy, you always seem to be short on cash. Does Small have you on an allowance or something?"

"Murt?"

"I'm simply asking. How can you walk around all day like that without any cash?"

"I do have cash. I just don't have enough."

Cool couldn't take it anymore. "Oh, for Christ's sake." He reached into his pocket, pulled out a fifty dollar bill, and handed it to the marshal. "Keep the change." Then he took the bolt cutters from the marshal and gave them to Virgil.

The locks were strong, but so was Virgil. It took some effort, but a minute later, the locks were free. Virgil dropped the bolt cutter, unlatched the door handles and lowered the ramp on the trailer. When he saw the Mini Cooper with Florida plates, he turned to Cool and said, "You son of a bitch. You might have just done what the feds have been trying to do for over five years."

"I like my other nickname better," Cool said.

"Looks like it's going to be a long night," Murton said.

Virgil nodded. "It is." Then he turned to Cool. "The Huntington County crime scene people are stretched to their limit. Can you run back to Indy and pick up Chip and Mimi? I'll call and get them headed to the airport."

Cool looked at his watch. "I can, but I'm going to be bumping up against FAA regs on duty hours."

"Can you make it work?" Virgil said.

"Yeah, but I'll be stuck here until morning."

"Don't worry about it. Go get Chip and Mimi. I'll see if I can get us some rooms."

Murton snorted. "Shouldn't be a problem. The way everyone was trying to get out of here? We'll probably have the place to ourselves."

Virgil took out his phone, called Becky and brought her up to speed, then asked her to get Chip and Mimi headed to the airport. "If you could go with them, I'll have a laptop and a burner for you to take back. It might help you get a line on Duncan somehow."

Becky said she would, then asked to speak with Murton. Virgil handed his phone to his brother, then looked at Cool. "Give me five minutes. I've got some evidence you need to take back. You can give it to Becky at the airport."

"Good enough. I'll get the chopper ready."

Virgil turned to run back inside to get the computer and phone. Then he stopped, turned back to Cool and said, "Nice job, Rich. Really."

Cool smiled. "Thanks. And don't forget, you owe me fifty bucks."

Virgil shook his head. "Nice try. The marshal only wanted forty. The extra ten is on you."

"Why is it the wealthy are always puckered up so tight? Consider the extra ten the vig."

"Ten on fifty?" Virgil said. "What have you been doing...taking lessons from Jonas?"

"The next number that comes out of my mouth is going to be sixty, so I'd think long and hard about the whole thing if I was you."

Murton was still talking to Becky, but he heard what was happening. He also knew the damage his brother could do to himself when it came to monetary negotiations. He told Becky to hang on, then said, "Virgil. Stop."

Virgil looked at Murton and said, "He's trying to take me for—"

"Virgil...*stop*."

CHAPTER TWENTY-FOUR

Murton's earlier statement proved to be true...it was a long night. Cool made the round trip, got the phone and laptop to Becky, then had Chip and Mimi back at the hotel. Virgil arranged rooms for everyone, and then, with nothing better to do except wait for the MCU and Huntington County crime scene people to complete their work, he and Murton and Cool went out to dinner.

After they'd eaten, Virgil called Sandy and told her he wouldn't be home until the next morning.

"Sounds like things are breaking," Sandy said.

"They are. I'll tell you all about it tomorrow. Right now, I've got to check in with Chip and Mimi and keep coordinating with the Huntington County people. The boys doing okay?"

"Yes, they're fine, baby. We'll all miss you tonight."

"Me too," Virgil said. "I'll be back in twelve hours or so."

"Is Murton doing okay?"

"He's holding his own, for now anyway. I can tell this dream is wearing on him, though."

"I don't doubt it," Sandy said. "You take care of your brother, Virgil Jones."

"I will. I promise. Listen, before I go, I need to ask you something."

"Sure," Sandy said. She was munching on a celery stalk, and Virgil could hear it over the phone.

"What are you eating?"

Sandy laughed like a little girl. "A piece of celery. You're trying to track down a killer, and that's what you wanted to ask me?"

Virgil smiled. "Not exactly. Have you noticed anything unusual about Mac lately? He sort of snapped at me the last time we spoke, and it felt pretty out of character for him. Is he under some kind of unusual pressure over something?"

"Not that I'm aware of," Sandy said. "Want me to say something to him?" *Munch, munch.*

"No, no, I was just wondering. When I asked Cora about it, she acted like she knew what it was, but essentially told me to butt out."

"Well..." *Munch.* "Cora does tend to keep her ear to the rail, but if she's not talking, I don't know what to tell you." Then, with a little playfulness in her voice, she said,

"Maybe you should take her advice, Virg. You know," *munch, munch...* "Butt out."

VIRGIL CHECKED IN WITH CHIP AND MIMI, WHO TOLD him that the trailer had either been wiped or anyone who was ever in it wore gloves. "Same with the Mini," Chip said. "We did get one pretty good print from the back of the plate, but other than that, we don't have much."

Virgil was afraid of that. "Yeah, I get it. Run the print, but I think you'll find that it comes back to a guy named Alex Carver. He was part of this crew, but he's dead. What about DNA?"

Mimi gave Virgil a defeated look. "We're collecting samples right now. In fact, we're almost done. But you know how that goes, Jonesy. Unless you catch this guy...uh..."

"Duncan," Virgil said.

"Right. Unless you catch this Duncan guy, the DNA won't matter."

Virgil nodded rapidly. "I know, I know. Get whatever you can."

They told him they would, then Virgil went up to Snow's room to check in with the Huntington County techs. They were packing up their gear as he walked through the door.

"Anything else I need to know?" Virgil said.

"If there is, I can't think of it," the tech said. "We've collected the brass, took blood samples, got prints from the phone and computer—which your researcher, uh, Becky, is it?"

"That's right," Virgil said.

"She's got the prints, and I imagine the equipment, so that leaves DNA. Catch the guy and he'll go away for life. Other than that..."

"Yeah, I know. My people told me the same thing. Anyway, thanks for your help, guys."

"It's what we do," the tech said with a fake smile. "Have a good night, huh?"

"You too," Virgil said. Then, with nothing better to do, he found his room, took a quick shower, then flopped down on the bed and caught the last ten minutes of the late news. Five minutes after that, he was asleep.

MURTON WASN'T. IN FACT, EVEN THOUGH HE KNEW he'd pay for it later, he was doing everything and anything he could to stay awake. He took out his phone and called Becky, and was surprised to find her still working at the bar. "Thought you'd be home by now."

"I was going to, but since the bar is closed, and you're out of town, I thought I'd put in a little extra time tracking down Duncan."

"Any progress?"

"Nothing worth writing home about," Becky said. "Jonesy suggested that I concentrate my search in Florida —and I am—but even that is going to take some time. Meanwhile, I'm trying to crack this laptop, but that takes time too."

"What about the phone?" Murton said.

"That's one tiny bright spot. It only had two numbers stored in it. One is a total dead end. It comes back as no longer in service."

"Another burner?"

"Looks that way," Becky said.

"And the other number?"

"The line is still active but I think the battery is dead. Either that, or it's turned off. Goes straight to voicemail. Sounds like an older guy. All he says is, 'Please leave a message.' He sounds sort of foreign. Cuban maybe?"

"I'll bet it belongs to a guy named Alberto...last name unknown. Snow gave Virgil that information before Duncan killed her."

"Want me to take a peek?" Becky said.

Murton knew she was asking if she should hack into the phone's carrier and get the name listed on the account. "Yeah, but don't get caught."

Becky laughed. "So I guess we're insulting each other now."

"Ah, you know what I mean," Murton said. "I'd hate to have anything come back and bite us on this one because if what Snow said is true, this Alberto guy is probably dead."

"Well, I'll take a quick look and see what I can see. Who knows? It might lead somewhere."

"Good enough. Listen, you're not at the bar by yourself, are you?"

"You know better than that. Ross and Rosencrantz are downstairs helping Robert clean up what they can."

Murton was relieved and pleased. Other than himself or Virgil, he wouldn't want anyone besides Ross and Rosencrantz watching over Becky if he wasn't around. "Let me talk to Rosie for a minute, will you?"

"Sure, hang on."

"Hey, Becks?"

"Yeah?"

"I love you."

"I know you do, baby. I love you too. I'll see you tomorrow, huh? Hold on, I'll get Rosie."

Becky set the phone down, opened the office door and called out to Rosencrantz.

Thirty seconds later he was up the stairs and in the office. "What's up?"

Becky handed him the phone. "It's Murt."

Rosencrantz looked at her and said, "He does know that I have one of these too, doesn't he?"

Becky tipped her head at him and pushed the phone into his hand. "Maybe he thought you needed the cardio."

Rosencrantz gave her a look and took the phone. "What up, dreamcatcher?"

"That," Murton said, "is not funny. In fact, it's not even accurate. A dreamcatcher is a small hoop containing horsehair mesh, or something similar, like string or yarn. They're decorated with feathers and beads, and they are supposed to give its owner good dreams...not the kind I'm having."

"Maybe you should get one. Have you been reading Wikipedia again?"

"Can it," Murton said. "I need a favor."

Rosencrantz could tell Murton was serious. "Sure, what do you need, buddy?"

"You're not going down to Shelby County tonight, are you?"

"No, Carla takes the night patrol once or twice a month. Tonight is one of those nights. That's why I'm here helping clean up your bar. I'm also keeping an eye on you know who." He turned and winked at Becky, who promptly punched him in the shoulder.

"How'd you like to spend the night at my place tonight?"

Rosencrantz smiled. "Does that mean I'd get to—"

"In the guest bedroom."

"I know, I'm just messing with you. Something I need to be aware of?"

"If there is, I can't put my finger on it. But something

is chewing at the back of my brain, and I don't know what it is. That means Becky gets protected."

"No worries, Murt. I've got your back. Get a good night's sleep."

"That's the goal," Murton said, then he ended the call.

Rosencrantz turned to Becky. "What side of the bed do you sleep on?"

"Why?"

Rosencrantz laughed. "Just kidding. You're going to have a house guest for the evening, and I'm the winning contestant."

Becky rolled her eyes. "Rosie, I appreciate it, but—"

Rosencrantz held out his hands, palms out. "It's a done deal. Orders from the second-in-command."

"You better not snore."

"I don't. C'mon, it'll be fun. We'll play canasta or something."

Becky made a rude noise with her lips. "Canasta? How old are you, anyway?"

Rosencrantz put one of his hands against his chest in a very feminine way, then said, "Haven't you heard it's not polite to ask a detective that question? Anyway, let me know when you're ready, and we'll make like a buffalo chip and hit the dusty trail." Then: "What? You live on a dirt road. It's funny."

"No, it isn't. I'll let you know when I'm ready. It might be a while. I'm working on a secret research project."

"What kind of secret research are we talking about?" Rosencrantz said.

"We're not. That's what makes it secret." Becky made a go-away motion with her hand, so Rosencrantz went away.

DUNCAN MADE IT BACK TO THE CONDO WITHOUT incident. He wasn't worried or panicked or even scared. But he was upset...mostly with himself. He'd stretched his story too far with Snow, and she'd somehow figured out everything he'd done. Taking the money back was one thing. He could have tuned her up until she decided to put it back in his account, but when he heard her talking to the cops, there wasn't enough time for any of that.

He reached into his pocket and pulled out Bert's roll of bills, and threw them on the table. Then he began going through Stout's, Potts's, and Bray's belongings, searching for cash. He took everything he could find, added it to Bert's stash and began counting. Total amount? A little over six grand.

He knew six thousand dollars wasn't nothing, but it was a far cry from the two million he'd had...for about five minutes, anyway. It infuriated him that Snow pulled the money back out of his account, and it made him even madder when he realized it was mostly his own fault. He poured himself a drink to try to relax, then took out a pen and pad of paper from the desk drawer and began to make notes on what he had to do next.

The drink helped calm him, so he had another, and that seemed to help even more. The list of supplies he'd need wouldn't be cheap, but he knew a guy who could probably get him what he wanted. And the money? It would have been nice, but he'd never gone into any of this for the money. No...this was about something else altogether.

He took another sip of his drink, then made the call. When the man on the other end of the phone answered, Duncan said, "Hey buddy, remember me?"

There was a very long pause at the other end of the line. Duncan simply smiled and waited it out. Finally, after almost two full minutes had passed, the man said, "Oh, shit."

"Oh shit is right. Get a piece of paper and a pencil. You're going to need to write this down."

"Thought you was dead, man."

"You and anyone else that matters," Duncan said. "Now get the paper and pencil."

There was another pause, then the man said, "I'm not sure I can help you, Cap."

Duncan smiled into the phone. "See, that's the difference between you and me. I am sure. You either help me, or I'll hunt down your entire family and make them my next set of victims. Don't forget, I know where your parents live." Then Duncan slid into a lie, one he knew would push the man over the top. "As a matter of fact, I'm parked outside their house right now. Want me to demonstrate my seriousness?"

"No, no, man. Not my parents. They old and ain't never done nothing to no one."

"Then get something to write with, and I mean right fucking now."

"I got it already. What you need?"

Duncan picked up his list and said, "Listen carefully..."

CHAPTER TWENTY-FIVE

The next morning Murton woke, once again covered in a cold sweat. His hands were shaking, his brain felt like it was misfiring, and for a moment he didn't know where he was. Then there was a loud pounding noise on the door of his room, and he remembered he was at the Comfort Inn outside of Warren.

He went to the door, checked the peephole, and saw it was Virgil. He pulled the door open, and Virgil rushed in.

"Murt? You okay?"

Murton looked at him and said, "No. What time is it, and why were you trying to beat down the door?"

"It's a little after seven, and I was trying to wake you up. I could hear you screaming through the wall."

Murton walked over and sat down on the bed. "I'm not surprised. And please don't ask, because in case the answer isn't obvious...yes, it was the same dream."

Virgil sat down next to his brother. "Any new insights?"

Murton shook his head. "No." They sat quietly for a few seconds, then Murton turned to Virgil. "I'm beginning to think I might be in real trouble here, Virgil."

"You're the toughest guy I've ever known, Murt. You'll get through this, whatever it is, and I'll be right there with you every step of the way like you always have been for me."

"But that's not entirely true, is it?" Murton said.

"What do you mean?"

"I wasn't always there for you. We spent a long time apart and at odds with each other after the war."

"That's ancient history, Murt. It's all in the past."

"Yeah, just like this dream. It's all in the past. It's me, but it's not me. I've never flown a plane in my life, but for some reason I keep having this damn dream where I'm flying a World War Two aircraft, and I kill a bunch of guys on a boat, all while your maternal grandparents watch it happen. I can't figure any of it out."

Virgil stood from the bed, walked over to the window, and opened the curtains. He wasn't only trying to brighten the room, he didn't want his brother to see the worried look on his face. When he spoke, it was to Murton's reflection in the glass. "I know you know about the problems I've had myself...the feelings I sometimes have in the morning when I wake up."

"This isn't that, Virg."

"Maybe it is, but it's showing itself in a different way. PTSD is serious, Murt. Anyway, hear me out, will you?" Virgil turned around and faced Murton. "The last time I went through it, you and I went to Jamaica and got my head straight, mostly thanks to Wu, and everything he had us do."

"I know," Murton said. "I was there, and I don't think that type of thing can fix this."

"Maybe not, but it's worth keeping in your hip pocket if nothing else works. We could try it if we have to, but in a way, I think you're right...there's something else going on. Dad said it isn't the dream that can hurt you. He said it's what's behind the dream."

Murton rubbed his face with his hands. "I know. In case you've forgotten, we've already had this conversation."

"I haven't forgotten, Murt, but I think it's worth taking a harder look at the whole thing. Dad said every-thing that happened after Grandpa Jack ended up on his own is part of this...that he did what he had to do to survive, and that's what your dreams are all about."

"What are you trying to say?"

"I'm simply wondering if your dreams aren't exactly what they appear to be," Virgil said.

"In what way?"

"I'll let you answer your own question. No, no, wait, hear me out. Give me three words—and I mean only three—that describe your dream."

Murton thought about it for quite a while, then said, "Death, destruction, and despair."

"I can see how it would land on you like that," Virgil said. "But here are three other words that fit as well: Survival, selflessness, and responsibility."

"Look, I know my mind isn't firing on all cylinders lately, but you're starting to lose me, Virg."

"Your description of the dream is all about the events that take place during the dream, and I think that's a natural response. But what I said? I don't think anyone could come up with three better words that describe who you are as a person, Murt. You're a survivor. You always have been. You're selfless...sometimes to a fault, and you carry the weight of yourself and others like a badge of honor. You're one of the most responsible guys I know. The dream might be showing you your own sense of selflessness and responsibility so that others could survive."

"So, where does all that get us?"

"I'm not sure yet, but I do know this: There is an end to everything that's happening with you and these dreams, and I think we'll know it when we see it."

"So we're supposed to take a wait and see attitude? When have we ever done that?"

Virgil smiled. "Never, and we're not going to start now. Haven't you ever noticed that the only time Dad speaks to me is when we're working a difficult case?"

Murton nodded. "Yeah, I have noticed that. Are you saying what I think you're saying?"

"Yep. Dad said it's all connected, and I believe him."

————

THEY MADE IT BACK TO INDY BY NINE, AND SINCE Virgil's truck was still at the bar, they stopped there first. When they walked in, Delroy and Robert were in a meeting with an insurance adjuster who tried his best to drag Virgil and Murton into the conversation but neither man had the time, much less the patience to turn their thoughts in that direction.

Virgil looked at the adjuster and said, "Look, I know you've got a job to do, and I appreciate your position, but Delroy and Robert not only run this bar, they are co-owners. Anything they say is fine with me and Murt. Do you need us to sign a form to that effect, or something?"

The adjuster shook his head. "No, I—"

"Good. Carry on, then," Virgil said. Then he and Murton headed up the stairs to Becky's office.

Murton took one look at his wife and said, "Just as a casual observation, you look as exhausted as I feel."

"That's because I am," Becky said. "We've been here all night. Never made it home." She kissed her husband, then gave Virgil a hug.

"Why not?" Murton said.

Becky evaded the question by pointing at the sofa. "When he snores it sounds like he's giving birth to a cow."

Virgil nudged Rosencrantz awake, and once he was up

and about, he told him to go home and get some rest. "We're down to a basic manhunt now. I'll call if anything develops."

Rosencrantz rubbed the sleep from his face. "Thanks, man. I'll catch you guys later."

He turned to walk out of the office, but Murton stopped him. "Hey, Rosie?"

"Yeah?"

"Thanks for staying."

Rosencrantz thought about the last case they'd worked and how Murton had come to their rescue. His quick thinking and medical training had saved both Ross's and Rosencrantz's lives after they'd been shot and seriously wounded. "For you guys? Anything. You know that." Then he turned and was gone.

After Rosencrantz was out the door, Virgil turned to Becky. "What'd you come up with?"

Becky thought, *Plenty,* but she kept the secret part of her research to herself. She didn't want to deceive her husband or brother-in-law, but for the moment, it couldn't be helped. Now simply wasn't the time. Plus, there was still more to do. "I got the laptop open. There isn't much on it in terms of evidentiary value." Then she held up her finger and said, "Wait, let me rephrase that. A good forensic accountant could probably make the case that the money in the accounts Snow had set up was ill-gotten gains from the robberies over the last five years. But I'm not a forensic accountant, and I don't know how much good it would do anyway since Snow is dead."

Virgil completely understood. "Okay, you're probably right." He pointed at the laptop with his chin. "Unless there's something else on that thing that helps us, let's turn it over to the feds."

Murton sat down on the sofa and said, "Speaking of feds, have you heard from either Franklin or Parr?"

Becky nodded. "Franklin is on his way back as we speak. He's been coordinating with Parr, who, as you know, has been in Louisiana looking into Carver. Between the two of them and what they discovered, they've tied Carver to Stout, and Stout to Potts and Bray. Given what we know about Snow, her bar, and how often they all frequented the place, I'd have to say the original crew is all accounted for."

Murton nodded. "Yeah, the hard way. They're all dead."

"So, that leaves Duncan," Virgil said. "I'd like to get my hands on him. We know for a fact that he killed Potts and Bray, and there's really no question he's responsible for Snow's death as well."

"Don't forget Carver, and our mystery man, Alberto," Murton said.

"I haven't," Virgil said.

"Neither have I," Becky said. She looked at Virgil and said, "Murt and I talked a little about this last night. The burner that Snow had? I took a look at the carrier's records for the number stored in the burner. It came back to an Alberto Alvarez, out of Naples, Florida. Parr is on the way there from Louisiana. If he can follow that chain, it might give us a lead on Duncan."

Virgil smiled at her. "Man, Becks, that's some great work. We're going to look like heroes to the feds. That should buy us some future cooperation whenever we need it."

"Hope so," Becky said. "By the way, you might want to get an after-the-fact subpoena for the carrier. I covered my tracks, but why make trouble for ourselves when we don't have to?"

Virgil nodded. "I'll get it done this morning."

Murton looked at Virgil and said, "Now what?"

Virgil looked at nothing for a few seconds, then said, "Good question. Until and unless we can get some solid intel on Duncan, we're sort of drifting."

Becky looked at both men and said, "That's a polite way of saying you're up Shit Creek without a paddle." Then, "What? I'm tired. I've been up all night."

Virgil looked at Murton and said, "Take your wife home. I'll do the paper at the MCU."

Murton clapped his brother on the back. "Thanks, man. Catch you later tonight or something, huh?"

"You got it," Virgil said. "C'mon over around happy hour and I'll fire up the grill."

Becky and Murton looked at each other, their faces a mixture of shock and mock horror. They both knew the kind of damage Virgil could do to a perfectly good chicken on the grill.

Virgil waved them off. "Yeah, yeah. Don't worry. I'll do steaks."

Duncan met his man near an abandoned warehouse on the west side of the city, north of the airport. When he saw Duncan's gloves, he said, "That truck hot?"

"Yeah. Why do you think I'm wearing gloves? Can you move it for me?"

"Probably. What's the split?"

"Half and half," Duncan said.

"That'll work. Still gonna need the cash for the supplies."

"You bring everything I asked for?" Duncan said.

"Yeah, it's all there. Gonna cost you though."

"How much?"

"Five ought to do it."

"Let's see what you brought," Duncan said.

The man opened the back of his van and pulled a blanket from the tops of the guns and ammunition. He looked at Duncan and said, "Two M4A1 5.56mm Carbines. They're full auto, air-cooled, magazine-fed, with a collapsible stock."

"Save the description for the brochure," Duncan said.

"In case you've forgotten, I'm familiar with military hardware."

"I ain't forgot. You asked, and I answered is all."

"What about ammo?"

"In the box. Five hundred rounds."

"Where's everything else?"

"Up front with the uniform. I know you wanted more, but I could only get two grenades. Who you going after, man?"

Duncan got right in his face. "Don't ask questions you don't want answered."

The man took a step back and held his hands up. "Hey, hey, we on the same side here. How about it on the cash?"

Duncan smiled like he'd momentarily forgotten who his friends were. "You're right. I guess you could say I'm a little wound up lately."

"I can see that. So...the cash?"

"In my truck. Hold on, I'll get it." Duncan walked over to his truck, grabbed a large paper grocery bag that held the HK45 with the Dead Air Ghost tactical suppressor still attached. When he got back to the van, he said, "I can't tell you how much I appreciate this. How long before they realize this stuff is missing?"

The man shrugged. "You know how it is. Stuff falls off the truck every once in a while. Paperwork can get lost too. It's all good, but I hope we don't have to do this again."

Duncan smiled. "Don't worry, we won't." Then he reached inside the bag and fired three quick shots into the man's chest. Once he went down, Duncan put one in the back of his head to make sure he was gone. Then he closed up the van, climbed in, and drove off, leaving the dead man and the Dodge dually behind. He'd find a similar van, swap out the plates, and be good...for a while, anyway.

CHAPTER TWENTY-SIX

L ater in the day, as Virgil was getting ready to leave for home, Franklin walked into the MCU and up to Virgil's office. Betty tried to stop him, but Franklin brushed past her like she didn't exist.

Virgil heard the commotion and stepped out into the hall. "Betty, it's okay. This is Agent Franklin with the Department of Homeland Security. He's welcome here anytime."

"Well, perhaps if someone would have told me that, there wouldn't have to be such a fuss about every little thing that goes on around here. I honestly don't know how you state people get anything done, what with all the helicopters, and comings and goings."

Virgil let his shoulders sag. "Betty, don't you have some reports to file or something?"

"I already did that. If it's all right with the two of you

big shots, I'll be on my way. My daughter called and invited me over for dinner. It sometimes happens twice a year."

That's probably because she's afraid of you, Virgil thought.

"What was that, Mister?"

"I said, that's good for you. Have a nice time. See you on Monday."

Betty shook her head, then walked away. Franklin turned to Virgil. "You don't let her carry, do you?"

Virgil's eyes got wide. "Are you kidding? She does enough damage with her attitude. Put a little ammunition into the mix and we'd all be dead by noon."

Franklin turned the corner of his lip up, then said, "Anyway, you got a minute?"

"Sure," Virgil said. "C'mon in."

Once they were seated, Virgil looked at Franklin. "What's up?"

"We have a problem."

"What sort of problem?" Then, before Franklin could answer, Virgil's phone buzzed at him. He glanced at the caller ID, then gave Franklin an apologetic look. "Just a second. It's one of my guys."

Virgil pressed the speaker button and said, "Hey, Ross. I'm in a meeting with Franklin. What's going on?"

"I'm over at an abandoned warehouse on the west side, right across the line in Hendricks County."

"What's going on over there?"

"We've got a dead guy...black male, mid to late thirties, shot in the chest and head."

Virgil was a little confused. "How'd you get the call?"

"Well, it's Friday, and it was my turn on the phone duty roster. I guess Betty switched it over to me before she left. Hendricks County put the word out, so I rolled over to take a look."

"Anything I need to know?" Virgil said.

"That would be why I'm calling," Ross said. "Chip and Mimi should be here any minute. The dead guy is face-down in the dirt about ten feet from a pickup truck. It's a white Dodge dually with Florida tags."

"Text me the address. I'm on my way."

Ross said he would, then ended the call. Virgil looked at Franklin. "I guess our boy Duncan isn't done yet."

Franklin stuck his tongue in his cheek. "So it would seem. Mind if I follow you out there?"

Virgil stood from his chair. "Not at all. What was it you wanted to tell me? You said there was a problem."

Franklin stood as well, then said, "On second thought, maybe you should ride with me. I'll fill you in on the way."

Virgil shrugged and said, "Let's roll."

———

ONCE THEY WERE ON THEIR WAY, VIRGIL TURNED TO Franklin. "So...you said there was a problem?"

Franklin shook his head. "Actually, no. I said, 'we have a problem.'"

"Hair-splitting isn't really my style, Franklin."

"Sure, make fun of the bald black guy. It's okay, I get it."

"Franklin?"

After a deep breath, Franklin's voice took on an official tone. "My partner, Agent Parr, sent all his intel to Becky."

"I'm aware," Virgil said. "We talked about it this morning. Between what he found on Carver, and what you got from Stout's residence, we've tied everything together on the crew. Everyone is dead, except for the new guy...Duncan."

Franklin looked at Virgil out of the corner of his eye. "Did I mention after I was done at Stout's, I flew down and had a little chat with the Manatee County sheriff?"

"Laun, right?"

"That's the guy," Franklin said.

"No, you didn't mention it. What'd he have to say?"

"It seems his crime scene people were able to put together the VIN on the burned-out van at Slips. Guess who it belonged to?"

"My first and only guess would be Duncan," Virgil said. "For some reason, he systematically took out the entire crew."

"Yes, he did, didn't he? And as a point of fact, your

guess would be correct. But it shouldn't be your only guess."

"Why not?"

"That van had been around for a while. I got in touch with my people and had them run it back through Florida's DMV. Duncan didn't buy the van when it was new."

"Who did?" Virgil said.

"I'm getting to that. I simply want you to follow my logic, and challenge my thinking if you believe I'm headed in the wrong direction."

Virgil looked out the front windshield and said, "I can do that. In fact, if you don't take the next exit, I'm certain you'll be headed in the wrong direction."

Franklin shook his head. "Very funny." Then he cut across three lanes of traffic. Once he'd cleared the off-ramp, he had them headed west toward the address Ross had provided. "Anyway, as I was saying, Duncan wasn't the first owner. As it turns out, there were three individuals who owned that van...the last being Duncan, who did, in fact, purchase it from Alberto Alvarez."

"Look, don't take this the wrong way, Franklin, but it sort of feels like you're dragging your explanation along behind you like a dead mule."

"Interesting choice of words."

"In what way?" Virgil said.

"Alberto Alvarez has spent half his life muling drugs up from Cuba and Jamaica."

"How does that fit into the crew who spent the last five years knocking over banks and credit unions?"

"Kelly Snow's father was a guy named Fred Snow. He worked with Alvarez and let a few kilos of pure, uncut coke float through the bar a few times a month. Fred got caught, thanks to an addict who happened to be his wife. She squealed on Fred to keep herself out of prison. Fred Snow did ten years and the very same day he was released he murdered his wife."

Virgil was beginning to see the bigger picture...or so he thought. "You're saying with both parents dead, Kelly Snow takes over the bar and gets recruited by Alvarez?"

"That would seem to be the logical chain of events. Except he didn't recruit her to keep the coke flowing. Alvarez got out of the drug trade, and into the bank robbery business."

Virgil, nobody's idiot, asked the next logical question. "You said that Duncan was the third owner of the van, and that he bought it from Alvarez. Who bought it originally?"

Franklin gave him a sad smile, then pointed out the front windshield. "In a minute. Looks like we're here."

Virgil looked out the window and saw Ross taking notes as he leaned against his squad car. Chip and Mimi were working the crime scene. Franklin parked a respectful distance from the body, then killed the engine. When he moved to open the door, Virgil touched him lightly on the arm. "Franklin, what is going on?"

"In a minute, Detective. I promise. But let me ask you this: How's the governor been acting lately? Seem his usual self, does he?"

When Virgil didn't answer, Franklin pushed his door open and said, "I figured as much."

VIRGIL CLIMBED OUT OF THE CAR, RAN AROUND THE back of the vehicle and blocked Franklin from getting near the scene. "Franklin, we've always worked well together, and it's my hope that our mutual cooperation continues. But the next words out of your mouth better be the rest of the story."

Franklin sucked on his cheeks for a second, then nodded and walked back over to his car. He parked his butt on the front fender and crossed his arms. "Do you remember Agent Thorpe?"

Virgil hadn't heard the name in a number of years, and had to think about it for a few seconds. "Yeah...he was your counterpart out of Portland, Oregon, I believe."

"That's correct. He was also Agent Gibson's direct supervisor."

Virgil looked off into the distance, trying to put the pieces together. "Gibson was killed while working undercover with Murt."

Franklin nodded. "That's right. Go on."

Virgil noticed that Ross was headed their way, so he

held up his hand, palm out. Ross nodded, turned around and went back to his squad car. Virgil turned back to Franklin. "What does a Portland, Oregon DHS supervisor have to do with any of this?"

"Well, for one thing, Thorpe is no longer with the DHS. After the operation that got Gibson killed was over, he got a letter of reprimand and was transferred to a different federal agency."

"Which agency?" Virgil said, even though he thought he knew the answer.

"Treasury...and not in DC, either. They sent him down to work out of the Miami field office. The Manatee County sheriff's office took Alvarez's house apart. They found records of conversations—emails and phone calls—between Alberto Alvarez and Thorpe."

Virgil was having a hard time believing it all. "Thorpe struck me as a solid guy."

Franklin nodded in a noncommittal way. "That's because you're not looking far enough back into the over-arching storyline."

"Meaning?" Virgil said.

"Meaning Thorpe had Gibson under his thumb for a long time." Then Franklin said something that surprised Virgil. "Did you know I was at Pam Donatti's funeral?"

"No, I, uh, was pretty upset. I don't remember seeing you there."

Franklin tipped a finger at Virgil. "And you had every

right to be upset. Your wife was almost murdered, and you almost lost your son, Wyatt, as well."

"What's the larger point, Franklin?"

"It's not that I was there. It's what you said during the service. It was all very eloquent. If memory serves, you said everything matters, spoke of choices made in the past, and something to the effect that everyone was where they were supposed to be. Do I have that right?"

"That was the gist of it, yes," Virgil said.

"I couldn't help but notice that Murton Wheeler wasn't present for the service. Why was that, Detective?"

Virgil squinted an eye. "He had other pressing matters that didn't allow him to attend. Why do I get the feeling you know where he was?"

"Because I do. Not only do I know, but Gibson made an audio recording of the entire event, presumably under orders from his boss at the time, Agent Thorpe."

Virgil rubbed his face with his hands. "Murton told me the governor was there and waiting outside in the limo when he killed Decker."

"He was. As I said, we have the entire conversation on tape."

"You're saying Thorpe was playing both sides of the fence and using Gibson to do it?"

"That would seem to be the case. Did you know that Thorpe was former CIA?"

"Yeah, I remember hearing that from the SWAT commander, Jon Mok."

Franklin lifted a shoulder. "Once a spook, always a spook. I don't think that sort of lifestyle ever fully lets one go. Do you?"

"I wouldn't know," Virgil said.

"Well, food for thought, anyway," Franklin said. "I'm pretty sure that Thorpe is hanging that audio recording of the night Murton shot Decker over the governor's head."

Virgil wasn't buying it. "That doesn't make sense. Was Mac outside in the limo? Yes. Did he have prior knowledge of Murton's actions? No. In fact, based on what Murton told me, once he was in the limo with Gibson and the governor, Decker was never mentioned."

"Look at it this way, Detective: Alvarez was getting his intel from Thorpe. Snow's crew knew which banks to hit and when, all courtesy of Agent Thorpe at the treasury department. Isn't it logical to assume that Thorpe could use that tape to implicate both your brother and the governor as co-conspirators in Decker's shooting?"

"Earlier you asked me to challenge your thinking," Virgil said. "Let me do that now. Snow and her entire crew are dead, with the exception of Duncan, who we will catch sooner or later. That means the whole thing is all but over. From my perspective, the audio recording that Thorpe has is useless. I've personally witnessed Mac come through on worse things than this. If Decker wasn't ever mentioned in Mac's presence, he's in the clear."

Franklin nodded thoughtfully. "I can see how you would think that."

"Why wouldn't I?" Virgil said.

"Good question," Franklin said. "Thorpe is all but finished, but there's still one more piece of the puzzle."

"Which is?" Virgil said.

"I'll answer that in about ten minutes. I want to see who the dead guy is before we start playing pin the tail on the federal donkey."

CHAPTER TWENTY-SEVEN

Virgil and Franklin walked over and said hello to Ross, then asked him what he had.

"Not much more than what I told you on the phone. The truck, as you can see, is a white Dodge with Florida tags. Chip and Mimi are doing the photography first. Said they'll start doing the prints next. I called Murt. He's on his way over as well."

Virgil shook his head. "That wasn't necessary, Ross. He's pretty wiped out lately. Why don't you call him back and tell him not to bother?"

Ross tipped his chin over Virgil's shoulder and said, "Too late. Here he comes now."

Virgil turned and saw Murton pulling into the lot. He walked over to his brother. "We've got this, Murt. No need for you to be here."

"It's not like I had anything better to do. Besides,

you said you were going to grill some steaks, and until you're ready to do that, I'm free. What have we got?"

"Does that look like the truck you saw?"

Virgil and Murton walked over to the truck but stayed far enough back not to contaminate the scene. "Yeah, that's the one. Florida tags?"

"Yep," Virgil said.

Murton looked at the body on the ground. "Who's the victim?"

"Don't know yet. Chip and Mimi are still doing the photos. We'll find out soon enough." Virgil walked his brother away from the scene, out of earshot of Franklin, then said, "I've been having an interesting talk with our favorite federal agent."

"About what?"

Virgil took ten minutes and brought Murton up to speed. "That doesn't make any sense," Murton said. "Mac was there when I killed Decker, but he was outside and waiting in the car. He had no prior knowledge of what I did, and once me and Gibson were in the car with him, no one spoke of it. I'm certain. If Thorpe is crooked, he's going to have to do a lot better than that to take Mac down."

"That's what I told Franklin. But you know what's bothering me?"

"What?" Murton said.

"Franklin asked me how the governor has been lately. I

know something is going on with Mac, and apparently Franklin does too."

Murton frowned. "Like what?"

Franklin had walked over and caught the tail end of the conversation. "My best guess is he's trying to protect you," Franklin said. "Both of you."

Murton gave Franklin a curious look. "Protect us from what?"

"Let's go look at the body," Franklin said.

Virgil and Murton followed Franklin over to where the dead man was lying face down in the dirt. He looked at Virgil and said, "Your crime scene girl...Mimi is it?"

"That's right," Virgil said.

Franklin got Mimi's attention and waved her over. "Mimi, darling, I know this isn't proper procedure, but is there any chance you could pull this man's wallet from his back pocket?"

Mimi smiled at Franklin, and with a voice that sounded like a stick of butter—if a stick of butter could talk—said, "I love it when big handsome black men ask me for favors. Wait here. I'll get everyone some gloves."

Franklin turned away for a moment, adjusted himself, then looked at Virgil and Murton. "What?"

"I didn't say anything," Virgil said.

"Me either," Murton said. "But simply as a casual conversation starter, it looks like you're about to fly the flag, if you know what I mean."

Franklin shook his head. "It's that voice. My god."

Virgil waved him away. "You get used to it."

"I don't see how," Franklin said.

Mimi returned with the gloves and told everyone to put them on. With that done, she reached into the dead man's back pocket and gently extracted his wallet. Once she had the driver's license free, she dropped it into a clear plastic baggie and handed it over.

Franklin took the baggie, looked at the name and said, "Tom Ford." Then he looked at Virgil and Murton. "Ring any bells, guys?"

"The face is vaguely familiar, but I don't think I've ever heard the name," Virgil said.

"Same here," Murton said. "I've seen this guy somewhere, but I don't know when or where."

"Maybe this will help," Mimi said. She handed them another baggie. Inside was a military ID that listed Ford as an Army Supply Sergeant. Virgil and Murton both shook their heads.

Franklin thanked Mimi, then let her get back to work. Murton looked at the body, then said, "If Ford was an Army Supply Sergeant, this must have been Duncan's work."

"No, it wasn't," Franklin said.

"What makes you so sure?" Murton said.

Franklin began walking back to his car and motioned for Virgil and Murton to follow. Once there, Franklin looked at Murton. "I take it your brother has brought you up to date on our conversation?"

"He has," Murton said.

Franklin looked at Virgil. "I told you there was one more piece of the puzzle."

"You did," Virgil said. "And I still haven't heard it."

"Actually, there are two," Franklin said. "The first is this: Army CID has had their eye on Ford for quite some time, and they've kept us—via the ATF—in the loop. They knew he'd brokered guns in the past, but they couldn't prove it...not that it matters now."

"What's the other piece of your puzzle, Franklin?" Virgil said, his impatience growing.

"I know for a fact that Jeff Duncan did not kill this man."

"How?" Murton said.

Franklin—who had something of a dramatic flair he liked to pull out of his pocket every once in a while—paused for effect, then said, "Because Jeff Duncan is dead. Thorpe killed him over two weeks ago."

FRANKLIN LOOKED AT VIRGIL. "THORPE'S BEEN IN federal lockup since the night it happened. Treasury knew he was up to something, but they didn't know what. They ran a sting on him, but it was too late. He ended up killing a prison guard who worked at the Florida State Hospital for the criminally insane."

"And the guard was named Jeff Duncan?" Virgil said.

Franklin nodded. "That's right." He pulled his phone from his pocket, brought up Duncan's picture, and held it out for Virgil and Murton to see. Both men looked at the photo, but neither recognized the man, and they told Franklin as much.

"Why did Thorpe kill Duncan?" Virgil said.

Franklin shook his head. "We think it was because Duncan had gotten friendly with one of the inmates. In fact, they'd become friendly enough that the inmate convinced Duncan to help him escape. When Thorpe found out what Duncan had done, he killed him."

"Why?" Virgil said.

"To cover his own butt," Franklin said.

"What was the inmate's name?" Murton said as he pulled his own phone from his pocket.

"I don't know. He was officially listed as John Doe, and his records were sealed by Thorpe before he was transferred out of DHS. Even I don't have access. Why do you ask?"

Murton held up a wait-a-minute finger, then spoke into his phone. "Yeah, Becks, it's me. Listen, can you look something up for me real quick? It should be pretty easy to find because it'll be filed in the MCU's system under closed cases."

"Sure," Becky said. "What do you need?"

"The initial reports from when we were looking at Charlie Esser's murder."

Becky paused for a moment, then said, "Okay. What are you looking for...specifically?"

"Virgil and I were down in Shelby County at the same time Mac called in the guard to assist when the troopers went on strike."

"I remember," Becky said.

"We had a little run-in with the National Guard. I need to know what unit it was."

"Okay. Give me five minutes, and I'll call you back."

"Thanks, baby."

Virgil looked at his brother. "Murt?"

"Just a second, Jones-man." Murton ran over to Lawless. "Do you have that sketch kit, or whatever it's called with you?"

Lawless nodded. "Yeah, it's in the van. Why?"

"Get it out. I'll explain in a minute."

Lawless got the kit out and set it up on the floor of the crime scene van. Once he was ready, Murton sent a picture to Lawless's phone and told him what to do. "It should be pretty simple...lose the hat and the mountain man beard, and give him shorter hair."

Lawless looked at him and said, "I can do that, Murt, but it won't be exact."

"I don't need exact. Your best effort will do it."

Lawless told him it would take about twenty minutes. Murton said that was fine, then called Becky back. "I need something else."

"Okay, but before you tell me, I've got the National Guard unit number."

She told Murton what it was, then Murton said, "Look into the Florida State Hospital for the criminally insane. It's located in Chattahoochee, Florida. They had an inmate go missing a few weeks ago. Get a name and a photo if you can and send it to my phone."

"You want me to backdoor it, or simply call and ask?"

"Backdoor, and make this one quick, Becks."

"It's what I do," Becky said, and then she was gone.

Virgil looked at his brother. "Murt? What's happening?"

"Let me see Ford's military ID," Murton said.

Virgil handed him the bag and when Murton saw the unit, he knew he was right. "Son of a bitch."

Virgil tried again. "Murt? What the hell is going on?"

Murton actually laughed. "And I thought the dreams were bad."

"What are you talking about?"

"If I'm right? I'm talking about my past coming back to haunt me...in more ways than one."

MURTON WOULDN'T SAY ANYTHING ELSE UNTIL HE WAS sure, and Virgil decided not to press him. Twenty minutes later, Lawless walked over with a composite and handed it to Murton. "Given what I had to work with, this was the best I could do."

Murton took the composite and walked away from everyone else before he looked at it. When he saw the face staring back, he sat down in the dirt, his knees drawn up, and placed his head across his forearms. Virgil walked over and said, "Talk to me, brother."

Murton's phone chirped at him before he could answer. Becky's text read, 'Oh my god. John Doe, records sealed by order of DHS prior to incarceration at Florida State Hospital. Current whereabouts unknown.' Murton brought the picture up and had he not already been sitting down, he might have fallen over.

Virgil looked at Murton and tried again. "Murt, you've got to tell me what's going on. Talk to me, man."

Murton wasn't quite sure he could get the words out. He stood, collected himself, then said, "The guy we've been looking for has been using Duncan's identity all along. Franklin is right. Jeff Duncan is dead."

"Then who killed Snow, the rest of her crew, and the guy out here?" Virgil said.

"Someone whose name I thought I'd never hear again," Murton said. Then he showed the picture to Virgil. "It's John Decker. He's alive. And he's here."

CHAPTER TWENTY-EIGHT

V irgil suddenly felt like he had way too much to do
and no time at all to get it done. He waved Ross
over. "Get Rosencrantz on the line. Right now." Then he
took out his phone and brought up the number for Emily
Baker, Sandy's detail driver who was a former military
fighter pilot turned state cop. As Baker's phone was ringing, he looked at Murton and said, "Where's Becky?"

"Still at the bar."

Sandy's driver was on the line in Virgil's ear. "This is
Baker. What's up, Jonesy?"

"Stand-by, Baker." Then to Murton: "Get her on the
phone and tell her to stay put." He looked at Ross. "Get
Rosie on the line, right now."

Ross nodded as he pulled out his phone. "I'm on it."

Virgil brought his phone back up and said, "Baker,
where are you?"

"I'm about halfway down your dirt road, heading home."

"Turn around and go back to my place. I'll explain as soon as I can."

"What do I need to know, right now?" Baker said.

"We have an imminent threat. Get back to Sandy and the kids. Call for backup. I want two troopers at the end of Murt's drive and two at my own. Get two others to block off access to the road. No one gets through except state cops. Call me back when you know everyone at the house is safe." Virgil hung up without waiting for a reply.

Ross had Rosencrantz on hold, the phone against his chest. He looked at both Virgil and Murton. "What is it?"

"It's Decker, and we're not taking any chances," Virgil said. "Tell Rosie to get Becky back to my place. Murt and I are on the way. Go to your place and grab Sarah and Liv, and come to my house. Watch your back."

Ross said he would, then told Rosencrantz what to do. Ten seconds later he tore out of the lot with his siren screaming at them in the background.

Murton ended his call with Becky and said, "Delroy and Robert are still at the bar. They'll ride with Rosie back to your place."

Virgil nodded and kept making calls. "Cora, it's Jonesy. Listen carefully. Where's Mac?"

"In his office. Why?"

"Get two state troopers up there right now. Once they

arrive, I need you and Mac at the airport. Cool will be waiting."

"Jonesy, what's—"

Then Virgil did something he'd never done before. He shouted at Cora. "Do it. NOW. Mac could be in danger. I'll explain later." Then he hung up and called Cool. "Rich, it's me. Cora, the governor, and two troopers are going to be showing up at the airport in about twenty minutes. Get them to my place as fast as you can."

Cool, who liked to live up to his name, didn't bother to ask questions. He simply said, "Roger that. I'll be ready." Then he hung up.

Virgil got in the driver's seat of Murton's squad car, then he and his brother left the lot the same way Ross had...with lights flashing and their siren screaming into the sky as dusk settled in.

Franklin turned to Mimi and said, "My goodness, those boys do know how to make an exit." Then, as if everything was right in the world, he pointed at Ford's body and added, "When you're finished with this nasty business here, would you happen to be free for dinner this evening?"

VIRGIL WAS PUSHING THE CHARGER HARD, THE TRAFFIC in front clearing out of his way. When his phone rang, he yanked it from his pocket and tossed it to his brother.

"This is Murton."

"Baker here. We're secure. I've got the lieutenant governor, the boys, Huma, and Aayla. Troopers are enroute as we speak."

"Good enough," Murton said. He looked at the nav display. "We're twelve minutes out. Stay tight, Baker."

"We're good," Baker said. She spoke in such a matter-of-fact tone that it helped to calm Murton. He ended the call and looked at Virgil. "Baker has it locked down. Troopers are on the way. Who else? We can't leave anyone hanging."

Virgil thought about it for a minute. "It wouldn't hurt to bring Mok up to speed. Ross was still with him when everything went down before. He's not in any real danger, but we may need him."

Murton nodded, spoke briefly with Mok, and ended the call as Virgil made the turn down his road. The two state troopers who had blocked the intersection heard them coming and backed their squad cars out of the way.

Virgil slowed, then rolled to a stop. He buzzed his window down and said, "No one gets through without a badge. Understood?"

"We've been briefed, Jonesy. We're here until midnight. Same with the troopers at both your houses. We'll all be relieved by another unit, but I'll make sure everyone knows the drill."

Virgil nodded, hit the gas, and took off toward his house, a little calmer.

Barely.

But he'd made a mistake. He *had* forgotten someone, and like Murton's dreams, it would come back to haunt him.

DECKER HAD A PLAN, ONE HE'D BEEN WORKING ON FOR years. And with Thorpe's help, he'd been able to gather all the intelligence he needed. Once he had that, it was simply a matter of getting free. The prison guard had handled that for him, the promise of the land and the money that was rightfully Decker's too much to resist. But the guard had been a fool, and once he'd let Decker escape, he died without ever seeing a penny, much less an acre.

Decker knew if he ever got out of the Florida mental institution, he'd go after the people who put him there, but he'd do it in a way that would keep everyone off-balance and scrambling to stay one step ahead of him. He knew he was close to his own end...that there'd be no coming back from this one, and that thought alone fooled his twisted mind into thinking he had an advantage.

The boy, Jonas, his biological son, was out of the picture. He'd never wanted him anyway, but it would have been nice to have the money that came with the kid and the land. No matter, that door had closed long ago, and it was one that'd never be opened again. This was about payback, and now that he was free, he knew he'd have to make his moves as soon as possible. He pulled the list from his pocket and looked at the names and addresses Thorpe had given him so long ago. There were only two, and sometimes Decker felt it wasn't enough. But the dish had grown cold over the years, and he knew when the time came, his revenge wouldn't only make him feel like he'd gotten part of his life back, it'd make him famous for a long time. And that, Decker thought, was the only way to go out. You had to do it with style. There had to be some meaning behind the action.

The first name on his list was nothing more than a way to send a message...to let them know he was out there. He rubbed the tightness out of his shoulder and wondered if they'd be able to put it together. It was hard to tell with the cops because they weren't always as smart as they liked to think they were.

The second name was who he really wanted...the man who'd pumped three bullets into his chest. Murton Wheeler. Too bad Wheeler never knew it had been Thorpe's men who took him away. Decker knew if it weren't for that, he would have died on the spot. He almost died anyway, but they got the bullet's out and even though he spent nearly six months in prison hospital, and had to undergo several surgeries, it was still better than the alternative.

He looked at the two names for another minute, then put the list away and got to work. There was still plenty to do before the fun started. He showered, cut off his beard, and used a pair of clippers to give himself a high-and-tight military haircut. He dressed in his uniform, made sure everything was squared away, and when he checked his watch, he thought, *Time to rock and roll.* Then got into Ford's van and headed out.

CHAPTER TWENTY-NINE

Virgil waved to the troopers who were positioned at the entrance of his drive, then drove up to the house and parked Murton's squad car right by the front door. When they went inside, they found everyone safe... and curious.

Sandy gave Virgil a quick kiss, then leaned back. "What's going on?"

Before Virgil could answer, Baker walked over and said, "We're secure. Delroy, Huma, and their child are in their wing of the residence with Robert. Sarah and Becky are downstairs playing with Liv and the boys. Ross is outside on patrol. Rosencrantz is making sure Murton's place is locked up. The governor and Cora just arrived at the airport. They should be here shortly."

Virgil nodded. "Thanks, Baker. Coordinate with the troopers, and keep an eye on the back of the property."

Baker said she would, then Sandy touched her husband on his arm. "Virgil?"

Virgil turned to his wife and looked her right in the eye. "It's Decker."

Sandy visibly swallowed, then said, "How is that possible? Decker is supposed to be dead."

"That's what we were led to believe," Virgil said. "It's a long story, and I'll fill everybody in as soon as we're all together."

Murton looked at Virgil. "I'm going to go check my place out, set the alarms, and get Rosie back here." Then he looked at Sandy and said, "I'm sorry."

Sandy gave Murton a hug. "This is not your fault, Murton Wheeler. Stop taking on weight that isn't yours to carry."

"I put three rounds in his chest at point-blank range. I don't understand."

"It happens," Virgil said. "We've all seen it before. Sounds like he got lucky."

Murton nodded, then walked through the kitchen and out the back door.

DECKER HAD DONE THIS KIND OF THING BEFORE, though admittedly, last time had been on the fly. This time would be easier because he knew where Ford's parents lived. When he thought about it, the whole thing seemed almost too simple. But regardless of the level of difficulty, or lack thereof, it had to be done. He needed a fresh set of wheels and a place to stay.

Ford's parents owned a nice little bungalow north of the city, on a quiet street in an aging subdivision. Decker turned into their drive, pulled his hat down low, walked up to the front door, and rang the bell.

Ford's father, an ancient relic of a man opened the door, then took note of Decker's squared-away appearance. "May I help you, Captain?"

Decker stood at attention and said, "Sir, my name is Captain John Decker, military police. May I step inside, Sir?"

The old man nodded and pushed the door open. Once he was in, Ford said, "What is it, Captain? Is my son all right?"

"Is your wife home, Sir?"

"She's in the kitchen. We just finished our dinner."

"Perhaps you should ask her to come out, Sir."

Ford always feared this day would come. His son had been hurt or killed somehow, and now the military was here to inform them. He felt a tear escape the corner of his eye. He turned to the kitchen and said, "Sweetheart, you'd better come out here."

The woman came around the corner slowly, wiping her hands on a dishrag as she did. When she saw Decker, she put a hand to her throat. "Is it about Tommy?"

Decker gave her a tight nod. "Yes, ma'am, but I want

to inform you that your son is alive. He's been injured...
quite severely, but the doctors say with time, he'll make a
full recovery. Your son and I are friends. I volunteered to
make the drive over to inform you, and escort you to the
hospital."

"What happened?"

"A stack of crates slipped off a forklift. Your son was
supervising the movement, but he was standing too close
and couldn't get out of the way in time. The crates were
heavy and landed on top of him. He has a fractured leg
and a couple of busted ribs. But I want to emphasize that
he will be okay. He is awake and alert and asked me to
pick you up. Something about your night vision, I think
he said. If you could grab your belongings, I'll give you a
ride to the hospital, courtesy of the United States Army.
My van is right outside."

The Fords looked at each other with a mixture of
shock and relief. Once they had everything they needed—
which, to Decker's relief didn't amount to much—they
climbed into the van and left.

Thirty minutes later Decker turned off the highway
and down a quiet country road. When the Fords asked
why they were stopping, Decker killed the engine, then
turned in his seat. "I think something is wrong with the
transmission. I'm going to check the fluid level. If I have
to, I'll get a replacement vehicle headed our way." He
climbed out of the van, raised the hood, and stood there
for a moment.

Then he ran to the side of the van and yanked the door open. "Sir, Ma'am, you'd better get out. There's smoke coming out of the engine compartment. Let's get away from this vehicle."

The Fords climbed out, and once they were clear of the van, Decker pulled his gun and shot them both in the back. He pulled their bodies across the road and rolled them into the ditch. With that done, he lowered the hood of the van, climbed in, and started back to the Ford's house.

He smiled the whole way there.

WHEN HE GOT BACK TO THE FORD RESIDENCE, DECKER parked the van on the street, left it running, then went inside the house. He found the car keys hanging on a peg near the inside garage door. When he entered the garage, he discovered that the old couple only had one vehicle, a black Chevy Impala. Decker punched the button for the garage door opener, then pulled the Impala out, and got the van tucked away, and out of sight.

With that done, he grabbed what he needed from the van, closed the garage, and headed back out. His first move wasn't going to be very complicated. He'd find a black Impala, swap the plates, which would give him a little security. Then he'd start the fun with a little shock and awe.

That'd get everyone's motor running.

THE PLATE SWAP WENT OFF WITHOUT A HITCH. THERE were only about a million black Impalas around the city. With that done, Decker took his time driving. There was no real hurry. As he drove he spent some time thinking about the last time he'd come this way...about how he was going to get his boy and make a run for the border. But the Jones bitch, even in her pregnancy, had fought him like a tiger. The fight had delayed him, and the delay had been long enough that he ended up getting shot by a state cop who flew the governor's helicopter. The shoulder wound had almost killed him. In fact, the more he thought about it, he realized that if he hadn't been carted away so quickly by Thorpe's men, he would have died from the infection. The irony of the whole thing was almost karmic. Two cops tried to take him out, but he was saved by a crooked fed.

When he got to the intersection of the dirt road and Highway 37, he saw the state troopers parked at the intersection. From the looks of things, he had them running scared, which is precisely what he wanted because as any good hunter would say, first you get your prey moving as one, then you divide and conquer. He drove past the troopers without giving them a second look and headed toward his destination. When he got to the stoplight, he looked over at the passenger seat and tipped the lid from the small box. The two hand-grenades were nestled in the wood shavings like a couple of baseballs waiting for the game to begin. The light turned green, and Decker drove on, headed for the opening pitch.

COOL SWUNG THE CHOPPER INTO THE WIND, THEN gently touched down on the pad in Virgil's backyard. The governor, Cora, and two state troopers climbed out and headed for the house.

When they got close to the back deck, Ross, who was hiding by the bushes on the side of the house, said, "Detective Ross on your left. The house is secure."

One of the troopers grabbed the governor's arm and stopped him, then drew his sidearm and let it hang loosely by his thigh. "Step out, please, Detective."

Ross slung his long gun over his shoulder and stepped forward so the troopers could identify him. Once they were sure it was him, they nodded, walked up the deck, and into the house. Ross followed them in and locked the door. He turned to Virgil and said, "You want me in here, or back outside?"

"You should stay," Virgil said. "You're a part of this too."

Cora looked at Virgil. "A part of what, specifically?" Then before Virgil could answer, she continued with,

"Jonesy, you'd better have a grade-A, one hundred percent, ultra-phenomenal explanation for all this...whatever it is."

The governor looked at Cora. "Don't worry. If I'm right, he does. And even if he doesn't, I'm pretty sure I do. Why don't we all sit down?"

CHAPTER THIRTY

When Decker arrived at his first destination he made a slow pass in the darkness to make sure no one was outside walking a dog, or some other damned thing. What he was about to do was a risk, but it was necessary, and even though he didn't see anyone, the thought of the whole thing made him nervous as hell. To get caught now before he ever got to Wheeler would amount to a total failure on his part. And more than that, if he was captured, there wouldn't be any more sealed records or crooked feds to keep him from spending the rest of his life in a Super Max prison.

So, he'd have to be quick...and careful.

He turned and went around the block, and when he got to the last Stop sign before his final turn, he reached up and flipped the switch to keep the car's overhead interior light from turning on when he opened the door. Then he removed the lid from the box on the passenger seat. With that done, he looked both ways for oncoming traffic, and when he didn't see any, he turned down the street and drove toward the target house. He killed his headlights when he was one house away, then coasted to a stop and parked on the wrong side of the street. He'd need to make a quick getaway because the hand grenades—two M67's—only had a delay of somewhere between four and five seconds.

Fortunately, the house sat close to the street, so with a little luck, he'd already be rolling away when they went off.

And that's exactly how it happened. He popped the car door, moved two steps up the lawn and pulled the pins, making sure to keep the handles depressed. Then one right after the other, he threw both grenades through the large plate glass window. As he ran back to the car he counted the seconds off in his head. By the time he got to three, he was jumping in the vehicle. By the time he got to four, the car was in gear and rolling, the door not even closed yet, the Impala screaming down the street.

By the time he got to five he heard the blasts, and when he looked in the rearview mirror, he saw the front door of the house fly out into the street.

He made a quick left, then a right at the next intersection, then another left, zigzagging away from the crime scene. He had to force himself to drive the speed limit.

Five minutes later he was sitting in line at a Taco Bell

drive-thru when he heard the first sirens. The whole thing gave him an appetite, and when he thought about it, he hadn't been this hungry since he'd murdered his old man years ago.

The killings always made him hungry. So, with the pilot who'd shot him now dead or dying, that made one down...and one to go.

RICHARD COOL'S LIVE-IN GIRLFRIEND, JULIA EVANS, AN orthopedic doctor with dusty red hair, big brown eyes, and an unusually playful personality for a surgeon had just stepped out of the shower when the grenades crashed through the window and blew the front half of the house apart. Fortunately for Evans, the master bath was at the back of the house, and while the explosions scared the hell out of her, she wasn't injured by the blasts.

It's what she did next that almost got her killed.

With nothing more than a towel wrapped around her body, she ran from the bathroom, grabbed the fire extinguisher next to the bed and headed to the front room. There wasn't much fire, and she thought she could get the flames knocked down, but when she stepped on the broken glass that was everywhere, she cut the bottoms of both her feet, and fell, hitting her head on the edge of the kitchen counter.

The blow knocked her out...and the flames started to take hold.

———

VIRGIL AND MURTON TOOK TURNS BRINGING EVERYONE up to speed on what had happened. When they were finished, Virgil looked around the room and said, "This guy is a total nut. That's why I wanted everyone here, at least for the time being."

Cora nodded at him, the nod at once an apology and an acknowledgment of a job well done. The governor looked at Murton and said, "This is mostly on me. I had no idea that Thorpe was crooked or that he was using Gibson. I never should have gotten you mixed up in that business with your father."

Murton shook his head. "Mac, you had no idea what was happening. None of us did."

"That's not entirely true, is it?" the governor said. "I heard the gunfire coming out of that building, and I knew you shot Decker. I'll tell you what I should have done. I should have kept my mouth shut. What was it I said? Something to the effect of 'Let's get out of here before the cops show up?'"

"I don't think we need to get too far down in the weeds on this one, Mac," Virgil said. "Thorpe's been locked up, we've got Franklin on our team, and he'll take care of the recording Gibson made. Our main concern right now is finding Decker."

Sandy looked at her husband. "Do you think it's a good idea that we're all sitting in the same house where he tried to kill me and Wyatt, and kidnap Jonas?"

The governor touched eyes with Virgil and tipped his head toward the kitchen. "Would you mind showing me where you keep your beer?" Then he glanced at Cora.

Despite the situation, Murton laughed. "Jesus, Mac, that was about as subtle as a sledgehammer. I'm pretty sure he keeps his beer in the fridge."

Virgil and Cora followed the governor into the kitchen. Ross was standing near the back door, and Virgil asked him to go join the others in the main room. Then he turned to the governor. "Mac?"

"The legislature is not in session," the governor said. "That means Sandy's workload is fairly light at the moment. In fact, I'm thinking that since the state has an ongoing agreement in place with the Popes regarding the drilling operations in Shelby County, perhaps a quick trip down to the island is in order. I'm sure there are enough things to talk about to justify the expenditure. The state will charter a plane. Sandy and the boys, along with anyone else—and I mean anyone—outside of the MCU's operational personnel should go along as special envoys." He turned to Cora and said, "Set it up with a departure as soon as possible."

Cora gave the governor a nod and took out her phone.

Virgil looked at the governor. "Mac, I don't think Sandy will want to go."

"That's one of the benefits of being the boss, Jonesy. She doesn't have a choice. I'll order her to go if I have to. Besides, what's better? Sitting around waiting for this idiot to make another move on her, or a little surf, sun, and sand in paradise?"

Murton had walked into the kitchen and caught the last part of the conversation. "Decker's not after Sandy. He's after me."

"And he'll do anything and everything he can to get to you, Murt," the governor said.

Virgil looked at his brother and nodded. "I'm with Mac on this one." Then to the governor: "But you get to tell her."

"My goodness," the governor said. "I believe Betty may have turned you into something of a sissy."

Virgil shook his head and walked over to the main room, with Murton and the governor on his heels. "Our fearless leader has a plan."

"I thought you were our fearless leader," Ross said.

Virgil gave the governor a dry look and said, "Apparently I've been demoted to sissy."

"I thought Betty was our fearless leader," Rosencrantz said.

"Is it always like this with you guys?" the governor said. "It's a wonder any criminals get captured at all."

Cora stepped into the room with her phone to her

chest. "The charter company says they can go tonight, but it won't be cheap. The only plane they have available at the moment is a Gulfstream G-650."

The governor waved the notion of money aside. "Tell them we'll take it, and that you'll call back shortly with a passenger list." Then to no one in particular: "How many people do we have?"

Virgil did the math in his head. With Sandy and the boys, Robert, Delroy, Huma, Aayla, Sarah and Liv, he came up with nine. He turned and looked at Becky. "I assume you're staying here with us?"

"I am," Becky said.

Virgil tipped his chin at Rosencrantz. "What about Carla?"

"I don't think she'll feel the need," Rosencrantz said.

"As a Shelby County official, it'd be nice to make her part of our delegation," the governor said. "The undersheriff could handle things for a few days. I'm sure I could convince her."

Rosencrantz took out his phone and made the call. A few minutes later, he hung up and said, "As it turns out, no convincing was required. She'll meet us at the airport."

"So that makes ten," Virgil said. "Rich? What about Julia?"

Cool shrugged. "I'm not sure of her schedule. Let me check." He took out his phone and tried to call, but didn't get an answer. "I know she had to work later than usual today. She's probably in the shower. I'll try her back in a few minutes."

"Well, let's count her for now," Virgil said. He looked at Cora. "Tell the charter company eleven people total. Seven adults and four children."

The governor cleared his throat. "Make that twelve total. I'll be going as well."

"Personal business with Nichole, Mac?" Virgil said.

The governor put his hand to his chest. "I would never use the taxpayer's hard-earned money for personal gain. The Shelby County Cultural Center's funding was put in place after a series of tense negotiations between the Pope's charitable foundation and the state. It's only natural that I attend and make sure everything is running smoothly."

"Are you prepping that statement for the lawyers or the press?" Murton said.

"Probably both," Ross said.

Everyone—even the governor—had a polite chuckle over Ross's direct observation. But when Cool's phone rang, the look on his face as he listened to the caller told everyone that something was terribly wrong.

CHAPTER THIRTY-ONE

Cool hung up and looked at no one. When he spoke, his voice shook with fear and rage. "That was the hospital. Someone tossed two grenades through my front window. Julia's in surgery. I gotta go. I have to get over there right now."

He began to move toward the kitchen and the back door that would take him out to the helicopter.

The governor said, "Rich?"

Cool kept going. "I gotta go, Mac."

The governor put a little gravel in his voice and said, "Stand your ground, Trooper. That's an order."

Cool spun around and said, *"What?"*

"You're in no condition to fly," the governor said. "I won't allow it."

"I'll take him," Murton said. "C'mon Cool, I'll have you there in fifteen minutes." He gave Becky a quick kiss, then grabbed his keys and phone. "Let's go." Ten seconds later they were out the door and screaming down the driveway.

Virgil looked at Mac and said, "It's started."

DECKER MADE IT BACK TO THE FORD'S HOUSE WITHOUT incident, and as a precaution, he'd parked the car one street over. If the cops happened to show, he could duck out the back, cut through the neighbor's yard and drive away.

He walked in and turned on the TV just in time to catch the evening news. When the report came up that a house had been bombed, he practically jumped with joy. But the joy soon turned to anger as he listened to the reporter tell the story. He'd missed the cop, and some woman he'd never heard of—presumably the pilot's girlfriend or wife—had only been injured by the grenades and was currently in surgery at Methodist hospital. The news footage showed the house was practically destroyed, but that did little to calm Decker. He flew into a fit of rage and began smashing everything and anything he could get his hands on.

When he finally wore himself out, he sat down to think. Maybe there was still a way to get to the pilot. If the woman in the house was at the hospital, the pilot would go there. It was a risk, but he'd done it before and gotten away.

It might be worth a look.

CORA HAD CALLED FOR THE GOVERNOR'S LIMO, AND BY the time it arrived, everyone was ready. The goodbyes were hurried and hectic, but everyone knew it would only be for a few days at the most. Once everybody was packed inside the limo, the state trooper motorcycle protection unit boxed the car and headed for the airport where the jet was ready and waiting.

When Virgil went back inside, the house—which only moments ago had been filled with people—now seemed eerily quiet. Everyone was gone except for Ross, Rosencrantz, and Becky.

"What now, Boss-man?" Rosencrantz said.

Virgil ran his fingers through his hair. "Good question. It's almost like we have to wait for Decker to make the next move."

"We could bait him," Ross said. "Why don't we pull the troopers? I could get up on the roof, and if he tries to make a run in here, he'll be dead before he gets out of the car."

"That's not a bad idea," Becky said. "But it could be a long wait. He's got time on his side."

"Speaking of time," Virgil said, "I want to make something perfectly clear. I don't know how all this will play out, but Decker isn't going to do any time in jail. Do I have to delineate that statement for anyone?"

Rosencrantz looked at Ross. "The definition of delineate is to describe something in a precise manner."

"I know what it means," Ross said.

Virgil barked at them. "Not now."

"Just trying to stay loose, Jonesy," Rosencrantz said.

Virgil held up his hands in an apologetic manner. "I know, I know. Me too. I'm sorry."

"I'll tell you who's sorry," Ross said. "I am. None of this would be happening if I'd been better prepared back when we were tracking Decker the first time...when I was still with SWAT."

Becky wasn't having it. "Knock it off with the apologies already. Everyone keeps trying to take the blame for something no one had any control over. Mac thinks it's his fault because of Thorpe and Gibson. Murton thinks it's his because he didn't kill Decker the first time, and you think it's yours because he escaped from a trailer through a back window you couldn't even see."

All Becky was trying to do was inject some perspective into the equation but her statement triggered something in Virgil's brain.

Becky saw the look on his face. "What is it, Jonesy?"

Virgil didn't answer...at least right away. Instead, he pulled out his phone and called Mimi. When she answered, he said, "Did you finish with the Ford crime scene?"

"Yeah, we finished hours ago. The body is at the Hendricks County morgue."

"Did he have any family?"

"He had an emergency contact card in his wallet. I gave everything to the Hendricks County guys since it was on their turf."

"Thanks, Mimi."

Virgil hung up, then looked at Becky. "Can you get me the number for the Hendricks County evidence cage? I need to talk to someone who can tell me something."

Becky took out her phone and did a quick search, then gave Virgil the number. When the call was answered, Virgil identified himself, then told the deputy what he needed. Five minutes later he had it. He wrote down the information, then asked to speak to the duty officer. When he had him on the line, he said, "Did you guys make the next of kin notification on the Ford case?"

There was a long pause, then the deputy said, "No...we thought you guys were going to handle that. They live in the city, outside of our county."

Virgil told him not to worry about it, and that they would take care of everything. Then he ended the call, looked at Becky, and finally answered her question. "Last time we were chasing Decker, the first thing he did was kill an old woman for her vehicle because he needed a different set of wheels."

"I remember," Becky said. "Murt told me that after the fact."

Virgil nodded rapidly. "When Ross got called to Hendricks County, Murt showed up. He recognized the truck that Decker had been driving because he left it behind. That means he took Ford's vehicle."

"Want me to get the info from the BMV?" Becky said.

Virgil shook his head. "Won't do any good. He was probably driving an Army car or truck. And if that's the case, he'd need to swap that out too."

"So where would he go to do that?"

Virgil held up the piece of paper he'd used to take notes from the Hendricks County deputy. "Ford's parents. I'd bet you any amount of money he's hiding out at their house and using their car."

Becky bit into her lip. "That means…"

Virgil nodded. "Yeah. If I'm right, Ford's parents are dead too." He looked at Ross and said, "The troopers stay. So do you. Becky does not get left alone for any reason. Got it?"

"No worries, Boss-man," Ross said.

"Now do you want me to get into the BMV?" Becky said.

"I do. Find out what kind of cars Ford's parents drive. Text me the info as soon as you have it."

"I can't do it from here," Becky said. "I'll have to go over to my place."

"I'll let the troopers outside know what you're doing. Ross?"

"I said I've got it, Jonesy, and I do."

"Okay. Watch your back. Don't get lulled into a false sense of security." Then Virgil turned to Rosencrantz. "Let's get to the Ford's and see what we can see."

"Think we'll get lucky?" Rosencrantz said.

Virgil shook his head in a sad way. "Probably not."

ONE OF THE SURGICAL NURSES CAME OUT TO THE waiting area and spoke with Cool and Murton. "She's in recovery right now, and she is awake and alert."

"When can I see her?" Cool said.

"In a few minutes. They're getting her hooked up to the equipment and settled in. It won't be long."

"What's her condition?" Murton said.

"The neurologist says she's going to be fine. The blow to her head didn't cause any damage other than a minor concussion, which we'll keep an eye on. There was nothing on the brain scans, and that's about the best news you could hope for. But the fall did cause a disk to herniate at the C7-T1 junction. The surgeon did a microdiscectomy, and everything went very well. She'll have to wear a collar for quite a while, and there will be some physical therapy involved but the bottom line is this: She's okay, and unless she gets an infection, she'll make a full recovery."

Cool let out a breath and looked down at the floor for a few seconds. "What's the rate of infection?"

The nurse shook her head. "I won't kid you. It happens. But they loaded her up with antibiotics before they went in, and she'll be on them for a few more days, so I wouldn't worry about it. They'll keep an eye on her sed rates, and the second they get out of whack, they'll get right on it. Don't worry, okay? She got lucky."

Murton put his arm around Cool's shoulders. "Relax, buddy. This is the best news you could have hoped for."

"I think I need to sit down," Cool said.

Murton nodded. "Go ahead. I'm going to call Becky and have her pass along the good news."

Murton reached into his pocket, then remembered he'd left his phone in his squad car. "I'll be right back. My phone is in the car. You want a coffee or something?"

"That would be great. Thanks, Murt. You're the best. Anyone ever tell you that?"

Murton smiled, but there was no light in his eyes. "All the time." *And maybe one day I'll believe them.*

DECKER COULDN'T BELIEVE HIS LUCK. HE'D JUST turned into the main parking area of the hospital and was sitting in his car when he saw Wheeler walk outside. A valet attendant pointed at Murton's squad car—which was still parked haphazardly at the front entrance—and said something, though Decker couldn't hear what because he was too far away. He watched as the attendant pointed again toward the far corner of the lot. Then Wheeler clapped the man on his back and moved to his car.

Decker dropped the Impala in gear, left his headlights off, and quickly drove in the direction the attendant had pointed out. Since he was closer, he'd be in position before Wheeler ever got there.

WHEN VIRGIL AND ROSENCRANTZ GOT TO THE FORD residence, they made a slow pass and went by without stopping. "TV is on," Rosencrantz said. "I can see it flickering through the curtains."

"Me too," Virgil said. "Take the next left and let me out on the side street. Go around the block, then take the front. That'll give me time to get in position at the back."

"You got it. Watch your ass, Jonesy."

Virgil popped the door, and as the car slowed he looked at Rosencrantz and said, "You too. Ring the bell once, then kick it. I'll be coming in hard through the back." Then he jumped out and ran through the neighboring yards. He stopped one house shy of the Ford's, and waited until he saw the lights of Rosencrantz's car.

Virgil moved through an aging hedgerow, then ran

across the lawn and up to the back porch. He quietly turned the knob, and to his surprise, he found the door unlocked. He cracked it, and when he heard the bell ring, he pushed the door open and let his Sig 226 lead him through the back of the house. He followed the sounds of the TV and when he got to the front room, he stopped dead in his tracks.

Rosencrantz stood there, his gun in both hands, sweeping the room. He touched eyes with Virgil, then tipped his head to the left, down a dark hallway. Virgil nodded and followed him that way. Both men checked all the rooms together, and when the house was clear, they walked back to the front.

"Someone sure did a number on the place," Rosencrantz said. "Look at this mess. Check the garage?"

"Yeah. Let's go together. Watch yourself, now."

When they entered the garage, they found a dark green army van but no other vehicles. They checked the inside of the van and saw that it was empty. Virgil shook his head. "I knew it. Decker was here."

They moved back into the house and closed the front door. "What about the Fords?" Rosencrantz said.

"The Fords are gone, man. They're dead."

"The front door was unlocked."

"Yeah, so was the back."

"Why would he trash the place?" Rosencrantz said.

"This guy is nuts, Rosie. I mean that in the clinical sense. He is literally insane. Something riled him up."

Rosencrantz moved to the TV and clicked it off. "I've had enough of this thing." Then, "Do you think he'll come back here?"

"I'm not sure," Virgil said. "He's got a plan of some kind. Look what he did at Cool's house."

"He's going after the people who hurt him. Cool shot him in the shoulder as he was leaving your place after Sandy was attacked. He'll go after Murton as soon as he can." Then Rosencrantz looked around the room again. "What's our next move, Jonesy?"

Virgil thought about it for a few seconds. "I know we should call the city on this and get the crime scene people out here, but if he comes back we could take him on the spot."

"I'm willing to wait it out if you are," Rosencrantz said.

"Let's do it. Get your squad out of sight. Put it one street over and cut through the backyard. I'll take the kitchen. You take the hallway. Stay out of sight, and don't hesitate. When he walks through the door—"

"Don't worry, Jones-man. I get it. This is a shoot first and ask questions later type of thing."

"You've got that right," Virgil said. "Move your car, and we'll get set up. This whole thing could be over in a few hours."

Except it wasn't.

CHAPTER THIRTY-TWO

Murton walked out through the hospital's front entrance and toward his squad car. The valet attendant saw him going that way and called out to him.

"Excuse me, Officer? I was hoping you could move your car into the main lot. You're sort of blocking things up around here."

Murton nodded at the attendant. He knew the young man was only trying to do his job. "Sure. My mistake. We had an urgent call, and I sort of dumped the car without thinking. I'll get it out of your way right now."

"The lot's pretty full, this being Friday night and all. It's always our busiest night of the week." He pointed off in the distance. "I think there are a few spots in the back."

Murton clapped him on the shoulder. "Don't worry,

I'll find something." Then he walked over and got into his Charger, pulled away from the entrance, and headed to the rear of the lot.

———

DECKER PULLED INTO AN OPEN SPOT, POPPED THE trunk lid, then hurried out of the Impala. He moved to the rear of the car and put one hand on the lid to keep it lowered, but unlatched. He had his gun out and held it across his chest. The suppressor made the gun a little cumbersome, but in situations like these, it was necessary. He got down on one knee with his back facing the oncoming squad car.

Murton turned into his own parking space one row away and climbed out of his car. When Decker heard Murton's door shut, he rested his forearm and head against the rear of the trunk, then let his shoulders heave up and down as if he was stricken with grief.

It'd either work or it wouldn't. But one way or another, Wheeler was going down.

———

IF MURTON HAD TO PUT A NUMBER TO IT, HE THOUGHT over the past week or so—ever since the dreams started— he was averaging maybe three hours of sleep a night. He was worn down, exhausted, and not thinking clearly at a time when he knew he needed to be on top of his game. But the stress and sleepless nights had taken their toll, far beyond anything he'd ever experienced in his life.

He glanced up at the hospital and thought about how lucky Julia was...that her injuries weren't life-threatening and that she would make a full recovery. When he saw the grieving man a few yards away, it made him think of his adoptive mother, Elizabeth, and how alone he'd felt as she was dying. He'd made a mistake that night...the last time he saw her in the hospital room. He was grieving himself and wouldn't let anyone comfort him. And right here was a brother soldier in his presence, suffering his own loss of some sort. Why not do a good deed?

Murton stopped a few feet away from the man's back. "Is there anything I can do for you, soldier?"

The man mumbled something unintelligible, his face buried in the crook of his arm. Murton stepped closer and said, "Excuse me, I don't mean to intrude. I didn't hear what you said."

Decker stood slowly and kept his free hand on the trunk lid, then he let go and the trunk popped open. When the lid came up, it distracted Murton for a half second, but that was all Decker needed.

He spun around, pointed his gun at Murton, and fired, hitting him in the shoulder. The shot spun Murton, and Decker rushed forward, grabbed him by the back of his shirt, and held him upright, the gun now pointed at his ear. Then he pulled him back toward the car, turned him around, and clubbed him on the back of his head with the butt of the gun.

Murton was out cold. Decker pushed him into the trunk, then yanked the handcuffs from Murton's belt. Once he had him restrained, he stripped him of his weapons, keys, and cell phone, and tossed them under another car. Then he slammed the lid on the Impala, jumped into the driver's seat and took off.

Wheeler was his.

VIRGIL'S PHONE BUZZED AT HIM, AND WHEN HE checked the screen, he saw it was Becky calling. "What have you got, Becks?"

"The Indiana BMV shows the Fords only have one vehicle. It's a late model black Chevy Impala. I'll text you the plate."

"Do that. Probably won't matter, though. Decker is smart enough to swap the plates."

"Why are you whispering?" Becky said.

"Rosie and I are set up inside the Ford residence. Decker was here. There's an army van in the garage, and the Impala is gone. So are the homeowners. We're hoping he'll come back."

Becky started whispering herself without realizing she was doing so. "Okay. Everything is quiet here. Ross and I are still at my place, and we'll stay in place. No sense in running back and forth."

"Got it," Virgil said. "Any word from Cool or Murton on Julia's condition?"

"Nothing yet. They're my next call."

"Keep me up," Virgil said.

"I will," Becky said, and then she was gone.

As Decker drove away, he couldn't believe how easy it'd been to take Wheeler. He was supposed to be some kind of tough guy, but he went down like a deer caught in the headlights. He stood there and practically let it happen. The more he thought about it, the more paranoid he became. Was it some kind of trick? Surely not.

But he couldn't let the thought go. He was halfway back to the Ford's place when he couldn't take it anymore. He pulled over on a quiet side street, got out, and popped the trunk. When he looked inside, Wheeler was still unconscious. Decker laughed at himself, closed the lid, and got back in the car. Twenty minutes later he turned down the street in back of the Ford's house, ready to park the car. He'd check the house to make sure it was still safe, then come back and put the car back in the garage. He had plans for Wheeler. He was going to watch him die from a gunshot wound to the shoulder, just as he almost had. But first things first.

As soon as he made the turn, he saw the unmarked state squad car parked directly behind where the Ford's house was. In a fit of panic, he slammed on the brakes and killed his headlights. Were they on to him already? Could they be waiting to ambush him? Only one way to find out. He left the headlights off and pulled away slowly, then turned the corner and parked at the intersection. The house was close enough to the cross street that he could clearly see it.

He watched for a moment, looking for signs of movement in the house, but didn't see any. Then he remembered that he hadn't bothered to turn off the TV before leaving. He watched for a few more minutes and still didn't see anything, but Decker was sure the TV had been turned off by someone. That meant only one thing: They were inside and waiting for him. He was sure of it.

He backed away from the intersection, turned around in an empty driveway, then took off. He had to think. He wanted Wheeler to die slowly.

———

BECKY TRIED MURTON'S PHONE BUT DIDN'T GET AN answer. She left a quick voice message and asked him to call back. She tried Cool's phone and got the same result. No answer.

She thought for a few minutes, then decided that they had probably turned their phones off because they were in the hospital. She didn't know why hospitals made people do that. It was as ridiculous as turning them off on an airplane. She spent some time on her other secret research project, but the thought of not being able to reach Murton or Cool nagged at her.

Fifteen minutes later she tried both men again and got the same result. She rubbed the sleep out of her eyes and thought about the definition of insanity. Enough already. She called the hospital's main switchboard and asked to be connected to the surgical nurse's station. After a minute or so, a nurse came on the line and said, "How may I help you?"

"My name is Becky Wheeler. My husband is Detective Murton Wheeler with the state's Major Crimes Unit. He's there with another state trooper, Richard Cool. Trooper Cool's girlfriend is Doctor Julia Evans. She was injured earlier this evening."

"Yes, I'm aware," the nurse said. "I spoke with both men once Doctor Evans was out of surgery."

"How is she?"

The nurse hesitated before she spoke. "Well, with the HIPPA laws, I'm not really allowed to give out any patient information. I hope you understand."

Becky rolled her eyes into the phone. "I do, but it's

not like I'm asking to see her chart. I'm simply wondering if she's okay."

The nurse lowered her voice and said, "You didn't hear it from me, but yes, she's fine. The doctors expect a full recovery."

"Thank God," Becky said. Then, "Listen, I'm trying to reach my husband. Is he around there?"

"I haven't seen either of them since we last spoke. Doctor Evans is still in recovery, and I know Officer Cool was going to go in to be with her. Your husband is probably still in the waiting room."

"Could you do me a favor and go check. I need to speak with him and he's not answering his phone."

"Sure, I can do that. Would you like to hold, or should I have him call you back?"

"I'll hold if you don't mind."

"One moment, please," the nurse said. Then there was a click, followed by the type of music that Becky thought probably made every single human being on the planet want to hang up after thirty seconds.

Becky waited the thirty seconds, plus an additional four minutes. Finally, the phone was picked up by Cool. "Becky?"

"Hey, Cool. How's Julia?"

Cool took a few minutes to give Becky the particulars, then finished by saying, "Bottom line, she's going to be okay."

"That's fantastic, Cool. How are you holding up?"

"I'm fine. A little pissed about my house, but I guess that's what insurance is for."

"Well, not to burst your bubble, but hand grenades? The carrier will probably call it an act of war and decline the whole claim."

Cool actually laughed. "Let 'em try. I have a gun, and I know how to use it."

Becky chuckled. "Listen, that's great news about Julia. I can't tell you how relieved I am to hear it. Is Murton around anywhere? I can't reach him on the phone."

"I haven't seen him for quite a while, actually. I've been in with Julia the whole time. He said he was going to call you."

Becky felt a tingling sensation on the back of her neck. "When was this?"

Cool checked his watch. "Uh, about an hour ago. He left his phone in his car. Said he was going to go get it, grab us a couple of coffees, then come back up. He didn't call?"

"No, Cool...he didn't."

Cool stayed true to his name. "Don't worry, Becky, I'm sure he's fine. I'll go find him, chew him out, and have him call you."

"Cool?"

"Yeah?"

"Decker tried to kill you. What are the chances he showed up at the hospital?"

"Becky, let me go look, okay?"

"Turn your phone on, and give me access to your location."

"I'm doing that right now. I'll call you back. Don't worry. I'm sure Murton is fine." And then Cool was gone...running hard toward the elevator.

CHAPTER THIRTY-THREE

Becky called out to Ross, who was in the room in less than ten seconds. "What is it?"

"Go notify the troopers that we might be on the move."

"What's going on?"

"Do it, Ross. Right now. I'll explain in a minute."

Ross gave her a tight nod, then ran outside. Becky brought the location app up on her computer and clicked on Murton's number. Fifteen long seconds later, the app connected to Murton's phone and showed him at the hospital. A full minute later it narrowed itself down and showed the phone near the hospital, but outside. Becky changed the overlay from the map setting to the satellite view and saw that Murton's phone was in the hospital's parking lot.

When she brought up Cool's phone, it showed him still inside.

———

COOL WASN'T INSIDE THE HOSPITAL, BUT HE WAS standing right outside the main entrance speaking with the parking attendant.

"Yes, Sir," the attendant said. "I spoke with him about...mmm...an hour ago? I asked him to move his car because it was blocking the entrance."

Cool was starting to lose his cool. "Yes, yes. Where did he take it?"

"I don't know which spot, Sir, but I pointed out to the back of the lot. It's pretty full out there."

Cool didn't bother answering, he just took off. When he got to the back of the lot, he saw Murton's squad car. He ran that way, hoping and praying that Murton was asleep behind the wheel. But prayers often go unanswered, and this time was no different. The car was empty and locked up tight.

He turned to run back inside when his phone chirped at him. When he answered, Becky said, "It's me. Where is he?"

"I can't find him, Becks. I'm standing right next to his car, but he's not here."

"Yes, he is Cool. He has to be. I'm looking at your location. You're right there."

"Hang up and call his phone, Becky. Do it right now."

Becky didn't bother to answer. She ended the call and punched Murton's number in. Five rings later it clicked over to voicemail. Becky slapped the desk with her palm, then redialed. This time she got an answer, and it was the one she feared the most.

"I'VE GOT IT," COOL SAID. "IT WAS UNDER A PARKED car."

"Where in the hell is Murton?"

"Becky, listen. Is Ross still with you?"

"Yes. Now answer my question, Cool."

"I don't know where he is. I've got his phone, and his keys, and, uh, both his guns. Everything was sitting under a parked car."

"Oh my god," Becky said. "It's Decker."

"I'm afraid there's more."

"What? *What?*"

"There's blood as well," Cool said. "And there's a lot."

Becky dropped the phone and screamed into her hands. Ross heard the scream and came running. "What is it, Becky? Talk to me. Becky?"

COOL CALLED VIRGIL AND TOLD HIM AS QUICKLY AS possible what was happening.

Virgil called out to Rosencrantz, then went back to Cool and the phone. "How long has he been gone?"

"We're not sure. Probably a few minutes either side of an hour."

"Stay put. We're on the way. Call it in, Rich."

"I'm on it," Cool said, and then he was gone.

Virgil told Rosencrantz what was happening as they ran from the house. They sprinted through the backyards and jumped into the squad car. Rosencrantz hit the lights and siren, and Virgil called Becky. When she answered, Virgil could hear another siren in the background. "Becky, where are you?"

"Where do you think? I'm in the car with Ross, and we're headed to the hospital."

"That's not a good idea, Becks," Virgil said. "This is exactly what Decker wants...all of us running around like crazy."

"Wrong," Becky said, her voice filled with fury. "He's got what he wants. He has my husband." Then before Virgil could say anything else, Becky ended the call.

Rosencrantz kept his eyes on the road when he spoke. "This is not good, man. Not good at all."

Virgil didn't say anything. He simply stared out the window and thought about his brother.

Decker wasn't sure where to go. His original plan had been to take Wheeler back to the Ford's house, chain him up, and watch him die a slow and painful death. But now that the cops knew he'd been there, he couldn't go back.

Then another thought occurred to him. He'd find a place where he thought no one would think to look. He'd go all the way back to the beginning, to the place where it all started on the day the cops made him look like a fool in front of his men. It was the place that should have been rightfully his all along. It's where they took his boy, and the land that came with him. The more he thought about it, he realized there was a simple sort of symmetry to the whole thing. He'd let Wheeler bleed out on the land that had cost him his own blood.

He took the back roads through the night, south...and down to Shelby County.

The hospital parking lot was locked down, and the crime scene had been taped off. Virgil and Rosencrantz beat Ross and Becky there, but only by a few minutes. Virgil didn't even have time to bring the responding officers up to date before he heard Becky running his way. She was yelling Murton's name over and over, and she managed to make it past two city police officers before Virgil wrapped her up in a hug and held her tight.

"This is as far as we can go, Becks. Any closer and we'll contaminate the scene."

She tried to pull free, but Virgil held on tight. Then he felt her body go slack, so he loosened his hold. He held her at arm's length and looked her in the eyes. "We will find him, Becky. I give you my word."

Becky pulled free, took a step back, and pointed her finger at Virgil. "Don't make promises you can't keep, Jonesy."

"I don't."

Becky looked away for a moment, then said, "It's too much blood."

Virgil sidestepped in front of her to block the view of the blood puddle. Cool walked over and said, "I spoke with one of the crime scene techs. He said it's not as much as it looks like. Not enough that he'd bleed out."

"Yeah, for now, anyway," Becky said. Then she bared her teeth at Cool and said, "Why'd you leave him alone? That was the plan, remember? No one was supposed to be alone."

Cool dropped his head. "Becky, I know it doesn't mean much to you right now, but I didn't think it was a problem. The car was less than ten feet from the entrance."

"Then why is it out here?" Becky said.

"The parking valet asked him to move it. For whatever

reason, he did it by himself. If he would have come back up to get me, I'd have gone with him."

Becky wiped the tears from her eyes and nodded. "I know, I know. It's not your fault. It's that damned dream he's been having. He's exhausted and not thinking straight. It probably didn't even occur to him to ask you to come down."

Virgil walked over to Ross and gave him a look. "You thought this was a good idea? To bring her here?"

Ross wasn't offended by Virgil's questions. "You've seen Becky in action. She's just like Murt. The woman is a force of nature. Do you think you could have stopped her?"

Virgil shook his head. "Probably not."

"What in the hell are we going to do, Virgil?"

Virgil looked at Ross with a sense of affection. It was the first time he'd ever heard the young man call him by his proper name. When he answered, his voice cracked. "I don't know, Ross. I really don't. But we better think of something, and quick."

DECKER WAS IN A STATE OF MIND HE'D NOT FELT IN A long time. The action, the planning, the precise military-style execution of his plan...it amped him up like nothing else. But he was also tired and hungry. He found an all-night convenience store and stopped for coffee and snacks. Not the healthiest choices, but the sugar and carbs would keep him going for now. So would the coffee. He paid the attendant, then got back in the car and continued on his way. Then he realized that in the dark of night, he was a little lost.

He'd gone almost twenty miles, and the further he went the more unsure he became. Finally, in a fit of frustration, he turned the car around and made his way back to the convenience store. "Got a state map?" he asked the attendant.

"Right behind you, on the rack."

Decker turned, saw the maps, grabbed what he needed, then opened it up.

The attendant cleared his throat. "Sir, you have to pay for the map before you use it."

Decker reached into his pocket and threw a twenty on the counter. "That's a stupid rule."

"Not really," the attendant said. "If you think about it, I mean. People could come in, look at the map, then leave without paying."

"Yeah, yeah, I get," Decker said. "Where in the hell are we? Show me." He spun the map around so the attendant could see it.

"Where are you headed?"

Decker was losing patience. "Look, I'm not trying to make a new Facebook friend. Where I'm going isn't the issue. Now point out where the fuck I am, and I'll be on my way."

The attendant grabbed a pen, then made a circle on the map. "Right here. There's a rest stop a few miles down the road. Maybe a little sleep might calm your nerves."

The look that Decker gave the attendant shut him up. "Keep the change, asshole."

As soon as Decker was outside, the attendant hurried from behind the counter, locked the door, then watched him drive away. He still held the pen in his hand, and with little forethought he wrote the plate number down on the inside of his wrist. If the guy came back, he was going to call the cops.

But as it turned out, the guy never did, and when morning rolled around, the attendant's shift was over, and his replacement showed up. "How'd it go last night?"

The night shift attendant gave him a shrug. "Same ol' same ol'...bunch of idiots. Had one guy who sort of scared me. He was pretty wound up. Wanted to look at a map without paying."

"You make him pay?"

"Yeah, but I almost let it go. This guy had a look about him, you know? I got his plate and wrote it in the log. He was driving a black Impala. If you see him, which you probably won't, I'd dial 911 and keep my finger on the Send button, if you get my drift."

"I'll do that. Go home and get some sleep, huh?"

"I'd love to," the night shift guy said. "But I'm headed

down to Evansville. Gonna catch the big airshow down there. I'll sleep when I get back."

"That's cool. Have a good time."

The day shift guy went behind the counter, turned on ESPN, then settled in for the duration.

CHAPTER THIRTY-FOUR

Before they'd left the hospital, Virgil had done two things, both borne out of desperation. First, he called Cora and gave her an update on everything that had happened. When he finished, she said, "Tell me what you need, Jones-man. Say the word, and you'll have it."

"I need the last few hours back," Virgil said. He sort of growled it at her.

"I was thinking more along the lines of what I could actually do."

Virgil softened his tone. "I know, I know. Listen, I'd like to get a description of Decker and his vehicle out to every TV and radio station in the state. Can you make that happen?"

"Consider it done. It'll be the lead story on every station, I guarantee it. What else? Are you thinking of a reward?"

"No, that will only clog up the lines with useless information."

"I'll have it all set by morning. Anything else?"

"Not that I can think of," Virgil said.

"Okay. Listen, Mac called a little while ago. Everyone arrived safe and sound at the Pope's. Sandy said she didn't want to bother you because she knew you were busy."

"Maybe you could call them back and fill everyone in on what's happening. I can't think straight right now."

"Got it. Hang in there, Jonesy. Murton is tougher than a hickory stump. If anyone can make it through this, he can."

"I hope you're right," Virgil said. Then he ended the call and walked over to Cool. "I need to ask you something, and it's going to be hard to say yes, but I need it anyway."

"What is it?" Cool said.

"We're getting ready to roll, and I need you to stick with us. Decker could be anywhere, and we may need you in the helicopter."

Cool shook his head. "That idiot put two hand grenades through my front window. Julia could have been killed. What if he shows up here? I can't leave her alone."

"She won't be alone, Rich. I'm going to have Ross and Rosencrantz stay here, right outside her door until this is over. No harm will come to her, I promise you."

Cool didn't like it, but he knew Virgil was right. "Let me go up and tell her. I'll be right back."

Virgil grabbed him by the arm and said, "Hold on a second." Then he turned to Ross and Rosencrantz. "Ross, Rosie...you're with Cool. He'll explain. Go now."

As the three men started back across the parking lot, Virgil looked at the crime scene techs and said, "Bag the guns, phone, and keys. They're coming with me."

The lead tech looked at Virgil and said, "We can't do that, Detective. We're not done processing the—"

Virgil ripped the crime scene tape in half, walked over to where Murton's belongings were, then picked them up. "There's nothing to process. We know who did this. See that blood on the ground? It came from my brother. You don't like the way I'm doing things, file a fucking report." Then he turned and walked away.

————

THAT HAD ALL BEEN OVER SIX HOURS AGO, AND NOW, with nothing better to do, Virgil, Becky, and Cool were all pacing around Murton's house, waiting for the morning news to come on. Virgil checked his watch and thought if the parking valet at the hospital had been correct, Murton had been missing for far too long already. He knew every second counted, and as they ticked off he felt further and further away from his brother.

When the news program came on, Becky grabbed the remote and turned up the volume. The three of them stood there in front of the TV and watched the fancy graphics with multicolored light effects flash across the screen. The report showed a picture of Decker along with a stock photo of a late model black Chevy Impala. The anchor stated that Decker was wanted for questioning in the abduction of a state police officer late last night. She went on to say that his whereabouts were unknown, he was considered armed and extremely dangerous, and should anyone see him they were to call the local authorities immediately. Then a picture of Murton came on the screen, and Becky moved toward the TV as if that act alone could put her closer to her husband. She reached out to touch the image, but just as she did, Murton's picture went away and the anchor was back, a smile on her face, saying they'd be right back with the weekend forecast, along with a furry friend from the local pet adoption center who needed a loving home.

Virgil was so mad he was vibrating. "Fucking news. They spent more time showing their fancy graphics and talking about pet adoption than Decker and Murt."

Cool put his arm across Virgil's shoulder. "Take it easy, Jonesy. The report is out. Someone will see him. He can't hide forever."

Virgil spun away from Cool. "I need some air. I'm going for a walk." He went out the back and started toward the pond.

Once Virgil was gone, Cool looked at Becky. "You okay, Becks?"

"No."

"Where is Jonesy going?"

Becky looked out the window and saw Virgil pulling a chair close to Mason's cross. "In search of answers."

DECKER WOKE, AND FOR A MOMENT HE DIDN'T remember where he was. Then it all came back to him in a rush. He'd taken the convenience store clerk's advice and pulled into the rest area off the highway. He sat quietly and listened for any movement from the trunk. When he heard none, he rubbed the sleep from his face, started the car, and got back on the road.

The daylight helped him remember the route better, and the map guided him right where he needed to go. A short twenty minutes later, he was there. At first he thought he might have been in the wrong place. The co-op building was gone, replaced by a modern-looking structure with a sign at the entrance that read *Shelby County Cultural Center*. Beyond the center were small housing units, a park, and far off in the distance, a large pole barn. When he scanned the area beyond the pole barn he saw drilling rigs of some sort, but had no idea what they were for.

He was surprised by the changes that had occurred over the years. The land that was rightfully his had been transformed into something almost unrecognizable. The area was quiet, there were no cars at the Cultural Center, and the park was empty. Decker looked at the pole barn for a minute, then decided—depending on what was inside—it might be as good a place as any.

He didn't want Wheeler to die in the trunk, after all. Decker, whose mind wasn't really his own anymore, wanted to watch it happen. He dropped the car in gear and headed toward the barn.

———

VIRGIL LOOKED AT THE CROSS FOR A LONG TIME, hoping his father would show. He sat for over an hour, waiting, asking, pleading, but if Mason could hear him, he didn't respond. Virgil was tired, mad, and hadn't felt so alone since his mom had died. He stood from the chair and began to walk back toward Murton's house.

"You're not going to give up that easily are you, Son? Your brother needs you."

Virgil spun around and saw his father sitting in the chair he'd just vacated. "Dad, tell me what to do."

"I can't, Virg. It doesn't work that way."

"Where is he? He's every bit as much your son as I am."

"I know that, Virg. But that's all I know."

"He's probably bleeding out as we speak, and you're going to tell me that you don't know where your own son is?"

Then Mason said something that surprised Virgil. "Do

you know where Jonas is right now? He's your son, just like Murton is mine."

"Dad, Jonas doesn't have anything to do with this."

"Doesn't he?" Mason said.

Virgil turned away and looked out at the pond. He knew that the conversations with his father held a meaning that was often difficult to grasp. He forced himself to calm down and listen, not only to Mason's words, but any hidden meaning they might hold. "Why did you ask me where Jonas is?"

"I was simply trying to make a point. You didn't answer, either."

Virgil stepped closer to his father. "I do know where Jonas is. He's in Jamaica."

"Yes, but where?"

"At the Pope's. He's with Sandy, Mac, and everyone else."

"But tell me...right now, in this moment, where he is, and what he's doing."

Virgil shook his head in defeat. "I can't. I don't know."

"The same is true with me and Murton, Son. Don't you see?"

"Yeah, I do, Dad. Except the difference is, if Jonas was hurt and in the hands of a madman, I'd move heaven and earth to find him. I'd think you'd want to do the same for your adopted son."

"What do you think I'm doing now?"

Virgil paused to think. "That wasn't the only reason you asked me where Jonas is."

Mason nodded without speaking.

"Jonas doesn't know it, but Decker is his biological father."

"I'm aware," Mason said.

"Dad, what am I missing?"

"Haven't you been listening, Virg. I've been telling you all along that everything is connected. *Everything*. You've got to go back to the beginning to figure it out."

"The beginning of what? Time?"

Mason tipped his head. "In a manner of speaking, yes. What did I tell you the night that Jonas came into your lives?"

"Dad, I'm tired. I don't remember."

"All you have to do is go back to the beginning, Son. The simplest things are sometimes the most significant. If nothing else, remember this: The answers are written on stars."

Virgil looked out across the pond again, trying to understand what his father meant, and how Jonas and Murton were connected...at least beyond the obvious. When he spoke, he didn't look at his father. "Dad, you've got to help me, here. I'm begging you."

When he didn't get an answer, Virgil turned to face his father, but Mason was gone.

DECKER GOT THE BARN'S DOORS OPEN AND DISCOVERED there was more than enough room to pull the Impala inside. And not only that, there were plenty of places he could restrain Wheeler and watch him either bleed out or die of infection from the gunshot wound.

He pulled the car into the barn, then closed the doors behind him. Since it was Saturday, he thought he wouldn't have to deal with any interruptions from outsiders, and even if he did, what did one or two more victims matter? Answer: None.

He popped the trunk lid, and when he got to the back of the car, Wheeler was curled into the fetal position, and the trunk was covered with blood. He nudged him with the gun's barrel and used the same words Murton had said to him. "Time to wake up, sleepyhead."

Except Murton wasn't asleep. He wasn't unconscious either.

GENE WALKER WAS LOOKING FORWARD TO HIS DAY. The sky was clear, the winds were calm, and this would be the last flight of the season for him and his Hellcat. The airshow in Evansville was one he always looked forward to, and even though what he'd told Mason's adopted son not long ago—the insurance and operating costs that came with the Hellcat were expensive—the flight and the performance he put on for aviation fans was worth every penny.

He hooked the tug up to the aircraft's tow bar, then carefully pulled it from the hangar. With that done, he called for the fuel truck, told the lineman to top the tanks, then went back inside to file his flight plan.

He woke the computer, logged in to the FAA's system, and clicked the tab labeled: NOTAMs & TFRs—acronyms for Notice to Airmen, and Temporary Flight Restrictions. The NOTAMs and TFRs would provide any and all relevant data regarding his flight down to Evansville. When the information came up, he chuckled and shook his head. Walker wasn't the only one going to have some fun today. The military was doing flight maneuvers out of Terre Haute, and the airspace restrictions they had in place meant that Walker would have to take an indirect route down to Evansville. In truth, he didn't mind. It'd give him a little more stick time. He'd go straight south, then cut over to the west.

He printed off the flight restrictions, then filed his flight plan. With that done, he went to sign for the fuel. He had a little spring in his step, and he liked it. When he checked his watch, he saw that his scheduled departure wasn't for another hour. But the anticipation was part of the fun.

CHAPTER THIRTY-FIVE

When Decker moved closer to pull him from the trunk, Murton lashed out with his leg and kicked Decker in the face as hard as he possibly could. Decker staggered back and howled with shock and pain... and Murton, who really was as tough as a hickory stump, rolled himself out of the trunk, ready to fight, even with his hands cuffed behind his back.

But when Murton hit the ground, he landed on his wounded shoulder, and the impact—together with the blood loss he'd already suffered—caused his head to swim, and his eyes went out of focus. Before he could even move or stand, Decker was right there on top of him, his fists hammering away at his face and ribs.

And then Murton went away again.

It was Becky who figured it out.

Virgil walked back inside the house and found her and Cool almost exactly as he'd left them. In other words, worried sick and pacing like they were trying to lay grooves into the hardwood flooring. Virgil knew that the conversations he had with his father were unusual, to say the least, and he often found it difficult to speak with someone who didn't know much about it. He caught Cool's eye.

"What?"

"I was wondering if I could have a minute alone with Becky?"

Cool shook his head. "C'mon, Jonesy. I'm in the loop. Did he say anything or not?"

"Who told you?"

"It doesn't matter. Word gets around. So, yes, or no?"

Virgil nodded. "Yeah, now all I have to do is figure it out."

Becky walked right up to Virgil and put her hands on his chest. "Tell us, Jonesy, and don't leave anything out. Not one single word."

They all sat down and that's what Virgil did. When he was finished, they both looked at him and shook their heads. "I wasn't even there that night," Cool said. "I'm at a loss."

Becky got up and began pacing the room again. "I've seen that video. It's one of the most amazing things I've ever witnessed. But I don't understand what he meant by go back to the beginning."

"I don't either," Virgil said. "I've watched that video so many times I can close my eyes and see the entire thing. Dad said to go back to the beginning. But the beginning is when you guys were, uh, frozen in time, or whatever."

"Can I see it?" Cool said.

Virgil shrugged, brought up the video, and tossed his phone to Cool. A few minutes later, Cool gave him the phone back, and when he did, his hands were shaking.

"It'll have that effect on you," Virgil said.

Cool simply nodded without speaking.

"I don't get it," Becky said. "He told you to go back to the beginning. He must have meant that night. But I was there the whole time. What are we missing?"

"I don't know, Becks. I can't think straight."

Becky was circling the room when she suddenly stopped. "What happened during that moment, Jonesy?"

"You already know what happened."

"I'm not talking about what's on the video. I'm talking about the beginning. What made you pull out your phone and make the recording?"

"I thought you guys were playing a trick on me," Virgil said.

"But we weren't. So what I'm asking is this: What did we miss before the video?"

Virgil thought about it for a minute, then stood up so fast he heard his knees click. "I don't think I ever told anyone. I was looking up at the night sky and I saw two shooting stars, side by side."

"And Mason told you that the answers were written in the stars," Cool said.

"No, he didn't," Becky said. "And I know how to find Murton. God, I can't believe I didn't think of this already." She ran to her office and woke the computers. Her fingers were already flying across the keyboard by the time Virgil and Cool were in the room.

"Becks?" Virgil said.

"Hold on."

"Becky, what are you doing?"

"Probably setting myself and the state up for a huge lawsuit. I'll deal with that later." She kept typing as she spoke. "What's the one thing that Murt and Jonas have in common?"

"They were both adopted," Virgil said.

"Exactly," Becky said.

Virgil and Cool looked at each other, their faces a mask of confusion. Becky didn't even have to look at them to know they didn't understand. "What kind of car are we looking for?"

"A Chevy Impala," Virgil said. "You already know that."

"Right. A late-model Chevy Impala, to be exact."

"So?" Cool said.

Becky looked at Virgil. "Get Nicky or Wu on the phone right now, Jonesy. I need their help."

Virgil knew better than to ask why. He simply did what he was told. As Virgil was waiting for the call to go through, Becky said, "Mason didn't say the answers were often written in the stars. He said the answers are often written on stars. Not 'in.' 'On.' Chevy's have a system called OnStar. If we can get into their network, I can track that car because I've already got the VIN from the BMV."

Before either man could respond, the phone was answered, and Virgil put it on speaker. "Hello, Virgil. It is Wu. You are well?"

Virgil felt like they didn't have any time to waste. He set the phone in front of Becky, who took the lead. "Wu, it's Becky. I need you and Nicky right now."

"We are aware of your troubles. Nicky and I are in the computer lab right now. What do Wu need?"

"I need a brute force attack on Chevrolet's OnStar system. I'm sending you the VIN right now. I don't have enough computer power or time to do it on my own."

"One moment, please," Wu said. He sounded like an Asian customer service representative. Two long minutes later he was back. "This can be done. It will require approximately thirty minutes. Please allow us access to your equipment."

Becky typed in a series of commands, then leaned into the phone and said, "Execute."

"Keep this line free. Wu will text coordinates when we have location."

Virgil turned to Cool. "Light that chopper up."

Cool ran from the house and across the backyard. Thirty seconds later Virgil could hear the rotor blades coming up to speed.

Virgil picked up the phone and said, "Wu, we're going airborne. Make it quick. Becky will coordinate with you from here."

"Fuck that," Becky said. "I'm going." Then she grabbed Virgil's phone and ran outside.

Virgil knew Ross had been telling the truth the night before. You couldn't tell Becky no. He still had Murton's keys, so he ran to his brother's gun safe and pulled out a Colt M16A4 rifle, along with two fully loaded magazines.

If Decker wanted a war, Virgil was about to give him one.

COOL GOT THEM UP, BUT WITHOUT A LOCATION HE didn't know where to go, so he flew an ever-widening pattern above Virgil's house.

Virgil leaned forward and said, "Keep us low, Rich. We need the cell signal."

"Roger that," Cool said. Then, "We also need satellite phones."

"We'll have them after this, I guarantee it."

TEN MINUTES INTO THE CIRCLING, VIRGIL HAD A thought. He turned to Becky, who was gripping the cell phone so hard Virgil was afraid it might crack. "What else do Murton and Jonas have in common?"

Becky shook her head without taking her eyes from the phone.

"Listen, Becks, it's a risk, but I think it's one worth taking."

"What is it?"

"Decker knows that Jonas is his biological son. He also knows that the land down in Shelby County would have been his if he ever got his hands on Jonas. There's a good chance that's where he's taken Murt."

"It's a hell of a risk, Jonesy. If they went north, we'd be wasting time heading south."

"Becky...trust me on this. He's my brother."

"And he's my husband."

"What does your gut say?"

Becky hesitated, but only for a few seconds. When she gave Virgil the nod, her jaw quivered.

Virgil told Cool to turn south and head for Shelby County.

GENE WALKER CHECKED HIS WATCH AGAIN, MADE A quick pitstop to the men's room, then walked out to the Hellcat. He pulled the wheel chocks, climbed the ladder, and slid into the cockpit. Once the line tech had the ladder out of the way, he fired the engine and let it come up to temperature. Then, after he was strapped in tight, he put on his headset, radioed the tower, and told them he was ready to taxi.

DECKER HAD MURTON HANDCUFFED TO A VERTICAL steel support beam inside the barn. He sat in a chair off to the side so he wouldn't get kicked in the face again. The kick didn't do much damage…he'd have a black eye, but Wheeler was too weak to do any real harm. He took the barrel of his gun and pressed it into the bullet wound on Murton's shoulder.

Murton groaned in pain, then opened his eyes. Decker put a mocking tone in his voice and said, "Even minor gunshot wounds will kill you if you don't tend to them right away. You've got to get the bullet out and all the little bits of fabric that follow it in. Sound familiar, asshole?"

Murton grinned through his pain. "You know what today is, Decker?"

"What's that?"

"The day you die."

"Big words from the guy handcuffed to a beam. Maybe I'll put three into your chest right now like you tried to do to me. Too bad you never noticed I was still alive when they carted me off. But Thorpe's guys were good, and they kept me alive. Anyway, I think you'll be the one dying today, not me."

"You might be right about my death, but I'll have the satisfaction of knowing you'll be right behind me. You think Jonesy won't square this? He'll hunt you down like a dog and gut you like a deer. If you had half a brain, you'd get in that car right now and never look back."

"Oh, don't worry. I am going to get in the car. As it turns out, I'm famished. I'm going to go get something to eat. But don't worry. I won't be gone long." He stuffed a rag into Murton's mouth and wrapped it with duct tape. "Stay right here, now." Then he laughed and walked over to the barn doors and slid them open. With that done, he got in the car and drove out the door.

BECKY YELPED, THEN SAID, "GOT IT." SHE THRUST THE phone at Cool, who put the coordinates into his navigation system.

Virgil leaned forward and said, "How long?"

WALKER LIFTED OFF AND LESS THAN TWO MINUTES later the tower handed him over to departure control. He acknowledged the handoff, then switched frequencies.

"Indianapolis Departure, Hellcat Seven Bravo Mike, with you level three thousand, southbound."

"Roger Hellcat Seven Bravo Mike, Indianapolis Departure. Fly heading one-eight-zero, climb and maintain five thousand feet. Be advised there is an active police search and rescue in progress along your flight path."

Walker didn't watch the news, so he didn't know anything about Murton's situation. He keyed the microphone and said, "Heading one-eight-zero and up to five. Permission to call the landline?"

"Granted."

Walker took out his cell phone and punched in the departure center's number, then stuck the phone between his ear and the left side of his headset. When it was answered, he said, "Gene Walker in the Hellcat. What's going on with the police search and rescue?"

The controller had known Walker for years and didn't hesitate to fill him in. Besides, the story had been on every news channel all morning long. When Walker heard they were looking for Mason's adopted son, he asked for the proper frequency to reach Cool in the helicopter, thanked the controller, and ended the call. Then he keyed his microphone and said, "Indianapolis Departure, Hellcat Seven Bravo Mike... canceling flight plan and dropping down out of controlled airspace."

The controller, who was the same man he'd just

spoken with on the phone said, "Roger that. Flight plan is canceled. Be careful, Gene."

"Wilco, and out," Walker said. Then he changed frequencies and called Cool in the helicopter. "State One, Hellcat Seven Bravo Mike. Standing by to assist. How can I help, Rich?"

Cool grinned into his headset. He gave Walker the coordinates and told him to start a search pattern. "We're almost there."

Walker had the Hellcat screaming through the sky at top speed. He keyed the microphone and said, "So am I."

———

THREE MINUTES LATER, VIRGIL POINTED OUT THE window. "There he is."

"I've got him," Cool said.

Becky pointed at the pole barn. "The barn doors are open. I'll bet that's where Murton is."

"He's turning around," Virgil said. "Becky's right. We can't let him get back to that barn, Rich. Take us in hot."

Cool poured the power on, lowered the nose of the chopper, and headed straight for the barn.

———

DECKER HADN'T EVEN MADE IT OFF THE CULTURAL Center's land when he heard the beat of the helicopter's rotor blades. He looked out the window and saw they were headed right for him. He turned the car around and began heading for the barn, but he knew it was too late. The helicopter had already flown past and was touching down right next to the building.

He slammed on the brakes, then reached into the backseat and got the automatic rifle out. Then he got out, took cover behind the car and started firing.

———

VIRGIL SAW THE FLASH OF AUTOMATIC FIRE FROM Decker's gun. He reached into his pocket and gave Murton's handgun and keys to Becky. "Go get our man, Becks." He pulled the charging handle back on his rifle. "I'll take care of this asshole."

Becky jumped from the chopper and disappeared into the barn. Virgil leaned forward and said, "Take us up, Cool."

———

COOL GOT THEM BACK UP AND OUT OF RANGE OF THE gunfire. Decker had burned through his first clip, and was reloading as the chopper circled overhead.

Virgil saw Decker struggling to reload. "Now, Cool. Give me one quick pass."

Cool dove toward Decker, and when they were in

range Virgil leaned out the open door and put a full clip through the front of the car. The radiator let go, and the air filled with steam and smoke. Cool yelled to Virgil: "Hang on!" Then he banked the chopper away and pulled up hard, taking them back out of range.

With all the steam and smoke coming from the car, Decker was afraid it might explode. He left the cover of his vehicle and started running toward the woods line at the edge of the property. It was a long way off, but if they tried to make a run on him, he'd turn and cut them right out of the sky.

And it almost worked.

BECKY FREED MURTON, THEN HELPED HIM TO HIS FEET. She racked the slide on his gun, then handed it to him. "Are you going to be okay?"

Murton nodded. "It's not as bad as it looks. The pain helps me focus. But we've got to get back to the chopper. We might not be out of the woods yet."

They moved toward the door, and when they saw Decker off in the distance, Murton shook his head. "What the hell is he doing?"

"Looks like he's making a run for cover. I think he's trying to draw Cool in closer."

"Won't work," Murton said with a matter-of-fact tone. He had calmed down because he knew it was all but over.

"C'mon, let's go." He took Becky's hand and they walked out the door in complete safety. Decker was so far away he couldn't have hit them with a guided missile.

Cool took the helicopter up to fifteen hundred feet and stayed far enough away that Decker wasn't a threat. "Now what?" Virgil said.

Cool shrugged. "That tree line is only about twenty yards thick. He'll eventually run out of ammo. Either that or Shelby County's finest will take care of him."

Except that didn't happen either.

———

DECKER FINALLY PUT IT TOGETHER THAT HE WASN'T going to be able to lure the chopper in, and that the tree line would only delay the inevitable. He changed plans and ran back toward the pole barn. If he could keep the chopper at bay, he might be able to get to Wheeler before they cut him down. He was so focused on keeping the chopper in sight he never knew what happened next.

———

MURTON STOPPED AND POINTED WITH HIS GOOD ARM. "Dear God, look at that."

Becky turned and said, "Murt...it's your dream. It's happening."

Walker had brought the Hellcat right down on the

deck, its engine screaming, its wheels up, the belly of the plane no more than ten feet off the ground, the tips of the propeller dangerously close to the pavement. When the prop hit Decker, there was a spray of pink mist, and then he simply disappeared. Walker pulled back on the stick, slid the canopy open, climbed and rolled at the same time until he was inverted, then made a pass right over Murton and Becky.

He smiled and waved as he went by.

CHAPTER THIRTY-SIX

Murton spent three days in the hospital. The surgery to remove the bullet went well, he was pumped full of antibiotics to keep a minor infection under control, and was on a morphine drip to keep the pain at bay. He drifted in and out of consciousness the first day after the surgery, and Becky was there the entire time, her laptop at her side, her research project almost complete.

On the second day, Virgil, Ross, Rosencrantz, and Cool kept coming in to bother him, and Becky had to keep shooing them away. They finally got the message and decided they'd leave him be...for now. "We've got better things to do, anyway," Rosencrantz said.

"Good. Go do them," Murton said.

"Where are you off too?" Becky said.

"Going out to the airport to pick up everybody," Virgil said. "They're inbound as we speak."

"Please don't let them visit me," Murton said. "I'm exhausted."

"When do you bust out?" Ross asked.

"The doctor said tomorrow as long as my sed rates are okay."

"Julia's getting out tomorrow as well," Cool said.

"Where are you guys going to stay until your house isn't broken anymore?" Rosencrantz said.

Cool gave him a look and said, "Not with you."

Rosencrantz shrugged. "I wasn't offering...just wondering."

Virgil walked over and kissed Murton on the forehead. "Thought we'd lost you, brother."

Murton laughed, then winced with pain. "I knew you'd show, Virgil. Never had a doubt." Then, "Christ, the pain from the surgery is worse than getting shot."

"Yeah, but it's a healing pain," Virgil said. Then he pointed his finger at Murton. "No pills."

Murton nodded. "I know, I know. Listen, I can't thank you guys enough...all of you, so please don't take this the wrong way, but get the hell out of here, will you?"

No one took it wrong at all, and they left Murton and Becky alone. Once they were gone, Becky went back to her laptop.

"What are you working on?" Murton said.

"Oh, nothing really. Just doing a little research.

Trying to get to the bottom of why your dream hasn't gone away, especially after everything that happened."

"I don't understand it," Murton said. "The whole thing with Walker and what he did? I thought for sure that would end it all, but it didn't."

"Maybe it's the meds," Becky said.

"I don't think so, Becks. It's something else. It must be."

"Get some rest, baby. We'll figure it out. I promise."

Murton thought there may have been something about the way she'd made the promise, but if there was, he was too tired and too drugged up to think clearly. He closed his eyes and tried to rest.

It didn't go well...and he sunk into the dream yet again.

Becky went back to her computer.

THE G-650 TAXIED OVER TO THE MILLION-AIR FBO, and once the engines were shut down everyone climbed out of the plane, the hellos much less hurried and hectic than the goodbyes had been. Virgil gave his boys a quick hug, then gave Sandy a long kiss. "I missed you guys," he said.

"And we missed you, Virgil Jones. Everyone at the Pope's said to tell you hello."

Virgil smiled, then looked around. "What's taking Mac so long to get off the plane?"

Sandy winked at her husband. "It seems there were some unresolved issues regarding the particulars of budgetary line items as they relate to the Cultural Center's ongoing operational status. Mac wanted to stay behind for a few more days and hammer out the details."

Virgil laughed through his nose. "Yeah, he wanted to stay and hammer something, I'm sure."

Sandy gave him a Becky-style punch to the shoulder and said, "Virgil!"

"So...that little speech you just gave me? It sounded awfully prepared."

"Good," Sandy said. "Guess who's in charge until Mac gets back?"

Virgil's smile went away. "Probably Betty."

TWO HOURS LATER, WHEN MURTON WOKE, HE WAS shaking and covered with sweat. He looked at Becky and said, "If this shit doesn't stop they won't have to release me. They can wheel me right up to the psych ward."

"Hang in there, Murt. I meant what I said. We'll figure it out."

THE NEXT DAY COOL MET WITH THE INSURANCE adjuster. "I don't know how to tell you this, Mr. Cool, but your policy clearly states that destruction of personal property resulting from an act of war, or any manufactured weapons used in warfare—such as military hand grenades—relieves us of any responsibility or recompense in the matter."

Cool nodded thoughtfully and gave the adjuster a toothless grin. "I completely understand. Listen, how much time do you have?"

The adjuster looked at his watch. "Well, plenty, I guess. I thought I'd be here longer but I didn't get a chance to read the report until I pulled up. Why do you ask?"

"I was hoping you could hang around for a little while. I need to make a quick phone call."

"Sure," the adjuster said. "I'll be here for about an hour, anyway. Even though we won't be paying, I still have to take some pictures and do the paper."

"Good, good," Cool said. "Take your time." Then he walked through the rubble of his house and stepped outside to make the call.

NICHOLE POPE REACHED FOR THE GOVERNOR'S PHONE, pressed the Answer tab and said, "Governor McConnell's office. How may I direct your call?"

Cool smiled into the phone. "Hey, Nichole. It's Cool."

"Not down here," she said with a giggle. "In fact, it's hot...and getting hotter by the second."

"Is Mac around? I need some help."

"Sure, hold on a second." She pushed the phone down near her stomach and said, "It's Cool on the line for you."

The governor shook the sheet from the bed, then picked up the phone. "What is it, Rich? I'm a little tied up at the moment."

Then Cool told him what he needed.

———

FORTY-FIVE MINUTES LATER THE INSURANCE ADJUSTER'S phone rang. He answered, then listened for a full five minutes without saying a single word. In fact, the only words he ever said during the entire call were, 'Yes, Sir, I understand completely.'

When he turned to Cool, his face was red, and there was a thin line of sweat across his brow. "That was my boss who just got off the phone with the director of the Indiana Department of Insurance. It seems I may have overstated the carrier's position regarding acts of war and whatnot. We'll be covering the entire loss, minus the deductible, of course."

Cool simply stared at him without speaking. The adjuster finally caved. "I almost forgot...in certain circumstances we do make allowances for the deductible of special claims. You'll have the check by the end of the week."

Cool smiled. "I know. My girlfriend and I will be staying in a suite at the Ironworks hotel for the duration of the repairs. I'll be sure to keep all my receipts for you."

MURTON WAS FINALLY RELEASED FROM THE HOSPITAL ON Monday morning. Becky got him home and settled in, then went back to work on the computer. Murton picked up the phone and made a call.

When the connection was made, the voice on the other end of the line said, "Hello, Murt. It is Wu."

"I wanted to call to say thank you," Murton said.

"Always a pleasure to assist in your time of need. It is what Wu do. You are well?"

Given the dream that still plagued him, Murton wasn't sure how to answer. In the end, as usual, he decided that the comfort of others was more important than his own. "I'll make it, thanks to Wu."

Wu chuckled, then asked about Virgil. "He is no longer troubled by his cerebral cyclones?"

"He's fine Wu. So far, so good."

"That is as expected. I will pass along your thanks to Nicky as well."

"Do that," Murton said. "Listen, about the brute force

attack on the OnStar system...will there be any blowback on that?"

"I thought you were calling to say thank you," Wu said with a laugh. "Now it seems you are insulting me."

Murton laughed too. "Naw, just wanted to make sure I didn't cause you any trouble."

"I believe at this very moment the cyber security people at General Motors are looking for someone in Slovakia. I do not believe they will find anyone, but Wu knows? There is nothing to worry about, my friend."

"Appreciate it," Murton said. "I'll be seeing you, huh?"

AT THE SAME TIME THAT WAS HAPPENING, BETTY walked into Virgil's office at the MCU and slapped a piece of paper on the center of his desk.

"What's this?" Virgil said.

"My letter of resignation. It turns out my daughter is pregnant and finally decided that she needs her mother after all. As for the letter, you can read it if you want, or I can recite it for you. I've got the whole thing memorized. In fact, I insist. It says, and I quote—Betty actually made little air quotes with her fingers as she spoke—'I quit. Effective immediately.' End quote."

Virgil tried very hard to keep the joy off of his face and out of his eyes. "Well, Betty, I know everyone around here will be sad that—"

Betty turned and walked out of the office without another word.

"—you didn't leave sooner," Virgil said.

———

LATER IN THE AFTERNOON AS VIRGIL WAS FINISHING UP his paperwork, Gene Walker knocked on his door. "Excuse me, I didn't see your secretary, but that gal downstairs? The one who sounds like, uh..."

Virgil smiled. "A stick of butter?"

Walker's eyes got wide. "Well, I was thinking more along the lines of whipped cream, but yeah, that's the one. Anyway, I told her who I was, and she said I could come up."

Virgil stood from behind his desk. "Have we met, Sir?"

"Not in the flesh, although I probably shouldn't put it that way after everything that happened. My name is Gene Walker. You're one of Mason's boys."

"That's right. Virgil Jones. Call me Jonesy. You knew my father?"

"That I did. Still miss the hell out of him."

"Me too," Virgil said, only because it was the polite thing to say. "How may I help you, Mr. Walker?"

Walker didn't beat around the bush. "That was me in the plane down in Shelby County. Am I going to be in any sort of trouble?"

Virgil walked from behind his desk and shook hands

with Walker. "You came to the aid of a wounded state police officer. You not only saved his life, but in doing so, you put your own life at risk in the service of other officers and civilians. As far as I'm concerned, you should get a medal."

"You've got that kind of pull?"

Virgil shook his head. "No, not really. But the governor is a personal friend of mine, and the lieutenant governor happens to be my wife. What you did will be in my report, and in all likelihood the report will be sealed due to national security concerns. I can't really talk about that part. I hope you understand."

Walker nodded. "I do."

"How's your plane? Did it suffer any damage?"

Walker nodded again. "I'm afraid so. I barely made it back to the airport. The prop is shot, the engine needs to be rebuilt, and some of the, uh, decedents body parts penetrated the fuselage."

Virgil dropped his shoulders. "Aw, geez, that's a shame."

"That's not the worst of it," Walker said. "The insurance company is refusing to pay for any of the damage. Something about the intentional unsafe operation of an aircraft resulting in the death of another."

"I might be able to help with that," Virgil said. "Hang on a second." He took out his phone and made a call.

This time when the phone rang, Nichole sighed and

didn't bother with any of the histrionics. "Jonesy's calling. It's for you."

The governor came on the line and said. "What is it, Jonesy? I'm sort of busy down here."

"I'll bet," Virgil said. Then he told the governor what he needed.

"Aw, for Christ's sake. What is it with you guys anyway?"

After the call, Virgil looked at Walker and said, "You'll get your check. I guarantee it."

Walker clapped his hands together. "I can't thank you enough, Jonesy. Seven Bravo Mike will live to fly another day."

"I thought it was Seven Boy Mike. Isn't that how you'd say the tail number?"

"No, you're thinking of the police phonetic alphabet. Pilots use a slightly different one. For example, you use 'David' for D, where we use 'Delta.'"

Virgil tipped his head and said, "Ah." Then he laughed out loud.

"What's so funny?" Walker said.

"Instead of Seven Bravo Mike, it ought to be Seven Bowel Movement."

"Why do you say that?"

Virgil was still laughing. "Because when Decker got turned to mist by the propeller on your plane, I about shit myself."

AT THE END OF THE DAY, VIRGIL WAS FINISHED WITH everything he needed to do, and was getting ready to leave when he had another visitor.

"Hey, Jonesy, got a second?"

When he looked up, he saw Sarah standing in his doorway. Her long red hair was pulled back and tied neatly in a bun, and she wore a professional-looking navy blue suit with an open-collar white shirt. She held a small briefcase with both hands in front of herself.

"Sure, Sarah. Come on in. What's up?"

"I'd like to know what I'd have to do to apply for the job of departmental secretary for the MCU."

Virgil was so happy he could have cried. "You're hired."

EPILOGUE

A week went by, and everybody settled back into their normal routine...except for Murton. He still woke every night, the dream haunting him more and more with each passing day. He knew if he didn't figure it out soon, he was going to lose his mind.

And then...this:

She traveled the dusty road, limo of black, hair of white, limbs brittle and thin. With a gait near falter and steps taken with care, she arrived with a lifetime of sorrow and regret. But now, for those not asunder, she knew it was finally time to lay her burdens down.

When she reached out to ring the bell, the door opened before her, and the young woman on the other side couldn't keep the tears from her eyes. "I wasn't sure you were going to come."

"I wasn't sure I could make it. The journey was arduous, no matter the modern conveniences of the day."

"Come in, please. He's in the front room."

Becky helped the old woman up the final step and guided her over to where Murton waited.

When Murton saw the old woman, he stood and said, "Hello. My name is Murton Wheeler. My wife told me we were going to have a visitor, but she wouldn't tell me who."

"I wasn't going to come at all," the woman said. "But your wife can be very persuasive. May I sit, please? The travel has left me somewhat unsteady."

"Of course," Becky said. She helped the woman into the chair facing Murton, then said, "I've made both tea and coffee, if you'd like."

"I think tea would be wonderful," she said. Then she looked at Murton and said, "I do hope you'll join me."

"I'm not supposed to have any caffeine for a while," Murton said. "I'm still recovering from a minor surgery."

The old woman gave him a kind smile. "I'd hardly call getting shot and having a bullet removed minor surgery." Then she looked directly into Murton's eyes and said, "My god, it's like I've gone back in time. You look just like him. Older, of course, but the resemblance is remarkable, even after all these years."

"Like who?" Murton said. "And you'll have to forgive me, but I don't believe I got your name."

The woman went on as if Murton hadn't spoken. "I'm here to ease your state of mind, dear. These dreams your wife has shared with me have an explanation. It might be one we understand, or it might be one we don't, but I believe in the most basic of statements."

"What statement is that?" Murton said.

"That the truth will set you free."

"What truth are we talking about?"

"I know about Virgil, and how you and he came to be brothers. Becky was kind enough to answer all of my questions. But now I have one for you. Do you know the story of your brother's maternal grandfather, Jack Bellows?"

Murton leaned closer and said, "Yes, at least most of it. Grandpa Jack never spoke much about his past, but we put the pieces together over the years. The death of his brother, Joe...the death of his parents at almost the same time, and how he ended up alone and on his own."

The woman nodded slowly. "Yes, that's how it all started. In some ways, it's how you came to be here."

Murton looked at Becky. She had tears running down her cheeks. She set a cup of tea on the side table for the old woman, then wiped her eyes and sat down next to her husband.

The woman sipped at her tea, then took a moment to

look around the room. "Such a wonderful home you've built for yourself."

"Thank you," Murton said.

"Now, where was I? Oh yes...you know how the story started, and how it ended. Your dream is real. I wasn't there, of course, but Jack and Hana were. The story made the newspapers all across the country. I cried for days when I heard the news." The woman looked at nothing for a few seconds, then said, "I always loved the way Hana called him Handsome Jack."

"I do know how the story started, and I definitely know how it ended. But I'm afraid I don't understand. What part of the story is missing?"

"Why, the middle, dear. That's usually where the answers can be found. When Jack set out on his own, he had to find a way to survive. Some might say he did wrong, but that's not true. He simply got mixed up with some people who themselves were trying to survive. Did you know that Jack was a war hero?"

"He never spoke much of the war," Murton said. "I do remember something about him saving a pilot who'd crashed his airplane on the flight deck of an aircraft carrier. Is that what you're referring to?"

"Yes, it is. One of those people I spoke of was the man he saved. His name was Howard Byrd. Oh, how I loved that young man...and what a fool I was to ever let him go."

"What happened?" Murton said.

"The truth is, I was a bit of a tart back then...young, carefree, full of myself, seeking my own path forward. I dallied some, I'm embarrassed to say, but Howard really was my one true love, no matter how poorly I treated him. He rode the train all the way across the country to find me, and when he did, I had him turned away."

"Why?"

"Because I was mad at the world in which we lived, mad at Howard, and raising his child. I had someone tell him I'd married even though I hadn't. If only I'd told the truth, he might have survived that awful event. You see, it was Howard flying the plane that day. He crashed it into the boat to save Jack and Hana's lives."

Murton looked at the woman and said, "Ma'am, I'm sorry, but I don't understand."

"Oh, but you do, if you'll just think about it. Don't you see, child?"

"I'm afraid I don't," Murton said.

"My name is Emma Ray. I'm your grandmother, dear."

And then she spent the next two hours and told Murton about the wayward strangers of his past.

As she finished, Emma Ray said, "I never knew you existed. Yet another mistake I made long ago. After Howard died, I eventually married and made a life for

Howard's child and myself. Our little girl turned out to be such a fine young woman."

Murton held a photo of Howard Byrd…one that Emma Ray had given him as she told her story. "The little girl was my mother," Murton said. It wasn't a question.

"Yes, but then she took up with that awful man, Ralph, and we shut her out of our lives. I'm so very sorry we did that. Look at what it cost me."

"But you're here now," Murton said. "And you're welcome anytime."

Emma Ray shook her head. "As is the story of the wayward strangers in my life, I'm afraid my time is short. If the doctors are correct, I'll die before the month is out. I intend to do so at home."

Murton now had tears running down his own cheeks. "What can I do?"

"You can make me a promise," Emma Ray said.

"Name it."

"Love your child."

Murton smiled through his tears. "I'm afraid we don't have any."

Emma Ray turned to Becky and said, "You haven't told him?"

Becky's jaw went slack. "Told him what?" She was genuinely confused.

Emma Ray looked at them both and said, "A mother can always tell." Then she stood, and Murton did as well. She gave her grandson a long hug, and at once a first and final kiss. "Love your child with your whole heart, Murton Wheeler. Make your grandpa Howard proud." Then she gave him a wink. "And sleep well tonight."

THE NEXT MORNING MURTON WOKE, AND FOR THE first time in weeks he'd slept without having the dream. When he rolled over in bed to tell Becky the good news, she wasn't there. He sat up, looked at the bathroom door and said, "Hey, Becks? Guess what?"

Becky opened the door, a pregnancy test in her hand, and a smile on her face. "Guess what yourself, mister..."

Thank you for reading State of Mind. If you're enjoying
the series, then there's good news:
Virgil and the gang will be back soon in
State of Need.

You felt the Anger.

You experienced the Betrayal.

You took Control.

You faced the Deception.

You accepted the Exile.

You fought for Freedom.

You understood the Genesis.

You held on to Humanity.

You braced for Impact.

You defined Justice.

You captured the Killers.

You lived the Life.

Now, it's time to feed the Need!

Stay tuned for further information regarding the Virgil Jones Mystery Thriller and Suspense Series. Visit ThomasScottBooks.com for updates.

— Also by Thomas Scott —

VIRGIL JONES SERIES IN ORDER:

State of Anger - Book 1

State of Betrayal - Book 2

State of Control - Book 3

State of Deception - Book 4

State of Exile - Book 5

State of Freedom - Book 6

State of Genesis - Book 7

State of Humanity - Book 8

State of Impact - Book 9

State of Justice - Book 10

State of Killers - Book 11

State of Life - Book 12

State of Mind - Book 13

State of Need - Book 14

JACK BELLOWS SERIES IN ORDER:

Wayward Strangers

Updates on future novels available at:
ThomasScottBooks.com

ABOUT THE AUTHOR

Thomas Scott is the author of the **Virgil Jones** series, and the **Jack Bellows** series of novels. He lives in northern Indiana with his lovely wife, Debra, his children, and his trusty sidekicks and writing buddies, Lucy, the cat, and Buster, the dog.

You may contact Thomas anytime via his website ThomasScottBooks.com where he personally answers every single email he receives. Be sure to sign up to be notified of the latest release information.

Also, if you enjoy the Virgil Jones series of books, leaving an honest review on Amazon.com helps others decide if a book is right for them. Just a sentence or two makes all the difference in the world. Plus, rumor has it that it's good for the soul.

For information on future books in the Virgil Jones series, or to connect with the author, please visit:

ThomasScottBooks.com

And remember:

Virgil and the gang will return soon in State of Need!

Made in the USA
Las Vegas, NV
16 January 2023

65713596R00246